ACCLAIM FOR ANDREW KLAVAN

"A thriller that reads like a teenage version of *24* . . . an adrenaline-pumping adventure."

—THEDAILYBEAST.COM REVIEW OF *THE LAST THING I REMEMBER*

"Action sequences that never let up . . . wrung for every possible drop of nervous sweat."

—*BOOKLIST* REVIEW OF *THE LONG WAY HOME*

". . . the adrenaline-charged action will keep you totally immersed. The original plot is full of twists and turns and unexpected treasures."

—*ROMANTIC TIMES* REVIEW OF *CRAZY DANGEROUS*

"[Klavan] is a solid storyteller with a keen eye for detail and vivid descriptive power."

—*THE WASHINGTON TIMES* REVIEW OF *THE LONG WAY HOME*

"I'm buying everything Klavan is selling, from the excellent first person narrative, to the gut punching action; to the perfect doses of humor and wit . . . it's all working for me."

—JAKE CHISM, FICTIONADDICT.COM

"Charlie teaches lessons in Christian decency and patriotism, not by talking about those things . . . but through practicing them . . . Well done, Andrew Klavan."

—*THE AMERICAN CULTURE* REVIEW OF *THE FINAL HOUR*

"This is Young Adult fiction . . . but the unadulterated intelligence of a superb suspense novelist is very much in evidence throughout."

—*CHRISTIANITY TODAY* REVIEW OF *THE FINAL HOUR*

IF WE SURVIVE

WE
SURVIVE

ANDREW KLAVAN

THOMAS NELSON
Since 1798

NASHVILLE   DALLAS   MEXICO CITY   RIO DE JANEIRO

Published in Nashville, Tennessee, by Thomas Nelson. Thomas Nelson is a registered trademark of Thomas Nelson, Inc.

Thomas Nelson, Inc., titles may be purchased in bulk for educational, business, fund-raising, or sales promotional use. For information, please e-mail SpecialMarkets@ThomasNelson.com.

Publisher's Note: This novel is a work of fiction. Names, characters, places, and incidents are either products of the author's imagination or are used fictitiously. All characters are fictional, and any similarity to people living or dead is purely coincidental.

Library of Congress Cataloging-in-Publication Data

Klavan, Andrew.
  If we survive / Andrew Klavan.
    p. cm.
  Summary: When revolutionaries seize control of a country in Central America where sixteen-year-old Will is serving at a mission, he and the other volunteers find themselves in a desperate race to escape the violence and return home.
  ISBN 978-1-59554-795-8 (hardcover)
 [1. Revolutions--Fiction. 2. Survival--Fiction. 3. Missions--Fiction. 4. Christian life--Fiction.] I. Title.
  PZ7.K67823If 2012
  [Fic]--dc23   2012020035

Printed in the United States of America

12 13 14 15 16 17 QG 6 5 4 3 2 1

This book is for John and Julie Nolte.

PROLOGUE

We were in the cantina waiting for a bus when Mendoza walked in and shot the waiter dead. It happened just like that, that fast. One second we were sitting around our table in the corner, drinking our Cokes, making conversation, eager to go home, looking forward to seeing our families again, to seeing America again. The next second the whole world seemed to explode with a deafening *blam!*

I jumped in my seat, shocked. I turned—and I saw the whole thing right in front of me, a sort of frozen tableau. There was Mendoza, in his rebel fatigues and red bandanna. His arm was extended. A wicked-looking pistol was in his hand. Smoke was still trailing upward out of the barrel.

The waiter was in front of him. Carlos—that was his name. A tall, round-bellied man with an easy smile. He didn't speak much English, but he liked to joke with us all the same, liked to flirt with the girls and nudge the guys as if to say, *You see, my friend, this is how you talk to the ladies. This is how you charm them.*

For one second—one second that seemed to go on forever—Carlos remained where he was—captured in the moment of reeling backward—a look of terror and sadness stamped on his features.

For that one second, that one endless second, we all seemed frozen, locked into that same terrible tableau. Pastor Ron, Jim, Nicki, Meredith, me. All of us motionless—frozen—as if we would never move again; all of us staring at the scene—our eyes wide, our mouths open.

Then Carlos fell. He began to take a step back as if the impact of the bullet was going to blow him across the room. But then—no—he just collapsed, his legs folding under him like pieces of string. I had never seen a dead man before, but somehow I knew from the way he went down that it was over for him.

The next second everything started moving again, moving very quickly. There was the sound of footsteps—a thunder of footsteps that seemed to come from all around us, shaking the floor and the walls. There were shouts from the street outside and then there were shouts in the cantina too. Deep, angry, threatening shouts. I heard a muttered curse from somewhere close to me. I heard a woman start to scream and then suddenly stop.

I looked around me. Men—all of them dressed like

Mendoza—all of them in fatigues with red bandannas tied around their heads—were charging through the cantina's swinging doors. They were spreading out around the room, flooding the room, lining the walls, blocking the exits. Every one of them was holding a gun—the sort of machine gun you always see in action movies and on the TV news with the bullet magazine curling out the bottom of it.

Two of the men posted themselves by the front door. Two others cut off the path to the back hall and the rear entrance. Another two blocked the stairway that led to the hotel rooms upstairs. They stood there with their machine guns raised to their chests and eyed the room, eyed all of us, with a look that said, *Just try to get past us. Just try, and see what we do to you.*

No one tried.

It was all over in a second. That fast, we were surrounded. Trapped.

What happened next—the bloodshed, the tragedy, the sheer terror—nearly defies belief.

But I guess I'd better start at the beginning.

CHAPTER ONE

There were five of us before the killing started. We had come to Costa Verdes to build a wall.

It was a poor country. A jungle country. A small country set on that narrow, twisting bridge of land that links Mexico to Colombia: Central America. The village we were in—Santiago—was a nothing of a place. Just a church in a flagstone plaza. A three-story-tall cantina-slash-hotel. A narrow street of shops and market stalls. And houses— little cottages really—trailing away up the road and into the mountains.

There were a lot of mountains in Costa Verdes. There were mountains everywhere, as far as the eye could see. They rose against the pale-blue sky in the morning, hunkered under black thunderclouds in the afternoon, and stood silhouetted beneath the stars at night. They were covered with forest, deep beryl green up close, blue-gray in the distance. And there was always mist rising out of the trees, spreading over the peaks and covering the horizon with an aura of mystery.

As for the wall we were building here in the village, it was the wall of a school—the only school for miles around. Not only the kids in the village used it, but all the kids from the farms and plantations on the nearby slopes: two dozen kids, maybe more, and of all ages. The wall had been destroyed somehow—I wasn't sure how exactly. *Los volcanes*, the natives kept telling us. The volcanoes. But that didn't make any sense. The only volcano I could see was miles and miles in the distance. I could only just make out its strange, flattened top, only just distinguish the trail of smoke that sometimes drifted from its ragged crater to blend with the mist hanging all around it. I didn't understand how "volcanoes" could have turned the school wall to rubble.

But rubble is what it was when we got there. And the school hadn't been much to begin with either. It was just a rectangular box made of cinder blocks with a long bench on each side for the kids to sit on, and a table and a blackboard up front for the teacher. Pretty pitiful when I compared it to my own school back home in California: Grove High, with its corridors and classrooms, its laboratories and library, its huge gym and football field and track and so on. Here in the Santiago cinder-block school, the kids barely had books to read and stuff to write with. Seriously: they used half pencils—pencils broken in half so there'd be enough to go around. They wrote on these little ragged notebooks, the blue covers nearly worn away, the pages full even at the borders because they had to use every inch of blank space they could find.

That's what it was like when they went to school, but they couldn't go much now with the wall demolished and one of the benches upside down on the floor amid the debris. Three cinder-block walls and a pile of gravel where the fourth one used to be—that was their schoolhouse now. *Los volcanes.* Whatever. We came to rebuild the place.

It was a church project. Or a church-slash-school project, to be more precise. The villagers here were too poor to buy the wall material themselves, and the local men were too busy working for their daily bread to take time to put the schoolhouse back together. So our church had taken up a collection for the cinder blocks and tools and mortar and so on, and then called for volunteers to come down here for a week or so during the summer break and slap the thing back up so the kids could get some kind of education. Grove High put up posters about the mission too, and Principal Hagen mentioned it during an assembly. In the end, some of us joined up in the name of Christian outreach and some of us came to get the Public Service credits we needed for graduation. Some of us had our own reasons too. Well, I guess all of us had our own reasons, when it comes down to it.

※

So who were we?

Well, let's see, there was Pastor Ron, first of all. Ron Collins, the associate minister at our church. He was a small, thin guy, with a bland, friendly face, eyes blinking out from behind his thick dark-rimmed glasses. He was young, mild-mannered, enthusiastic. Maybe a little *too* enthusiastic sometimes, if you ask me. Trying too hard to make things exciting and interesting to his teenage traveling companions. You may know the type. Always wanting everyone to think everything was *fun, fun, fun*—and then getting sort of quietly disgruntled and annoyed when anyone thought it was not, not, not. But I don't want to be unfair to him: he was a good guy, he really was. He always had time to listen to you and help you out if you had a problem. And his sermons were a lot more intelligent and interesting than the ones given by the head pastor, Pastor Francis. It's just that Pastor Ron was sometimes a little bit . . . *clueless*, I guess you'd say.

I'll give you an example. Once, shortly after we arrived in the village, Pastor Ron saw a little kid threatening a bigger kid with a stick. The little kid had his back against a cottage wall. The big kid—a big, fat hulking monster of a guy—was hovering over him, his hands balled into fists and his face darkening like a rain cloud. The little guy was holding a stick in front of him with both hands. He was so scared, you could see the stick vibrating as his hands shook.

Now, see, to me, it was pretty clear that the little kid was defending himself against the big kid in the only way he knew how. But Pastor Ron went hurrying over to the two of them and quickly pulled the stick out of his hands.

"No, no, mi amigo," Pastor Ron said in his flat, American-accented Spanish.

He knelt down between the boys and put a hand on a shoulder of each. He began talking to them in the quiet, patient, friendly way he had. I don't speak much Spanish myself, but I could make out some of what he was saying. He was telling the boys how wrong it was to do violence, and how it was especially dangerous to fight with sticks because you could take someone's eye out and leave him blind. He said the boys had to learn to be friends and give up fighting . . . and so on.

"Comprendez, amigos?" he asked. *Do you understand, my friends?*

The boys nodded, their big round eyes staring into the friendly stranger's face.

"Bueno," said Pastor Ron.

He patted them on the shoulders and stood up. And looking very satisfied with himself, he walked off to our tents, carrying the stick with him.

You can probably guess what happened then. In fact, I'm sure you can. The minute Pastor Ron ducked into our tent and was out of sight, the big kid—seeing the little kid had lost his only means of defense—hauled off and punched that poor little mite so hard, the boy literally left his feet before he thumped down to the ground in a cloud of brown dust. Man, that punch even made *me* see stars and hear the birdies sing, and I was standing nearly twenty yards away.

Happy then, the big kid went tromping off down the road, leaving the little kid sitting in the dirt, sobbing and rubbing his eyes with his fists.

That's all I'm saying about Pastor Ron. Nice guy. Good intentions. Just a little clueless, that's all.

※

Then there was Nicki—Nicki Wilson. Or—as I sometimes called her secretly, in my own thoughts—High School Barbie. Which was maybe a little unfair. I mean, Nicki had a lot of sweetness to her, she really did. And she was glamorous: pretty in a sort of flashy way with wavy blond-brown hair and big, deep-blue eyes that could blink innocently at you and send your heart reeling. Her makeup was always perfect, even out there in the middle of nowhere. Her clothes likewise were always neat and elegant, even in the wilting heat of noon before the thunderstorms started. When she walked up the little dirt path to our worksite, the people of Santiago actually stopped and stared at her with awe, as if she were a visiting princess or something. The little girls in the village—they loved her especially. And she was great with them, always ready to sit down with them on a bench and show them how to decorate their clothes with ribbons and rhinestones she had with her or how to tie up their hair in different ways.

So Nicki was sweet like that, but she was also just a little bit . . . what's the word I want? *Shallow*, I guess. She was seventeen, had just finished eleventh grade, and had left her Public Service credits till the last minute. She had come on this mission to Costa Verdes, as I overheard her say once, because she just *couldn't stand the horror* of having to *waste* her senior year doing some *dreary something-or-other in a homeless shelter* when *everyone knew* twelfth grade was supposed to be one long party.

She wasn't a lot of help with the wall either. It was a hard job. We had to dig a huge pit for the old debris, clear the rubble away, and cover it over. Then we had to haul the cinder blocks up the hill from the plaza where the truck had left them. We had to reset the big footer in the foundation, mix the mortar in a wheelbarrow, and so forth. And Nicki—well, just being honest here: she had a tendency to dog it a little, if you know what I mean. She'd sort of delicately lay some mortar on top of one of the blocks, wrinkling her nose at the yucky stuff as if it were a dead animal and handling the trowel as if it were the ten-foot pole she didn't want to touch it with. And then, the first second she thought she could get away with it, she'd heave a humongous sigh, blowing a stray curl off her pretty forehead, and she'd say, "I have to take a break! I'm *just* exhausted!"

On top of that, she had absolutely zero appreciation for how blessed we Americans are—you know, how nice our homes are, even the small ones, how much we have, even when we think we don't have that much. The people in Santiago—they had nothing. I mean, nothing. Their houses were clay boxes roofed in thatch. Most of them didn't have electricity or running water. The dads worked in the fields all day and the moms literally had to do the laundry at the river, down on their knees, scrubbing the clothes in the water.

"How could anyone live this way?" I once heard Nicki whisper under her breath. "You can't even get online!"

And okay, it was sort of weird—our cell phones didn't work and the Internet was only available at the cantina. We were all suffering Facebook withdrawal. But it didn't occur to Nicki that a whole lot of the world lives like that, you know. In fact, we in America, with all the stuff and gadgets and connections we have, we're the exceptions, the lucky ones—oh, and by the way, most of us didn't have a lot to do with making that happen.

Listen, I don't want to be all critical and pick on Nicki, because as I said, she was a sweet girl really, with a true depth of kindness in her . . . but I do have to tell this one story on her just because it makes me laugh.

One day, toward the end of our visit, when the wall was just about finished, the natives invited us to a ceremony. This was a big compliment—an honor really. The people of Costa Verdes are Christians—Catholics—but the country's original religion is some kind of ancient Mayan thing, and it still survives under the surface of the culture. That is, the people go to the church in the plaza every Sunday and all, but they still have a couple of festivals and ceremonies from the old days—part of that religion they surrendered when the Spanish explorers came and converted them.

Most of the time, they didn't let strangers come to these ceremonies. But I guess they were grateful to us for fixing their school and all, so they invited us along. And let me tell you, it was cool. I mean, hypercool, cool to the magnitude of awesome. We all gathered very solemnly in this cave—really, a cave hidden under vegetation in a side of one of the moun-tains. We sat against the cave wall and the only light was the flickering flame from a torch this old priest was carry-ing. The priest looked like he was about two hundred years old, he was so stooped and brown and wrinkled. He moved around the cave in front of us, lighting a bunch of candles with his torch so that the whole place glowed with this sort of wavering yellow light.

Then this big wooden statue was carried in by two of the men from the village. A carved, painted statue of some sort of grinning skeleton man. Very cool. Like some kind of Batman villain. I guess he was the god they were worshipping.

The men set the statue in the center of the cave. Then the priest—and I swear I'm not making this up—gave the god a cigar to smoke. No, really. He stuck the cigar in the god's grinning mouth and lit it for him with one of the candles! Then, when the god was comfortably enjoying a smoke, the priest moved around among the candles, swinging this balled cloth that spread a sweet smell everywhere like incense. And all the people clapped and sang and chanted, with their eyes shining and their faces looking kind of rapt and devout and happy. Very, very, very cool. Made me wish we did stuff like that in our church sometimes! Well, not really. But you know what I mean.

So anyway, this whole ancient, sacred ceremony went on, with all of us Americans being honored by being allowed to watch. And there we were, in this mystical cave full of candles and incense and chanting people. And finally, when it was over, the priest blew out the candles one by one, and the cave sank into a blackness that you could never describe, never even imagine, just a complete, lightless nothingness full of the fading echoes of the people's prayers.

Then silence. Total darkness. Total silence.

And out of that silent darkness came Nicki's voice—a sort of lazy, complaining whine.

"I am in such a *shopping* mood today!" she said.

I nearly pitched forward onto my face laughing. That was

Nicki all over, it really was. The natives honored us by sharing their most ancient secrets, and all she could think about was scoring a new pink T at A&F!

Sweet girl, just . . . shallow.

※

And then there was Jim Nolan. And you know the old expression, "If you can't say something nice about someone, don't say anything at all"?

Well, I haven't got much to say about Jim Nolan.

Jim was the smartest person in the universe—if, that is, the universe were his own imagination—which I think he believed it was. Jim was sixteen. Tall, very skinny, stoop-shouldered. Had kind of bugged-out eyes and very thin lips that he always seemed to be pressing together in disapproval of something. He really did know a lot—or he thought he did, anyway—about history and books and so forth. And whenever anyone said anything about practically anything, he was only too willing to correct them about it and give them a lecture on what he thought was the truth of the matter.

"We—we Americans, I mean—we destroyed this country, that's the fact of it," I heard him say once.

I was coming down the hill after helping Pastor Ron and the others drag tarps over our building materials in preparation for the afternoon storms. I heard Jim talking before I saw him.

"General Benitez was a great reformer," Jim went on. "There's just no question he would have redistributed the land more fairly. It's only because our CIA took it upon themselves to come in here and help the reactionaries overthrow him that you continue to have the poverty and unfairness you have today!"

Typical Jim. All the poverty and misery in the world was America's fault. Just as it never occurred to Nicki that poverty and misery were the default mode of the planet and we should be grateful for what we had, it never occurred to Jim that we didn't cause that poverty and misery; it was there long before we got here.

Anyway . . . I heard him talking like that and I came around a stand of thick-trunked evergreen trees and then I saw him. He was standing in a little clearing with a group of men. The men were sitting on the ground and Jim was standing over them as if he were a professor giving them an open-air lecture. He was pointing a finger at them as he spoke, driving his ideas home as the words tumbled out of him.

The men? They just sat there, gazing up at him with dull eyes. One of them I noticed looked particularly mean. A lean, broad-shouldered guy in his thirties. He had a craggy face, weatherworn and somber. A thin mustache, a cigarette dangling from the full red lips underneath. His eyes looked to me to be almost black. And the way he was looking up at Jim—with a sort of droll, distant, disdainful humor—well, it was the way someone might look at a spider who was just disgusting enough to hold his attention for a few seconds before he stepped on it.

That guy—that guy with the mean eyes? That was Mendoza, it turned out. I would see him again. Hanging out around the edges of the village. Talking to some of the men there. Talking to Pastor Ron once, as if they were having a philosophical debate of some kind.

And of course later, in the cantina, with his gun.

But that time—that time Jim talked to him—that was the first time I ever noticed him.

※

Enough about Jim. Let's move on to Meredith Ward. What can I tell you about Meredith? Not much really. She was a hard person to get to know—though she was not hard to admire at all. I sure admired her, at least. I admired her and I liked her—a lot.

Meredith was the oldest of us—except for Pastor Ron, of course. She was twenty or so—maybe twenty-one, I'm not exactly sure. She was not from my hometown, not from Spencer's Grove, like the rest of us. She went to Westfield College nearby and, like a lot of the kids from Westfield, came into town to attend our church on Sundays. I guess that's how she became part of this wall-building expedition.

Meredith wasn't pretty like Nicki. She wasn't pretty at all, really, not in what you'd consider a glamorous way. But to tell you the truth, after getting to know her for a day or two, I found her looks sort of grew on you. In fact, I started to think she was sort of beautiful. She reminded me of a painting or a statue or something: very tall, taller than I am, almost six feet, her back always straight and her chin always up, her face kind but serious, her pale brown eyes clear and direct. She had a very pale complexion—white with maybe a little rose just beneath the surface. And she stayed that way, even after the rest of us had turned brown from working in the sun. She had short curly hair, a sort of high forehead, a strong, straight nose—like I said, not pretty in any movie star way but really . . . *noble-looking*—I guess that's what you'd call her.

She didn't talk very much. I noticed that about her right away. Not that she was standoffish or anything. She'd sit with us and listen and laugh at all of our stupid jokes like everyone else. But everyone else *always* seemed to be talking about something or other: what they liked to do for fun or what music they liked or what video on YouTube cracked them up, their school plans, career plans, philosophy of life, and so on and so forth. Not Meredith. She listened. She asked a question sometimes, made a comment sometimes. But she almost never said anything about herself—what she liked, what she did, who she thought she was. Even when you asked her a direct question, she'd answer in a few words, very simply, and that was the end of it. After a couple of days around our campfire, I knew she came from Colorado originally.

And I knew she wanted to be a grade-school teacher after graduation. That was it.

I've told a story about everyone else, and I've got a story about Meredith too. It's a sad story, but it does tell you a lot about her.

While we were in the village—just the second day we were there—a baby died. I don't know what caused it, a fever or something. There wasn't any doctor in the village, and I guess the sickness just carried the kid off.

Anyway, the first thing I knew about it was just after I woke up. I was coming out of the Guy Tent when I heard the terrible sound of the baby's mother screaming and crying. She was out in the street, the dead baby in her arms. She was calling out desperately to the other villagers, to us, to God, to anyone who would listen. Like I said, I don't speak much Spanish, but I understood she was begging us—begging all of us—to make the baby come back to life, to make her nightmare end.

What happened next: the poor woman went sort of crazy with grief. She carried the infant's body back into her cottage and refused to come out. I caught a couple of glimpses of her in there through the open door. She was cradling the dead child in her arms as if she could somehow comfort it. She refused to let anyone come near it, refused to let anyone take the baby away for burial. Her husband went in and tried to talk to her, but she wouldn't listen. Some of the other women from the village tried as well—same result. The local priest—the Catholic priest—Father Juan, his name was—he went in and reasoned with her for half an hour. Then the old priest too, the guy from the cave ceremony—he tried. But the mother simply would not let the baby go, would not admit that the child's soul was gone now, that she was cradling nothing but the body that remained.

We—the other Americans and I—went to work on the wall, digging the pit, clearing the debris. It got to be almost noon. The woman was still in her house just down the road. Sometimes, when I would take a wheelbarrow of trash down to the dumping spot, I would see her in there, still clutching the corpse of her child and wailing—crying out in a way I could hardly stand to hear, a pure, steady, unending keen of grief. It just broke my heart.

At last, just as I was returning to the worksite after one trip, I saw Meredith. She was on her knees, using a small spade to work over the place where we were going to lay our new footer. Without saying a word to anyone—without even looking at anyone—she laid the spade aside and stood, brushing a strand of hair back off her forehead. She left the site. Walked down the dirt road to the grieving mother's house. Wove silently through the clutch of women who had gathered worriedly outside the door and went inside.

Ten minutes passed—and then, all at once, the mother's terrible wailing stopped.

Just like that—and for the first time that day—there was quiet in the village.

All of us building the wall stopped what we were doing. I don't think we really realized how awful that noise had been until it ended. We looked toward the mother's house. Another fifteen minutes went by. Then Meredith came out.

It'll be a long time, if ever, before I forget the sight of her. Walking straight and tall as she always did, her chin lifted, her expression set, her eyes clear—and carrying the little bundle of the dead child gently, tenderly in her arms. The mother followed just behind her, her head hung, as she went on crying quietly. The crowd of women outside parted as Meredith passed through them, silent and stately. She walked down the road to the church with the mother right behind her and handed the child over to Father Juan for burial.

"What in the world did you say to her?" I asked Meredith that night as we finished our dinner around the fire.

But Meredith only shook her head—and there was something about her that made you stop asking questions when you knew she didn't want to say more.

※

So I guess that's everyone—everyone except for me, that is. And there's not much I can tell you about myself because, frankly, I'm just not all that interesting. My name is Will— Will Peterson. I just graduated tenth grade this past spring. I just turned sixteen. I've lived in Spencer's Grove, California, my whole life and I am pretty much your standard-issue run-of-the-mill male-version kid. I don't love school but I like my friends. I like football but I'm too small to play, except an occasional game of touch in the park. I like video games—duh!—especially the first-person shooters—and especially the survival horror ones where you get to blow zombies away—and maybe *most* especially the ones that make my mom cringe because of all the blood. Bwa ha ha! I don't really know what I want to do with my life. Something about computers probably. Maybe have my own business of some kind. Anyway, I still have a lot of time before I have to figure all that out.

The only thing I should add, I guess, is that I had my own special reasons for coming to Costa Verdes, for joining this little expedition to Santiago to build the school wall. I mean, sure, I wanted to come for the church and to do good in the world and all that Bible stuff. And yeah, I also needed the Public Service credits to graduate like everyone else.

But there was also this: my mom and dad had been fighting a lot recently. As in: a lot of a lot. They were fighting about everything, it seemed like. Work, the house, money. Me. And I have to tell you: I hated it. Hated, hated, hated—you can add as many "hateds" to that as you want and still be in the ballpark. And even more than I hated to hear them fighting—or to *not* hear them when they lowered their voices and went right on fighting in a low mutter and hiss—I hated what I just knew was going to happen next. The we-need-to-have-a-little-talk-Will. The Dad-is-moving-away-just-for-a-little-while.

The it's-not-your-fault-Will. It'll all be just the same as always except now you'll have two houses to go to, won't that be nice?

Nice. Right. I mean, I would've rather they just shot me. All right, maybe that's a small exaggeration. I'm just saying: I hated listening to them squabble and I hated waiting for the Big Day and the Little Talk to arrive. The way I figured it: if I could get a week away in Central America and do my little bit to save the world and not have to listen to my parents fight all at the same time—well, good deal, right?

Absolutely.

So that was my story. That was me.

※

And that was all of us—five of us. Pastor Ron, Nicki, Jim, Meredith, and the illustrious Will Peterson, aka myself.

We came to Costa Verdes to build a wall.

I just wish I could tell you that all of us made it home alive.

CHAPTER TWO

We finished our work on a Friday. There it was, the little cinder-block box, the school, fully rebuilt. Benches all back in place. Debris all cleared away. It was a good feeling to know the kids here would be able to learn stuff again and that I'd had a little bit to do with it.

The villagers were grateful. That night, in fact, they held a celebration for us in the plaza in front of the church. They hung strings of colored Christmas lights like they did on market days and they lit sparklers. The children gathered in a chorus, wearing their best white shirts, and sang a song for us. Then a band played music and the women danced, waving colored handkerchiefs around. Father Juan held a special service on the church steps. He said a blessing on the school and included us in his prayers.

Like I said, it was a good feeling. I was glad I'd come.

※

In the morning, we rolled up our sleeping bags, folded our tents, packed our backpacks, and hoisted them onto our backs. We tromped down from our campground on the side of the hill to the cantina-slash-hotel in the plaza. That's where we had to wait for the van that would take us to the plane that would take us to the airport in the capital city of Santa Maria. From there, we would fly back to California.

We were all excited, all eager to get home. Even me. I guess I harbored some small hope that my folks would have worked things out while I was away. I know: fat chance. But I couldn't help hoping. And, anyway, I missed them.

It was just after noon when we entered the cantina. The place was almost never crowded—only sometimes when buses brought tourists through town to see the church. But there were some people there today, families seated at some of the tables eating lunch, men standing at the bar drinking beer. The cantina not only had the only Internet access, but it also had the only television in the village—a really old one—I think it was powered by coal or steam or something! Anyway, it was up on the wall over the bar with a blurry, fuzzy soccer game playing on it, and the men were all watching that.

Our group sat at a large round table in the corner up front. Pastor Ron bought us all some Coke and chips.

"Well, here's to the children of Santiago," said Pastor Ron in his mild, quiet voice.

He lifted his glass of Coke and we all clinked our own glasses against it.

"I want to drink to going home!" Nicki said loudly. "And to taking a bath and going on Facebook and having a phone that works! And sheets. Clean sheets! I cannot wait!"

"Well, I guess you've really learned something about the way other people live, Nicki," Pastor Ron said to her—so mildly I couldn't tell whether he was being sarcastic or not.

"Which I bet she'll forget the minute she gets to CPK," Jim Nolan muttered into his Coke.

"CPK!" said Nicki, sighing deeply. That's California Pizza Kitchen to you—the central place to hang in Spencer's Grove. "Don't even mention CPK until I'm actually holding a roasted artichoke and spinach slice in my perfectly manicured fingers!"

"I rest my case," Jim said, rolling his eyes.

"What's the one thing you've missed most?" Pastor Ron asked us. I think he was trying to start a friendlier conversation—you know, trying to keep Jim and Nicki from getting into some kind of brawl.

"What do I miss? I miss civilization," said Nicki immediately. "Which I define as any place where people have more than one change of clothes."

"For crying out loud—" Jim started to say.

I cut him off, saying, "I miss my Xbox. I was right in the middle of the new *Gears of War* when we left. And my mom wouldn't let me bring my Zune. She said it was 'inappropriate.' What does that even mean?"

"I have to admit, I do kind of miss a working cell phone," said Pastor Ron wistfully.

"My cell phone! Puleeze! The first thing I'm going to do when we get to Santa Maria is call every single human being I've ever met," Nicki cried.

"What about you, Meredith?" Rob asked.

And we all turned to her—because everyone always did that when she talked. Everyone always listened to whatever she had to say.

Meredith smiled. "That bath Nicki mentioned—that did sound good."

"Jim?" asked Pastor Ron.

Everyone turned to him. And you just knew—*knew*—he wasn't going to say anything that might make it sound like home was a good place. He shrugged. Knocked back his Coke so that the ice rattled. "I miss my books, I guess," he said, as if the whole idea bored him.

"Amigos, amigos!" This was Carlos, the waiter. He had come to our table and was standing over us, one hand resting on Pastor Ron's shoulder and another on Meredith's. "We are all very sorry to see you go." He then rattled off something in Spanish that I didn't understand. I guess it was something flattering about the girls because Meredith smiled up at him and murmured, "You're too kind, señor."

Well, that was all the encouragement Carlos needed. He started rattling away again and though I couldn't tell exactly what he was saying, I could tell it was something flowery and complimentary because first Meredith laughed and then Nicki rolled her eyes and said, "This dude is *such* a player!"

Carlos smiled at her and then wagged his finger at me. "You are paying attention, señor, yes? Now you learn: this is how you talk to the ladies so you will always have many beautiful girlfriends."

"Thanks for the pointers," I told him.

He winked at me.

Finally, giving Pastor Ron and Meredith each a friendly pat on the shoulder, Carlos asked, "Well . . . can I get you more drinks?"

"I don't think so, Carlos, gracias," said Pastor Ron. "Our driver should be here any minute."

"Well then, my friends, I will only tell you: go with God, yes?" And with that, Carlos wandered off to another table.

"All right," I said. "Now someone has to explain to me what he was saying. So I can learn how to talk to the ladies and have many beautiful girlfriends."

Nicki said, "If you talk to the ladies like that, you'll end up with many beautiful fat lips, believe me."

"Oh, now, I thought he was very chivalrous," said Meredith with a laugh.

"Chivalrous—that's a good thing, right?" I asked.

"Yes," said Meredith.

"Whatever," said Nicki. "Play-uh."

Then, with a sudden bang, the cantina door swung open—and Palmer Dunn walked in.

※

That's one more person I have to tell you about: Palmer. I didn't like Palmer very much. I don't think anyone did, not in our group, anyway. He was our driver—and our pilot. A week ago, he had flown us here from Santa Maria. It was a terrifying flight, all of us crammed into his tiny Cessna, thunderstorms tossing us around every five minutes. Then the landing: bouncing down onto an airfield that was nothing more than a strip of packed dirt on a flat plain of grass. And afterward, more sickening bumps as he drove us in his black van over jungle roads here to Santiago. Now he was here again to drive us to his plane and fly us back to the capital. I don't think anyone was much looking forward to the trip.

I'm not sure exactly what it was about the guy that bugged me so much. There was just something dark about him. He was an American, like us—older, but still young—maybe twenty-five. Tall and lean and muscular in his jeans and black T-shirt. He had sandy hair and a day's growth of stubble on a rough-looking serious face—serious, that is, except for his eyes. He had pale green eyes that always seemed to be laughing at you, laughing at everyone.

But let me try to clarify what it was about him that I didn't like. I didn't like the way he talked to us, quiet and droll and mocking, as if we were too stupid to be worth his time. I didn't like the way he looked at Meredith and Nicki when he first saw them, his eyes going up and down them slowly, his lips curled into a smirk. I didn't like the way he snorted laughter at Jim when the bumpy plane ride turned his face a sickly green. I didn't like the way he swaggered when he walked, his whole air of arrogance. And, maybe more than anything, I didn't like the fact that he frightened me. He was tough. You could tell just by looking at him. And I knew if we ever got into any kind of a fight, he would be able to pound me into the ground without even getting out of breath.

Just look at the way he was when he walked into the cantina. He glanced over at us in our corner and lifted his chin—just a little, almost imperceptibly, at Pastor Ron—just to let us know that he saw us, that he knew we were there. Didn't say hello. Didn't come over to talk. Just lifted his chin and then walked right by us to the bar.

Pastor Ron called after him in a friendly voice as he passed by. "Would you care to join us for a Coke, Palmer?"

Palmer didn't even answer him. Not a word. He stood at the bar. There was an old lady behind it, serving drinks. She came over to him.

"Cerveza," Palmer said. *A beer.*

Pastor Ron was twisted around in his chair, still looking at Palmer as if he expected an answer to his invitation. I could tell he wasn't happy with the way Palmer ignored him. He went on watching as the old woman set a bottle of beer on the bar in front of Palmer.

"I hope you're not going to have too many of those before

you pilot your plane," said Pastor Ron—still trying to sound more friendly than concerned.

Palmer's only answer: he turned to us, lifted the beer bottle in a sort of toast, watching us with his mocking eyes. Then he knocked back a slug and turned back to the bar, raising his gaze to watch the soccer game on the TV while he drank.

Pastor Ron sat twisted around in his chair another moment, as if still hoping for a better answer. Then, finally, he turned back to us. I could tell he was put out and embarrassed by the way Palmer treated him.

"Considering how rough the plane ride over was, I can't help thinking a drunken pilot won't help much," he said.

"No kidding," said Jim—and I could tell he was really worried about it.

"If he kills us before I get my bath, I will never speak to him again," said Nicki. "Ever."

I laughed. "That'll teach him."

"Don't worry, Jim," said Meredith. She reached across the table and touched Jim's hand. She could see he was afraid of the upcoming plane flight as well as I could. "I have a feeling Palmer could fly that plane safely in his sleep."

Jim took a deep, unsteady breath. "Yeah, well, I hope you're right because it looks like—"

And that's when it happened. Just like that, out of nowhere. The door to the cantina opened again—I didn't see it, I only realized later I had heard it.

And then the cantina—the world—our lives—exploded in a single gunshot—and I turned to see Mendoza holding the smoking pistol while Carlos the waiter tumbled down to the floor and died.

CHAPTER THREE

Then everything happened like I said before: the thundering footsteps, the armed men charging in and flooding the cantina, lining the walls, blocking the exits, blocking the stairs. A woman started to scream, then stopped. It was Nicki, her hand covering her mouth, her eyes starting to glisten with tears. The people at the other tables leapt to their feet. The men at the bar froze. The whole cantina went weirdly quiet—silent, except for the faint hiss of cheering coming from the soccer game on the TV.

And then I heard someone, a man, speak two words in a low whisper, his voice trembling with fear.

"Los Volcanes," he said.

The Volcanoes.

Then it was over. Really, it all took no more than a second.

Carlos was dead on the floor and the rest of us were completely surrounded by grim-faced men with machine guns. We were totally trapped before any of us could even react.

And then someone did react: Meredith.

She got up out of her chair. My hand went out to stop her, but too late. She was already moving quickly across the room toward Carlos.

Mendoza caught the motion out of the corner of his eye. He turned to Meredith quickly, fiercely, his craggy face pulled tight in a dangerous frown.

"Sit down, señorita!" he barked. "Don't go near him!"

Meredith ignored him—totally. She didn't even look at him. She didn't even pause. I sat there helplessly, as if nailed to my chair. My guts twisted as I watched her hurry to Carlos's side and kneel down beside him. She put her hand on the waiter's neck, searching for a pulse.

"I said sit down!" Mendoza shouted. His deep, rough voice seemed to make the walls shake.

And still, Meredith paid absolutely zero attention to him. As I watched—as all of us, even the gunmen watched—she knelt there pressing her fingers into the fallen man's neck for what seemed like a long, long time.

Then she looked up at Mendoza. Her face was calm and still, her eyes as clear and direct as ever.

"You've killed him, señor. He's dead."

Mendoza looked at her a long moment, as if trying to decide whether to answer her or to kill her too. Then, in a quick, businesslike manner, he slipped his pistol into the black holster on his belt. One corner of his mouth lifted in a sneer.

"He was an enemy of progress," he told her.

Slowly, Meredith removed her hand from Carlos's neck and lifted it to his eyes. The dead man's eyes were still open, still staring at the ceiling with that expression of terror and sadness he'd had at the end. Gently, Meredith pushed his eyes closed.

Slowly—as we all watched her—she rose to her feet, to her full height. She was wearing khaki slacks and a white blouse. She had a full, sturdy figure and she had never reminded me more of a statue than just then, as she faced Mendoza. She gazed at the killer for what seemed like forever. Then, quietly, she said one word:

"Progress."

Well, you had to have heard the way she said it, the tone of voice; so help me, she might just as well have slapped Mendoza in the face. It would've been less insulting.

At the sound of her contempt, the sneer vanished from Mendoza's lips. His dark eyes smoldered with rage. His hand went back to his holstered pistol. I caught my breath, nearly certain he was about to shoot Meredith the same way he'd shot Carlos. But instead, he stepped forward. He stepped up to Meredith—close to her—inches away. He was about her height, maybe six feet, and they were eye to eye.

He stared at her. And I probably don't have to tell you

that Meredith didn't flinch, didn't quail at all. Then, suddenly, Mendoza's hand flashed up. He grabbed Meredith by the hair—hard, so that she gasped with pain.

That broke the spell that held me to my chair. I leapt to my feet, ready to rush to Meredith's defense. Pastor Ron leapt to his feet at the same moment. So did Jim.

And on the instant, men with guns surrounded us, pointing their weapons directly into our faces.

No one had ever pointed a gun at me before. It's not the sort of thing that happens a lot around Spencer's Grove. It's an interesting experience too, if *interesting* is the word I want. Seeing that black barrel trained on you—knowing that sudden death could spit out the bore at any moment—it does something. It takes your will away. If this had been one of my daydreams, where I'm always the hero, I would've knocked the gun aside and rushed to Meredith anyway. In real life? The power to move seemed to drain right out of me. I stood there motionless, looking from the gun in my face to the place where Mendoza held Meredith by the hair, twisting his fist to make her gasp again with pain.

He looked at us—me and Pastor Ron and Jim—standing there helplessly under the machine guns. He flashed us a smile.

"What's the matter, gentlemen?" he asked. "Is chivalry dead? Does America have no more men in it? No one to help a lady in distress?"

"Let her go!" I said.

One of the gunmen standing next to me jabbed the barrel of his rifle into my forehead. The pain rattled me, knocked me back against the table.

"Easy, boy," Mendoza said to me through his gritted teeth. "You want to live to be a man, don't you?"

"Really—Mr. Mendoza, isn't it?" Pastor Ron said in his calm, come-let-us-reason-together voice. "There's no need to—"

"Shut up, priest," Mendoza said.

One of the gunmen emphasized the point by stepping closer to Pastor Ron, raising the barrel of his weapon to Pastor Ron's forehead.

Pastor Ron shut up. And I didn't blame him.

"What about you, Señor Dunn?" Still clutching and twisting Meredith's hair—so hard he nearly dragged her off her feet—Mendoza raised his eyes to Palmer. I turned to Palmer too.

And do you know what Palmer Dunn was doing? You are not going to believe this, but I swear it's the truth. Palmer was watching the soccer game. So help me. Standing at the bar. Drinking his beer. Watching the soccer game on the TV on the wall. Just as if nothing had happened. Just as if nothing were happening now.

When Mendoza spoke to him, Palmer glanced his way, pausing with the beer half lifted to his lips as if he'd only just noticed the other man was there.

"You talking to me?" he asked.

Mendoza laughed and shook Meredith in his grip, hard, the way a dog shakes a rabbit he's caught in his teeth.

"I asked you what you are going to do, señor?"

Palmer considered Mendoza—and then Meredith—as if he were trying to figure out what all the fuss was about. Then he reached out along the bar. There was a wooden bowl there, full of macadamia nuts. He took a handful.

"I think I'm gonna have some of these nuts," he said. He popped a few into his mouth and chewed. "Mm."

Mendoza laughed. It killed me the way he wouldn't let Meredith go, the way he went on gripping and twisting her hair, sort of pulling her this way and that, displaying her to his gunmen like some sort of trophy. "You surprise me, Señor Dunn," he said—but he was talking to his soldiers as much as to Palmer. He was entertaining them. They laughed as they looked on, cradling their guns. "You are big strong American soldier, no?"

"I was a Marine, actually," Palmer said pleasantly through his mouthful of nuts. "But not anymore."

"Big strong United States Marine," said Mendoza. "And you are not going to rush to the aid of your countrywoman in her distress?"

Palmer shrugged. He turned back to the TV, lifting his beer. "Your country, amigo. Your revolution," he said. "It's none of my business." Once again, he started to lift his bottle of beer to his mouth. But he paused. He glanced at Mendoza sideways. "Of course," he added, "you never know how these things are going to turn out in the end. Do you?"

With that, Palmer went back to watching the soccer game.

Suddenly—and for no reason I could tell—the expression on Mendoza's face changed. The white grin beneath his mustache disappeared. The light of cruel humor in his eyes went out and was replaced by something else, something that looked to me a lot like fear.

Without another word, he let Meredith go—that is, he tossed her away from him like a toy he was bored with. She lost her footing and stumbled, fell to one knee on the cantina floor.

I ran to her then. I forgot about the guns. Or maybe I figured, *Let them go on and shoot me.* Whatever: I ran to her. I stooped beside her. Took her by the arm and helped her to her feet.

"Thank you, Will," she said. I was shocked to hear how quiet her voice was—breathless, but still calm. She rubbed the spot on the side of her head where Mendoza had gripped her.

Holding her arm, I walked with her back to the table. Pastor Ron pulled a chair out and we both helped her to her seat.

I thought Mendoza might come after me next, angry at me for going to Meredith. But when I turned back to him, he was standing right where he'd been, still gazing across the room at Palmer Dunn.

Palmer glanced away from the TV for a moment, met his gaze, and smiled. Then, calmly, he turned away. Swigged his beer. Watched the soccer game. Something had passed between the two men—something important—but I couldn't understand what it was.

Now Mendoza looked around the room at his gunmen. His gunmen quailed, looking frightened. Easy to understand why. Mendoza looked angry now—really angry. He looked like a man who felt humiliated and was searching for someone to punish.

He stood there glaring a long moment. Then he made a quick, harsh gesture with his hand. "Vamanos!" he barked.

As quickly as they had come thundering in, the gunmen started to thunder out again, storming to the cantina door and through it, out into the plaza. Mendoza continued gesturing at them, continued barking orders in Spanish. Two gunmen broke away from the pack. One grabbed Carlos by one foot and one by the other. They dragged the dead waiter to the door and out.

More orders from Mendoza. Two more gunmen broke away from the pack as it filed out. Mendoza pointed this way and that, and one gunman took up a post at the doorway in back, while the other stood with his machine gun at the front entrance.

The thunder of footsteps faded. Aside from the guards at the exits, the gunmen were gone. Mendoza stood alone and finally quiet in the center of the room.

The killer looked around slowly—looked around at all of us—one, then another, then another. When his eyes passed over me, I felt dread blow over me like a chill wind. It made goose bumps rise on my flesh.

"No one is to leave this place," Mendoza told us. He gestured toward the guards at the doors. "These men have orders to shoot anyone who tries to get away. Or tries to use the Internet. Or the phone."

He paused as if he would say something else. But then he just gave Palmer one last angry glance.

This time, Palmer didn't even turn from the soccer game.

And with that, Mendoza made a sharp pivot on his heel and marched out of the cantina.

CHAPTER FOUR

Nicki fell apart. The moment Mendoza was out the door, the second the tension in the cantina broke, she let out a little hiccup sound, raised her hands beside her head, rigid and shivering as if she were suffering a massive electric shock. Tears streamed down her cheeks and her mouth opened and closed a moment without making a sound. And then she did make a sound: strained, tearful words coming out of her in little coughing bursts.

"What . . . is . . . happening? What . . . they . . . killed . . . they killed . . . What . . . ? What . . . is happening?"

I knew how she felt. It was as if, with Mendoza gone, we finally had a chance to feel just how shocked and scared we were. I know I felt my own heart suddenly speed up, as if it were going to break out of my chest and run for the hills in pure terror.

"No! I mean . . . no! I . . . I . . . I . . . ," Nicki said. "No . . ."

Meredith got out of her chair. Went to her. Put her hands on her shoulders.

"Ssh. Quiet, Nicki," she said—calmly like that, as if she hadn't just been roughed up by a murderer. "Quiet. It's going to be all right."

"All right??? They killed . . . that man! They killed . . . ! All right???"

"Well, what did you all think?" asked Jim. "This has been building for years. How long did you think these people were going to tolerate—"

"Not now, Jim," Meredith said quickly, and Jim's mouth closed into a tight line as if he could only hold back by force what he wanted to say. Meredith leaned down and set her cheek against Nicki's as Nicki hiccuped out another sob. "It's all right. It's going to be fine."

"No. I . . . I . . . What is happening?" said Nicki again. She was weeping steadily now. "What is happening?"

I looked from them to Pastor Ron. "What *is* happening?" I asked him. "What are we going to do?"

Pastor Ron stared at me, and I felt my racing heart drop in my chest. Pastor Ron—he was our leader. He was the only real adult we had with us. He was the one who was going to have to take charge. But the way he looked just then—his eyes big as dinner plates behind his glasses, his lips parted as if he wanted to speak but couldn't find the words—it was . . . well . . . not inspiring, to say the least.

But now another voice came from across the room.

"You oughta shut her up, for one thing."

Palmer. He had turned around, was leaning back against the bar, the beer bottle still in his hand. He gestured with the bottle at Nicki—Nicki, who went on sobbing and babbling out unfinished sentences and disconnected words.

"If you want to know what to do," said Palmer, "that'd be a good place to start."

I saw Pastor Ron blink—almost as if he were coming out of a trance. He looked at Nicki.

"Are we going to die now?" Nicki sobbed to no one in particular. "Are they . . . going to kill everybody? Are they going to shoot us?"

"Ssh," said Meredith.

"I mean it," said Palmer. "Shut her up and fast."

Pastor Ron licked his lips. "There's . . . there's no need to talk to her like that," he said. "She's upset."

"I don't care if she's the queen of England," Palmer answered him. "You oughta quiet her down before these clowns do it for you."

He gestured with his beer again. I followed the movement to look at the guards—the one at the front door and the one at the rear. They were watching us. Staring at us. Staring at Nicki. The looks on their faces sent that cold wind of dread through me again. They didn't look happy. Not at all. They looked annoyed. They looked angry. As if they wanted Nicki to stop crying. Fast. As in: Right now. And permanently.

The one at the rear door looked like he was about to lose his temper for sure. And everyone else in the bar—the local people, I mean—were sort of cowering together, as if they were expecting an explosion at any moment.

I saw Meredith look at the guards too, same as me. She gave a single nod. "Palmer's right," she said.

She was still holding Nicki by the shoulders, but she lifted her hands now to her face, to her cheeks. Gently but firmly, she turned Nicki's face toward her.

"Look at me, Nicki," she said very calmly. "Nicki, look at me."

"What?" asked Nicki. "What's happening? What's . . . Are they going to kill us now?"

Holding Nicki's face in her hands, Meredith gave her a soft shake. "Quiet. Look at me. I want you to be quiet now. I want you to stop crying and be quiet."

"But . . . I don't know . . . I can't . . ."

"Yes, you can," said Meredith. "Look at me." Now, finally, Nicki did look—her crazed, terrified eyes met Meredith's clear, steady gaze. Nicki sobbed again and trembled and then seemed somehow to grow more still. Her next sob was quieter. "That's right," said Meredith with an encouraging nod. Nicki took a breath. Then another breath. "That's right," said Meredith again. She wrapped her arms around Nicki and hugged her and Nicki held on to her—grabbed her as if for dear life—and was finally quiet, trembling in Meredith's arms.

I looked up to check on the guards again. I saw one of them—the one at the front door—draw a deep breath as if he were relieved the annoying noise had stopped. The other one—the angry one at the back exit—a sort of bloated, hamster-faced, mean-looking character—went on casting his baleful glance Nicki's way. But after another second or two, he seemed to lose interest.

Palmer turned from one guard to the other, lifting his beer as if in a toast. "Que típico de una mujer, eh?" he said. *Just like a woman.*

The guards liked that. It made them smile and nod. Finally, they looked away from us.

And I was relieved. I was. But I was angry too. Suddenly, in fact, I was really angry. I guess it was a late reaction to everything that had just happened. Suddenly, I was angry at everybody and everything. Angry at Mendoza for what he'd done to Carlos and to Meredith. Angry at the gunmen for imprisoning us here. Angry at Pastor Ron for not knowing what to do. And angry at Palmer—Palmer with his arrogant smirk and his insulting talk.

"Maybe . . ." Startled out of my own thoughts, I turned at the sound of Pastor Ron's voice. He was still blinking behind his glasses as if trying to wake himself up. "Maybe if we called . . . someone . . . The US embassy in Santa Maria . . ."

My eyes lifted to the phone at the back of the bar. I'd seen it there before, sitting on the bottom shelf under the bottles of wine and whiskey. It was the oldest phone I'd ever seen. An ancient squat thing that looked like a phone in some black-and-white movie. It actually had one of those curlicue wires on the handset.

"I wouldn't try reaching for that, if I were you," said Palmer Dunn. "Mendoza gave orders to kill anyone who tried. Anyway, the Volcanoes have probably cut the connection by now."

Pastor Ron nodded dully. "If only our cells worked . . . ," he murmured.

"If only," I heard Palmer mutter into his beer.

Somehow, that did it for me. His sneering tone of voice. His disdain for everyone. Somehow, that was the thing that made my anger boil over.

I found myself standing up out of my chair. I found myself taking a step toward Palmer.

"Well, what's *your* bright idea?" I shouted at him. "If you know so much. If you're so tough. If you're so tough, why didn't you do anything? Huh? You just stood there while he . . . while he . . . You just watched TV! So, I mean, what makes you so great?" I was so angry I didn't know what I was saying. I gestured wildly at Meredith. "You didn't even help her! He pushed her around like that, like . . . like . . . He hurt her. And you just stood there! You didn't do anything!"

I know. I sounded like an idiot. But I couldn't help myself. The words just came bubbling out of me.

And Palmer—he barely glanced my way. He took one

last swig of his beer before clonking the empty bottle down on the bar.

"Well, you did something, kid, didn't you?" he said. "And how did it help?"

I started to talk again, to shout at him some more, but nothing came out. He was right. What had I done while Mendoza dragged Meredith around the room like a rag doll? I just stood there. Watching. Helpless.

"You don't get any points for good intentions," Palmer said softly.

"All right." A chair scraped. Pastor Ron stood. He seemed finally to have overcome his shock, to have regained his senses. He stood next to me. "It doesn't do any good for us to fight among ourselves." He faced Palmer. "What *is* happening here, Palmer?" he asked—and I was relieved to hear him sounding more like his usual calm and thoughtful self. "Do you know? What exactly is going on?"

It was the first thing any of us had said—or that anyone had said—that Palmer seemed to take seriously. He actually seemed to give the question some consideration before he answered.

"It's an old-fashioned revolution, Padre. Most of the countries around here have gotten over this sort of thing, but in Costa Verdes, it's been building up for years. Mendoza and his guys—the Volcanoes—that's their nickname—they're reds— or progressives, or whatever you want to call them. They figure the people who own most of the land and plantations in the country ought to share them with the other people, the peasants."

"They should!" The words broke out of Jim Nolan. "Ninety percent of the country's wealth belongs to a handful of people. It's ridiculous!"

Palmer only shrugged in answer. "Whatever. My guess is the Volcanoes are planning to slaughter themselves a bunch of plantation owners. That's the usual progressive idea. Plus, they'll bump off all the poor slobs like Carlos who haven't supported them in the past. Then they figure everything will be peaceful and fair happily ever after."

"Wait a minute!" Jim protested. "You can't just reduce this to—"

But Pastor Ron waved at him to be quiet, and he was. The pastor continued to question Palmer. "Do you think it's just happening here in Santiago?" asked Pastor Ron.

"I doubt it," said Palmer. "Mendoza's just a local thug. The main fighting must be in the capital, in Santa Maria. That's where most of the government's army is. The rebels are going to have to defeat the army if they really want to take control of the country."

"That's why he let me go, isn't it?" asked Meredith suddenly. She still had her arms around Nicki, but she turned in her chair to look at Palmer. "That's why Mendoza let me go. You reminded him that the army might win, the revolution might fail . . ."

Palmer nodded. "The last time they tried this stuff, the

United States put a hand in to help the government hold on. When it was over, when the revolutionaries failed, the people who killed or mistreated American citizens found themselves on the end of some rough justice."

"So you scared him," said Meredith, thinking it through. "You scared Mendoza into leaving me alone."

Palmer shrugged.

"Thank you, Palmer," Meredith said.

"I just told him the truth, that's all," Palmer said.

"Thank you," Meredith said again.

Palmer shifted where he stood. *He looks uncomfortable,* I thought. He didn't answer Meredith. He spoke to Pastor Ron instead: "Anyway, none of that's going to do us much good, if the rebels take the capital. The Volcanoes are plenty angry this time. And they have long memories."

"You mean, if the Volcanoes win . . . ," Pastor Ron began to say.

"If the Volcanoes win, you can bet Mendoza will be back in here in a city minute. And this time, he won't be such a nice guy about it."

That got Nicki started again. She pulled away from Meredith. "You mean . . . You mean . . . he'll kill us! He'll shoot us!"

"Ssh, Nicki." Meredith put her arms back around her. "It'll be all right."

"I'm glad you think so," said Palmer. His lip curled and the sardonic humor came back into his eyes.

"What do you think, Palmer?" asked Pastor Ron. "I mean, what do you think we should do?"

Palmer looked over at the guard by the front door, then over at the other guard at the rear. They grinned back at him unpleasantly. "Well, Padre," Palmer said, "I'm looking at two men with AK-47s. Unless you're planning to roll up a 'Coexist' bumper sticker and beat them to death with it, I'd say we're going to pretty much do whatever they tell us to do."

"It's our fault! It's just what we deserve!" Jim Nolan—who else? On his feet. Leaning in toward Palmer. His lean cheeks pink. His finger pointing. His voice bitter. "General Benitez tried to bring reform to this country. Thirty years ago. He tried to redistribute the land and we, the US, the CIA, they came down here and overthrew him. And now we're paying for it. It's all our fault."

When he spluttered to a stop, Palmer looked at him—looked at him, I thought, with a look that said, *Who is this idiot?* He seemed about to say that out loud, in fact—or something like it. But the next moment, everyone in the cantina—Americans and locals alike—stiffened as a new sound reached us from outside.

Gunfire. Not far off either. Machine-gun shots rattling in the hills around us.

"I'm guessing that's some land reform going on right now," said Palmer. "Might be a good idea to change the channel on the television set, see if we can get some news, find out what's happening in the capital. Because if the capital falls . . ."

Everyone gasped and tensed as another round of gunfire exploded outside—louder, closer this time.

Palmer didn't finish his sentence. He didn't have to. We all knew what he was going to say:

If the capital fell, if the revolutionaries won, Mendoza would come back in here and kill us all.

CHAPTER FIVE

What happened next was like a dream. If by a dream, you mean a nightmare. If by a nightmare, you mean the weirdest and scariest thing that ever happened.

Palmer turned to the old lady behind the bar. He spoke to her in a quick burst of Spanish. The lady—a tiny, stooped creature with a face like a raisin—picked up a remote control from below the bar and pointed it at the TV. The soccer game went off and the news came on. You could tell it was the news because a serious-looking man and woman were seated behind a desk looking directly into the camera. There was a map of the country behind them.

The man spoke in rapid Spanish—I couldn't understand a word of it. After a couple of minutes, the picture changed and some film came on. The film showed angry people fighting in the city streets. I assumed they were the streets of Santa Maria.

What made it all so weird—so dreamlike—so frightening—was that we could hear the gunshots on the television and at the same time, we could hear the gunshots in the hills around us. And we knew that what happened on the TV would decide what happened here. It was like watching a zombie movie and suddenly hearing a slow, thudding knock on your front door . . . The life shown on the television and real life were becoming one dangerous thing.

I stared up at the TV screen. On one end of the street, men—most of them dressed like Mendoza in fatigues with red bandannas tied around their necks or foreheads—were firing machine guns or hurling hand grenades and flaming bottles. On the other side of the street, a ragged line of soldiers cowered behind riot shields or sometimes fired back with machine guns of their own. Sometimes mobs of other people, ordinary citizens, I guess, surged forward. They seemed to be supporting the rebels. They overturned cars and threw rocks and lit fires. Everywhere, buildings were in flames.

I felt my heart pounding hard in my chest. It looked like the rebels had the people on their side. It looked like the soldiers were being overwhelmed. And I knew that if the rebels won, Mendoza would come back here. And I would be killed. Me and Pastor Ron and Meredith and Nicki and Jim—all of us. All of us would be shot dead as brutally and suddenly as Carlos the waiter. I stared at the TV and I knew this was true—and yet somehow I couldn't really get myself to believe it.

The newsman went on talking rapidly over the pictures.

"What are they . . . ?" I had to swallow—hard—before I could get the words out. "What are they saying?"

"They're saying the fighting is intense in the capital but that the army has things under control and is moving steadily toward victory . . . ," Pastor Ron translated.

"The TV stations are run by the government," Palmer said. "They say the army's winning, but it sure doesn't look like that to me."

"What do you mean?" I asked. I tried to swallow again, but I couldn't. My throat was too dry. "What do you mean?"

"Well, look at the video," said Palmer. "The army's in complete disarray. They're right outside the government compound and they're not even up to full muster. It looks to me like the army is deserting and the rebels have got the people behind them."

Nicki let out a wail of misery. "Does that mean we're going to die?"

Meredith patted her shoulder, but no one answered. A fresh round of gunfire started up outside. It wasn't in the hills this time. It was closer.

I looked nervously toward the door. "It sounds like they're fighting in the village here," I said.

Palmer snorted. "That's not fighting, pal. The fighting

here is over. Those are executions. They're killing anyone who didn't support them."

I went on staring at the door. *Executions.* Something sharp and rancid roiled in my stomach. I thought of the celebration in the plaza last night. The children singing. The women dancing. The men setting off fireworks. The priest thanking God that we had come to their village and helped them rebuild their school.

I wondered which of them—which of those men, women, and children—were being lined up against a wall and shot to death as we stood in the cantina, waiting to learn our fates.

I turned back to the television. The video was over now and they were back in the studio with the newsman and newswoman. It was kind of an awful sight. The looks on their faces . . . They were trying to go on as if nothing catastrophic were happening. But the anchorman's brown skin had gone a funny off-color. He was licking his lips between words as if his lips were as dry as my throat. The anchorwoman had turned white and looked like she was on the verge of tears.

"What . . . what are they saying now?" I barely managed to whisper.

Pastor Ron's voice didn't sound much better than mine as he translated. "They're saying they will continue to bring us the news for as long as it's possible. They're saying they won't desert their posts until the very last minute and that they have full confidence the army will restore order soon . . ."

"But they're lying," I said. "Right?"

Pastor Ron nodded. "It sounds like it, yes. Now they're saying President Morales will speak to the nation very soon."

Palmer gave a short, cynical laugh. "Yeah. From his hotel in Los Angeles," he joked sourly.

I caught a movement out of the corner of my eye. Nicki. She had drawn back from Meredith. She was staring into Meredith's eyes. The expression on her face was pitiful beyond description. The fear. The helplessness. Like a child lost in a crowd.

"I don't want to die, Meredith," she said. "I'm only seventeen."

Palmer glanced over his shoulder at her. He gave a soft derisive snort—as if to say, *Who cares how old you are? You can die anytime.* Then he turned back to the TV.

And just at that moment, there were a few bursts of static on the screen—and then the picture went out. There was nothing, not even a test pattern. Just darkness.

We all stood there—we Americans and the locals just the same. We all stood there, staring at the blank screen.

Palmer made a gesture to the old lady. She lifted the remote again. Changed the channels. Nothing. More nothing. Then the soccer game. She cycled through the channels one more time. The soccer game was the only thing playing anywhere.

She shut the TV off. The cantina was silent.

"Well . . . what does *that* mean?" I asked. "The picture just . . . I mean, it just went off like that. It just went dark.

What does that mean?" I don't know why I bothered to ask—I knew well enough what it meant. The rebels had overrun the station. Which meant they had gotten inside the government compound. Which meant they were winning, if they hadn't already won. "What . . . what does it mean?" I asked again anyway. I guess I was just hoping someone would tell me I was wrong.

No one answered. No one had to. Pastor Ron put a hand on my shoulder and gave it what was supposed to be a reassuring squeeze. I was not reassured.

"This might be a good time to pray," he said quietly. He went back to his chair. He sank into it slowly, his eyes cast down, his lips moving silently.

"Is it over?" asked Nicki, turning from Meredith to him and back to Meredith again. "Did the rebels win? Are they coming now? Are they going to kill us?"

"Stop, Nicki," Meredith said. "We don't know what's going to happen. None of us knows."

But the way she said it—well, it sounded like she *did* know.

Long, slow seconds ticked away in silence. I took Pastor Ron's advice: I prayed. Hard.

Then—horribly—my prayer was cut short. The air in the cantina seemed to rattle as gunfire exploded—right outside now—right in the plaza beyond the cantina door.

Nicki let out a short scream at the sound of it, jumping in her chair and covering her mouth with both hands. The gunfire continued. And there was cheering too. Men cheering as they fired their machine guns. There was a small front window, but it didn't show much. Just a rectangular section of the square. Now and then I saw a figure running by, but other than that, I couldn't see what was happening.

I glanced over at the guard by the front door. He was looking out the door into the street. I couldn't see what he saw, but when he turned back to the room, he was smiling. He pumped his fist at the other guard, the hamster-faced guy at the door.

Hamster Face's hamster face lit up with a hamster-faced grin. All at once—no warning at all—he let out a high-pitched *whoop* of his own. He raised his rifle into the air and pulled the trigger.

Nicki screamed again. The gunfire was deafening. Plaster came pouring down from the ceiling like snow. Hamster Face let out another burst. And now Nicki lost control of herself, screaming and screaming.

"Stop! Stop! Make him stop!" she shrieked, covering her ears with her hands. "Please! Make him stop!"

Meredith could only hold on to her while she screamed. Finally, the pounding explosions of the gun fell silent. The last bit of plaster pattered to the floor. And Nicki, still covering her ears, stopped screaming and bent forward against Meredith, sobbing instead.

That was the only sound in the room. Nicki sobbing. Nothing else for I don't know how long.

I stood where I was, looking at—well, nothing really. Just sort of staring around the room, from corner to corner, from face to face. Thoughts were racing through my mind at a crazy speed:

Wait a minute . . . wait a minute . . . this is me here. The one and only me. Will . . . good old Will from Spencer's Grove. I just came to this country to help out. I just came for a week. To build a wall. For my church. To be a good guy. I'm supposed to be going home today. Back to school. Back to ordinary life. They can't just walk in here and shoot me. Can they? For no reason? Because I'm an American? Because they don't like the way people behave in this country? I never even heard of this place before I got here. What about my mom and dad? I mean, they may be angry at each other, but they still love me . . . We're a family . . . They'd be heartbroken if they just . . . I mean, they can't just . . . kill me . . .

Can they?

That's what I was thinking when the front door opened and Mendoza walked back in.

CHAPTER SIX

When I saw him—when I saw the look on his face—the light of triumph in his eyes—I felt as if a hand were closing on my throat. I couldn't speak. I couldn't swallow. I could barely breathe.

This can't be happening. Not to me.

Then two more gunmen entered behind him. The two already in the cantina—the ones guarding the exits—moved to join them. The four men flanked Mendoza, two on either side, holding their machine guns up at their chests at the ready. As Mendoza slowly moved his gaze over the room, over our faces, the gunmen's eyes moved right along with his.

Is this it? I thought. *Are they just going to do this? Are they just going to start shooting us? Right here? Right now?*

An image flashed through my mind: a policeman coming to my house . . . telling my mother that I had been killed . . .

the shock and grief on her face . . . It was an unbearable idea.

I could still hear shooting and shouting out in the streets beyond the cantina door. A figure running by the window sometimes. But in here, there was only stillness, silence. Mendoza seemed to study each of us—one frightened, staring face after another. Some of the villagers seemed to shrink under his gaze, as if they hoped they could disappear from in front of him.

Mendoza let out a short, sharp order. Nicki gasped and started in her chair. I felt myself stiffen too, afraid that he had just commanded the gunmen to kill us all.

But no. His next words were in English.

"Everyone out but the Americans. The Americans stay."

He didn't have to tell the villagers twice. Even before he translated, the cantina was loud with the scraping of their chairs and the rumble of their footsteps as they bolted from their seats and rushed to the front door. One of the gunmen held the door open for them, grinning sadistically at their fearful faces as they raced to get out of there, to get away from Mendoza. As they fled into the streets, we heard more shooting outside and more shouting. The rebels celebrating their victory and lording their power over the villagers.

Finally, all of the locals were gone from the cantina. The only people left were we Americans, Mendoza, and his four gunmen.

In the quiet, Mendoza went on studying each of our faces.

I saw his mouth curl underneath his mustache as, finally, his eyes came to rest on Palmer Dunn.

"Well, Señor Dunn," he said. "It is over, yes? The army is finished. The capital is ours. The question is settled."

Palmer regarded the rebel coolly. He nodded. "It looks that way."

"You hold out hope? You think your American spies will bother us now? Or your fellow Marines?"

"They're not my fellow Marines. I told you."

Mendoza ignored this. He went on. "That was many years ago, after all, you know. The Cold War is over now. Your country has no Soviet Union to worry about anymore. So who cares if the people of a tiny Central American country choose a government that treats them with justice?"

To my surprise, Palmer grinned. A great big grin, as if he thought this whole thing were just some kind of joke.

"Is that what's happening?" he asked.

"Yes! Yes! It is!" This was Jim. Still on his feet. His eyes urgent. He turned to Mendoza. "He doesn't get it, Señor Mendoza—but I do!" he said. "We talked about this earlier— out in the field—don't you remember? I agree with you! With your cause! I support what you're trying to do, I just—"

"Shut up," Mendoza said to him.

Jim looked surprised. "No, I'm just trying to say—"

"Shut up," Mendoza said again.

He gestured. One of the gunmen stepped up to Jim. I held my breath in fear. Nicki let out another gasp.

But the gunman only pressed the butt of his machine gun into Jim's chest and shoved him with it.

Jim staggered backward. The back of his legs hit the edge of his chair. He sat down into the chair, hard. The gunman stood over him, scowling down at him. Jim stared up at him, frightened into silence.

The exchange had turned Mendoza's attention toward our table—and his eyes fell on Meredith again. I could see something spark in his gaze, some unfinished business, some unexpressed rage.

The rebel leader hooked his thumbs in the sides of his belt—an arrogant posture—and came swaggering toward where Meredith was sitting. He moved past me as he went, casually knocking me aside with one elbow.

"Ah, yes," he said, looking down at Meredith. "The deaf girl. The one who cannot hear the orders that I give to her."

Meredith lifted her face to him where she sat. "I hear you very plainly, Señor Mendoza," she said.

"Oh? Oh yes?" said Mendoza. He looked around at his gunmen and gave them a laugh, and they laughed with him, sharing the hilarity. "You hear me but you do not obey my commands? Is that it?"

Meredith went on looking up at him, but she didn't answer.

Mendoza reached down and put his hand under her chin—an affectionate gesture a guy might make toward his girlfriend, only she wasn't his girlfriend and it wasn't affectionate at all.

"I am asking you a question, señorita . . ."

"Please take your hands off me, Señor Mendoza," Meredith said.

Mendoza hesitated—but he didn't take his hand off her. Instead he shifted it from her chin to her cheek. He stroked her cheek with one finger.

"I am afraid you do not fully understand the situation you are in," he said to her.

"I understand," said Meredith. "Please take your hands off me."

I held my breath as I stood there watching them. I can hardly describe what I felt. I was afraid. I don't mind admitting it. I thought they were going to kill us and I didn't want to die and I was afraid. But at the same time, I wanted to knock Mendoza down—I wanted to so bad, so bad. It made me sick in my heart to see him treating Meredith like this, taunting her and trying to humiliate her like this. And to just stand there, helpless to stop him—that was the worst— almost worse than the fear of dying—to stand there with all those guns around me and not be able to do anything to help her . . .

Mendoza went right on stroking her cheek as if he hadn't heard what she said. He looked around at his gunmen. Laughed as if to ask them: *Can you believe this woman?* I could tell he had no intention of letting Meredith boss him around—certainly not while his men were watching him.

Now, he took his finger from her cheek and crouched

down in front of her. He reached out to take her hand, which was lying in her lap. I saw Meredith try to pull her hand away, but Mendoza caught it in both of his hands and held it. Crouched down like that, his eyes were level with hers. He held her hand and looked into her eyes.

"Dear girl," he said quietly—almost gently. "I have to tell this to you: you are in terrible danger here. Do you understand this?"

"Yes," said Meredith. In the quiet cantina, her clear, ringing voice was startlingly steady and calm. "I understand completely."

"These are very violent times in my country, very dangerous times. At times like these, life becomes very cheap. A person can disappear very easily, causing much grief to everyone who knows them. You understand?"

Meredith didn't answer but only gazed at him, her face stony, expressionless, as he went on holding her hand in both of his.

And I watched the two of them. Everything inside me wanted to stand up for her, but I knew if I did, I would get myself badly hurt, maybe worse. I hated myself for being a coward, but I just couldn't bring myself to speak up or move.

"On the other hand," Mendoza went on, "there is a hope. A possibility. For a woman like yourself, an attractive woman. You might be able to make a friend, you know? A powerful friend who can protect you in times of need." He smiled at her. "Señorita," he said in a tone of appeal. "There is no reason for this animosity between us when instead you could improve your situation very greatly by showing me the kind of affection you—"

Meredith spit in his face.

The shock of it. Man oh man! It was as if a lightning bolt had gone through the room. It was as if a lightning bolt had gone through *me*—pierced me head-to-toe in a single instant like a spear hurled down from heaven. I could hardly believe what I'd seen, could hardly believe that Meredith would do it—and would do it here, now, when it was sure to bring misery and pain down on her like an avalanche.

But it was real. It really happened. She spit sharply right in Mendoza's eye—and he was so startled, he let go of her hand and fell back out of his crouch, dropped down—*bang*—onto his backside on the floor.

Instantly, he scrabbled up. Leapt to his feet. His rugged face was dark with fury as he wiped the spit off it with the heel of his palm. There was this moment then—this moment captured like a snapshot in my memory—when he stood there looming over Meredith like some enormous storm and she sat looking up at him, with her eyes as clear as ever, her face as calm, as if nothing he did could have any effect on her whatsoever.

Then Mendoza barked out a word in Spanish—a word I didn't know—some curse word, I'm sure. And with a growl of rage, he drew back his hand to slap her.

I grabbed his arm. I didn't know I was going to do it. I

didn't even think about it. I just leapt forward and grabbed hold of his wrist with both my hands to hold him back.

It was the first time I'd ever heard a note of fear enter Meredith's voice. "No, Will, don't!" she cried out.

But it was too late. One of Mendoza's gunmen smacked me in the face with the butt of his machine gun.

No one had ever hit me before, not ever. It was awful. An awful feeling. A jarring trauma through my whole body. It drove out everything, every other thought. I went stumbling backward helplessly, and the next moment the gunman—or maybe another gunman, I don't know—hit me again, driving the machine-gun butt into my stomach, knocking the air out of me.

I tumbled sideways to the floor, another shock going through my body as I hit. Someone screamed—Nicki, I guess. A chair scraped. I heard Pastor Ron say, "No more—please!"

Clutching my stomach, groaning, I looked up and saw Mendoza. From that angle, he seemed enormous, a looming tower of pure rage. His face contorted in fury. He had already wiped the spit off himself, but he did it again and then again, as if it were stuck on him and he couldn't get it off.

Then he let out a roar and he kicked me.

I tried to protect myself, covering myself with my arms, but the tip of his heavy boot drove into my gut and then pulled back and drove into my forehead. I felt a double explosion of pain, saw a double explosion of light and then sparkling darkness. I couldn't catch my breath. I couldn't think about anything except how much I hoped this would stop, how I would do anything—say anything—to make it stop.

When I managed to look again, tears blurred my vision. I saw Mendoza. I saw him pull the pistol from his holster. He was going to shoot me where I lay.

A new prayer flashed through my mind: *Please be with me, God*. I was pretty sure I was about to be making that request face-to-face.

But just then Meredith jumped to her feet. She made a move to rush to me where I was lying on the floor. I think she was going to throw herself between me and the bullet. But she never got the chance. Instead of shooting me, Mendoza pulled his pistol back as if he were going to smack her in the head with it.

This time it was Pastor Ron who stopped him. He got between him and Meredith and grabbed Meredith by the shoulders. He pushed her away from me and away from Mendoza. He settled her back into her chair, murmuring something to her I couldn't hear.

Breathing hard, the pistol still lifted in his hand, Mendoza turned back to me. I could see he was wild with rage. He still didn't shoot me, though. He turned away. He started stalking around the room, stomping here and there as if he weren't sure which way to go. He started shouting at everyone, turning from side to side.

"Is there someone else? Eh? Someone else who wishes to

defy me? Do you want to see what happens? Do you want to have a conversation about it? You will have a conversation with a bullet, I tell you. Who wants to?"

He stopped. His back was to me. He seemed to have settled on a target for his wrath.

"What about you, Señor Dunn?" he asked. "Do you have something to say to me? Eh? What do you have to say?"

There was a pause. I couldn't see Palmer from where I was lying. I couldn't really see anyone, curled up on the floor as I was with my arms wrapped around my throbbing stomach and blood dripping down from my forehead into my eye. But I heard Palmer's voice, all right. He sounded—well, he sounded exactly the same as he sounded before. It was exasperating. He still was all cool and comical—as if he didn't have a care in the world—definitely as if he didn't care about what happened to me or Meredith or any of the others.

"You're a tough guy, Mendoza," he drawled in that sardonic way of his. "For a minute there, I wasn't sure you and your four gunmen were going to be able to take that teenager. But you took him, all right. You surely did. Mucho macho, amigo. I salute you."

I managed to lift my head up from the floor a little and got a better look at Mendoza where he was standing in the center of the cantina, facing Palmer, his back to me, his gun hand by his side. I saw his shoulders rise and fall as he breathed heavily in his rage.

Then he looked around him. He seemed to be at a

loss—not knowing whom he should scream at next. Then he waved his gun in the air and shouted orders in Spanish.

Every time he did that, my guts turned to water: I didn't understand the words. He could have been saying, *Open fire* or *Kill them all*. I didn't know whether in the next moment the gunmen would spray the room with bullets.

But no—not yet.

Someone—one of the gunmen—grabbed the back of my collar. I felt myself choking as he pulled up on me, trying to haul me to my feet. I worked desperately to get my legs under me before he strangled me. My legs were weak and wobbly—but somehow I managed to stand.

The gunman who had me in his grip gave me a hard push. I stumbled across the room toward the bar where Palmer was standing. I staggered into the bar and hurt, dazed, dizzy, I started to fall again. Palmer grabbed my arm roughly and steadied me on my feet.

Breathing hard, leaning against the bar, I looked around and saw the others: Pastor Ron and Meredith and Nicki and Jim. The gunmen were standing over them, shouting at them, waving their machine guns in their faces, forcing all of them out of their chairs to their feet.

Now they were prodding them with their gun barrels, herding them toward the bar, toward where I was standing with Palmer. My head thick with pain and my eyes still blurring with tears, I saw my friends' faces as they hurried in front of the relentless guns. Nicki was weeping, her legs so weak under her she could barely walk. Meredith stood uncannily straight, her face uncannily still as she kept her arm around Nicki's shoulders, holding her as steady as she could as they were both jostled forward. Pastor Ron seemed dazed, in shock, his face blank, his eyes blinking rapidly behind his glasses as he stumbled toward me. Jim had his hands up in the air like a guy being robbed. He kept saying, "Okay, okay, I get it," as the gunmen pushed and prodded him—pushed and prodded all of them—with the barrels of their weapons.

Finally, we were all huddled together against the bar. Again, I thought this might be it, might be the end. I stood there helpless and dazed and bent over in pain, waiting for the gunfire to begin. I prayed God would comfort my parents, but I didn't know how much comfort they would ever find.

Mendoza stood in the center of the cantina and looked at us—a black look, his eyes murderous.

"Lock them up!" he shouted.

CHAPTER SEVEN

The next few moments were a terrifying chaos. The gunmen rushed toward us, shouting gruffly in Spanish,
prodding us in our backs with their gun barrels, striking
at our heads with their fists and open hands. Our backpacks—everything we had—were left piled up in a corner of
the cantina as they forced us out of the room, out the back
entrance, into a dark hall. I saw Palmer Dunn up in front
of me, moving at a quick but steady walk, keeping ahead of
the blows. But the rest of us were all bunched together, and
though I knew there were only four gunmen, they seemed
to be everywhere, on every side of us. Their shouts engulfed
me. My fear and pain engulfed me. I staggered along, hardly
knowing where I was.

Now there was a staircase. Now we were being chased up
the stairs. I heard Nicki wailing like a lost child. I heard Jim

saying, "Okay, okay, okay," over and over again. I stumbled and went down, cracking my shin against a riser. The next moment I was struck on the side of the head—by a fist or a gun butt, I'm not sure which. Panicked, I scrabbled to my feet, leapt forward, stumbled again, nearly fell again, but finally made my way up, following the feet of Pastor Ron above me.

Another hall. More running. More shouting. More blows. I was beginning to feel sick. My stomach, aching from Mendoza's kicks, was churning and turning. I know it sounds funny under the circumstances—I mean, the circumstances being we were probably all about to be killed—but I had this terrible fear that I was going to throw up and humiliate myself in front of Meredith. I guess that wasn't the way I wanted to spend my last minutes on earth.

The next thing I knew, I saw an open door in front of me. We were being pushed through it so fast that we all sort of collided together. I remember my shoulder went into Pastor Ron and I was jostled aside and hit the wall. Then Pastor Ron went through the door and one of the gunmen shoved me through it after him.

Through blood and tears, through the whirling confusion in my head, I saw a room—one of the rooms in the hotel above the cantina. I saw a window and a wooden bed and a bureau with a mirror on it. I saw the dim yellow light in the ceiling, a bulb protected by a frosted glass globe that was dark with the bodies of the dead insects trapped inside.

I saw it all swirling and turning around me. And then—
it was as if the world were a video and someone slowly turned
down the volume, then snapped it off—everything seemed
to grow dim and distant.

Then it was gone.

※

I had lost consciousness, I guess.

I opened my eyes. The first thing I saw was Meredith.
A sweet sight: her face looking down at me. Her pale eyes
were so clear, her face so calm, her smile so gentle, I thought
everything that had just happened must've been some kind
of dream. Really, that's what I thought—I thought maybe I
got sick or something, had a fever, you know, and had this
whole elaborate hallucination about how we were going
home and suddenly people were shooting people and beating
me up and . . . it couldn't have happened that way! Meredith
wouldn't be smiling down at me like that, wouldn't look so
calm, if it had happened that way.

Then I looked around me and realized: no, it had not
been a dream. It was a nightmare—and it was all true.

We were in the hotel room above the cantina, like I said.
I was lying on the bed, still in my clothes, still wearing my
sneakers. Meredith was sitting next to me, hovering over me.
I heard Nicki sniffling and crying somewhere. Guys talking
in low voices—Pastor Ron and Jim, I thought.

Meredith lifted a washcloth. Put it to my face. It was wet with warm water. She pressed it against the place above my eyebrow where Mendoza had kicked me. It hurt when she touched it—a lot. I flinched with the pain.

"All right," Meredith murmured. "Just let me clean it out so it doesn't get infected."

I let her. I tried to keep still and not show how much it hurt. I watched her face. She looked so pretty and so kind, I wanted to just lie there and look at her forever.

"What happened?" I managed to ask her after a while. "Did I faint or something?"

"Mm-hm." She went on wiping my forehead. I could feel the crusts of blood coming away. "Mendoza kicked you in the head pretty hard."

"Yeah." The whole thing was coming back to me. "I remember."

"That was a silly thing for you to do," Meredith told me. "Grabbing him like that. I don't want you to do anything like that again. Do you understand?"

I looked up at her. I wondered what color her eyes were. Kind of brown, but so pale they were nearly colorless, nearly clear. "I had to," I told her.

"No," she said. "You didn't."

"He was going to hit you."

"I can take care of myself."

"You can't beat up Mendoza."

"Neither can you," she said. She turned away to dip the

washcloth in a basin on the bedside table. I saw the blood come off the cloth and stain the basin water brownish red.

"Are you kidding me?" I said. "Didn't you see the way I pounded his boot with my head? The guy's gonna be limping for days."

She gave a short little snuff of laughter. Turned back and set the washcloth to my head again. "Ha-ha. Very funny. All right, I'm almost done," she added as I flinched again. "It was very brave of you, I know. And I'm grateful. But I'm serious: don't do anything like that again, Will. I'll be all right."

I didn't answer. I just lay there looking up at her as she cleaned my face. On the one hand, I wanted to do anything she asked me to do, everything she asked me to do. On the other hand, I knew if Mendoza or anyone else lifted a hand to her again, I'd do just the same as I did before. And the time after that. And the time after that. They'd have to kill me to stop me.

For now, though, I wanted to just go on lying there, just go on looking up at her, up at those pale eyes, feeling the warm cloth on my face. But after another second or two, I forced myself to push my feet off the bed and sit up.

The room tilted and turned a little as a fresh wave of dizziness washed over me.

"Lie back down," said Meredith, touching my shoulder.

"I'll be all right," I told her.

Finally, the room grew still. I looked around me.

I saw Nicki. She was sitting in a cushioned chair in one

corner. Slouched there with her head dropped back on the rest, her eyes closed. Her body was still heaving every now and again with sobs and she was trembling weakly, but she seemed barely aware of where she was.

Pastor Ron and Jim were standing by a window, the bright sunlight slanting in on them, turning their figures to hazy silhouettes. They were both looking outside, conferring with each other in low voices.

What about Palmer? I wondered. Where was he? I saw him. Just outside the window, there was a narrow balcony. Palmer was standing on it, his hands on the wooden railing. I could see the white wall of the plaza church just beyond him.

"What's happening?" I asked.

Pastor Ron glanced over at me. "They've locked us in here. Put guards outside the door and outside. They're deciding what they're going to do with us, I guess."

I started as a round of gunfire went off in the streets. There was cheering and shouting out there too.

"What *will* they do with us, do you think?" I asked.

Pastor Ron didn't answer, only shook his head. He turned to the window, to the balcony, to Palmer.

"What do you think, Palmer?" he asked. "You've spent more time in this country than any of us. You seem to know the way things are. What do you think the rebels are planning to do?"

Palmer glanced over his shoulder at the pastor, looking back into the room as if he'd only just now remembered the rest of us were here. He came off the balcony, stepped inside, gestured toward the street with his thumb.

"Right now, it looks like their plan is to get drunk and shoot the place up," he said. "By way of celebrating the victory of justice over oppression."

"Yes, well, no doubt. But I meant, what do you think Mendoza is planning to do with us?" Pastor Ron asked.

Palmer leaned his back against the wall, his hands behind him. He seemed to give the question some consideration. "It's not really up to Mendoza. That's my guess, anyway. My guess is if it were up to Mendoza, we'd all be dead right now." He lifted his chin in an ironic gesture at Meredith. "Especially after Lady Liberty over there spit in his eye like that."

"I'm sorry if I made the situation worse," Meredith said.

Palmer shrugged. Shook his head. "If I was you, lady, I'd've done the same."

We all jumped a little as another round of shooting and drunken laughter rose to us from the plaza below.

"Well, if the decision isn't up to Mendoza, who *is* it up to?" Pastor Ron asked.

Palmer thought some more. "Mendoza's right about the United States. Now that the Cold War's over, which group of thugs runs Costa Verdes doesn't mean a whole lot to us. We've got enough on our hands fighting the Islamos. I kind of doubt we'll get involved in any serious way down here. Still . . . a bunch of dead American missionaries, or whatever you guys are—that's gonna make headlines, make things uncomfortable for the rebels as they're trying to set up their new government. I don't think Mendoza wants to start that firestorm without an official go-ahead from Cobar."

"Cobar?" asked Pastor Ron.

"Fernandez Cobar. He's the leader of the whole business. He's the guy who'll make the speech from the balcony after they've chased President Morales out of the country."

"Wait," said Jim, suddenly perking up. "Fernandez Cobar? *The* Fernandez Cobar?"

"Only one I know," said Palmer.

"But he's terrific!" Jim said. He looked around at all of us, a new hope glowing in his eyes. "No, really. I read his book. *Soldier of Justice.* He's a great man. A genuine freedom fighter."

Palmer chuckled. "Well . . . I guess. If by 'genuine freedom fighter' you mean soulless psycho killer."

"Soulless . . . ? No!" said Jim. "No. That's not right. Not Fernandez Cobar. The man is brilliant. He writes op-eds for all the big newspapers!"

"Okay," Palmer drawled. "I'll split the difference with you. Let's say he's a soulless op-ed-writing psycho killer. He wouldn't be the first. And Mendoza's not much better. They pretend they're killing for the great cause, but it's the killing they love."

"So our fate is in the hands of a bunch of crazy murderers," I said.

"That's ridiculous!" said Jim fiercely. He gestured angrily

at Palmer. "He's just . . . he's talking nonsense. Racist nonsense. He doesn't know *what* he's talking about. I'm telling you: I've read Cobar's book . . ."

He caught his breath, steadied himself. Glanced at Palmer quickly as if he were afraid the pilot would get angry and attack him. But Palmer just went on leaning against the wall and watched Jim, smiling. Jim continued speaking more quietly.

"Look. This country has been the victim of foreign conquest and corporate greed for nearly five hundred years. All the land and wealth are in the hands of a few people. Thirty years ago, a man—a great man—named General Benitez tried to take power and change all that. But the United States claimed that it was all some kind of Soviet plot and we sent agents and soldiers down here to overthrow him. Kill him. That's why Mendoza's so angry at us. That's why they're *all* so angry at us and treating us the way they are. What? Don't laugh!"

This last part of Jim's speech was to Palmer, who stood pinching the bridge of his nose between two fingers as he shook his head and chuckled quietly to himself. After a moment, Palmer looked up, still smiling.

"Sorry," he said. "I guess I'm kind of starved for entertainment."

Containing his anger, Jim appealed to the rest of us. "These people—they're not just some . . . bunch of bloodthirsty savages from some primitive country, like he seems to think. These are committed men trying to bring justice to their people. If we reason with them . . . If we can explain that we understand their fight, that we . . . we sympathize . . . they're not going to just . . . kill us. Like animals. Why would they?"

Pastor Ron took a deep breath. He looked at Palmer. "He's right, Palmer. What reason do they have to kill us? How does it benefit them? We haven't done anything to them—we specifically, I mean."

Palmer only answered him with another shrug. "Hey, do what you gotta do, Padre," he said. And with drawling sarcasm he added, "You go right on downstairs and tell Mendoza you sympathize with his great cause. And don't forget to mention you read Cobar's op-eds in the newspaper."

"We will," said Jim defiantly. "That's exactly what we'll do." But I noticed he didn't move an inch.

Pastor Ron nodded. "Well, it *is* better than just sitting here, isn't it? Just waiting here for them all to get drunk and do something crazy." He looked around at the rest of us—Nicki and Meredith and me. I could tell he was trying to convince himself. "I mean, Jim's right, these people aren't monsters. They're human beings, right? They'll listen to reason."

Palmer sighed. "That's one theory," he muttered.

He came off the wall and stepped back out onto the balcony, looking down at the plaza below. We heard another shuddering round of gunfire from down there. We heard some women screaming. Another ragged round of shouts and cheering.

Pastor Ron looked around at us. "They're just getting drunker and drunker down there. Which means the situation is just getting more and more dangerous. I think someone has to go down and talk to them sooner rather than later, before they're too far gone to listen." He glanced over at Jim for support.

"I think you're right," Jim said. "I'm telling you: these are principled people. The way they've been treated—the way our country has treated them—they have every right to be angry. But that doesn't mean we can't appeal to their sense of justice. It's a hunger for justice that made them rise up in the first place."

Pastor Ron nodded as Jim talked, but when he turned my way I could see he was still undecided. His wavering gaze came to rest on Meredith.

"What do you think, Meredith?" he asked her. "What do you think we should do?"

She was sitting beside me on the edge of the bed. I turned to her, to her profile. She wasn't looking at Pastor Ron. She was looking past him, at the balcony, at Palmer.

"Palmer," she said.

He turned to look at her over his shoulder.

"You think they're going to kill us, don't you?"

He nodded slowly. "Seems the most likely outcome, yeah."

"You don't strike me as the sort of man who's just going to stand by and wait for that to happen."

He turned around, leaning back against the balcony

railing. He gave an easy, casual smile. "Well, now, that's interesting. Just what sort of man *do* I strike you as?"

There was a long silence. I watched Meredith as she studied him. But she didn't answer. She shifted her gaze instead to Pastor Ron.

"I think it might be best to wait, Pastor."

Pastor Ron lifted his hands from his sides. "Wait for what? Listen to them. Listen to what's happening out there."

As I sat watching her, I saw Meredith's eyes shift—from Pastor Ron to Palmer on the balcony and back to Pastor Ron again.

"If these men are as sadistic and murderous as Palmer says they are—"

"They're not," Jim insisted.

"If they are, trying to reason with them would be the worst thing you could do."

The pastor seemed confused by this. "How can it ever be wrong to try to reason with people, Meredith?"

"It's just human nature," she said. "When people are full of that sort of anger and"—she searched for the word—"*wickedness*, the sound of reason strikes them as an accusation. You'll only make Mendoza angrier still—especially if he's been drinking."

"It's ridiculous. It's ridiculous," said Jim. "I'm telling you, if you'd read Cobar's book as I have . . ."

"Well then, why don't you go?" I said to him. I probably should've kept my mouth shut. But, to be honest, Jim was beginning to annoy me. I'd seen Mendoza—we'd all seen him with our own eyes. Murdering Carlos in cold blood. Abusing Meredith. Threatening everyone. Maybe it was true there'd been injustice in his country—I didn't know. Maybe his friend Cobar wrote great articles in the newspaper. I hadn't read them. All I knew for sure was what I'd seen for myself—and if Mendoza was some kind of rebel saint, well, I was Spider-Man. "If you're so sure Mendoza's a freedom fighter who'll listen to reason, why don't *you* be the one to go talk to him?" I said to Jim.

Jim's mouth opened and closed once or twice before he answered me. But then he said, "All right, I will. I will."

But—lucky for him—before he could even take a step to the door, Pastor Ron put a hand on his arm to stop him.

"No," he said. "That's absurd. Jim's sixteen. I'm responsible here. I'm responsible for all of you. I'll go."

"Pastor . . . ," said Meredith.

"I'll just . . . I'll just talk to him, that's all. I promise I won't make him angry, Meredith. I'll just explain that we're not his enemies and that, you know, if he lets us go, it'll show everyone how merciful and just he is. It will help the rebel cause."

Behind him, I saw Palmer shake his head and turn around, back toward the balcony rail. He had stopped paying attention to us and was studying the plaza again.

Pastor Ron stood where he was another second. He looked around at all of us—as if he was hoping maybe one of us would talk him out of his idea. No one did. Finally, he walked to the door.

Meredith stood up and watched him go. "Pastor Ron—really—Palmer's right—don't," she said.

"C'mon, Pastor," I said. "Really. We saw what Mendoza did. These guys are nuts. It's too dangerous."

"They're not nuts," Jim said grumpily.

But Pastor Ron didn't respond to any of us. He took a deep breath, gathering his courage. Then he knocked on the door. A gruff voice barked at him from the other side. Pastor Ron murmured softly through the door in Spanish.

Meredith looked back at Palmer on the balcony. "Palmer," she said. "Don't let him do this. Stop him."

Palmer didn't even turn around, didn't even look at her. Just went on doing what he was doing, namely, looking down over the railing.

There was another burst of gunfire out there.

Then the door opened. A gunman—a guard—was there. He reached in and grabbed Pastor Ron roughly by the arm, dragged him out into the hall, and shut the door behind him.

CHAPTER EIGHT

The sound of the door locking was loud in the silent room. I looked at Meredith where she stood. I could see how worried she was.

"He'll be all right," I said to her.

I heard Palmer snort out on the balcony.

Meredith took a deep breath. She tried to smile at me, without much success. "I hope so," she said.

"They won't kill him, will they?" asked Nicki, in tears. She had lifted her head from the back of the chair. She was looking around as if she'd just woken up from a deep sleep. She looked awful. All her glamour and prettiness were gone. Her face was bloated and streaked, covered with makeup stains. "They won't kill Pastor Ron, will they?" And she started to cry again, putting her face in her hands. "I can't stand this anymore. I can't stand it."

"It's going to be okay," said Jim—but he didn't sound as confident as he did before when he was talking politics. He kept watching the door through which Pastor Ron had gone. Staring at it, as if he could see through it to what was happening.

Meredith turned around and faced the balcony. "Palmer," she said.

He glanced back at her. "What did you want me to do?" he asked her. "Knock him down? The man's an adult. He makes his own decisions."

Meredith didn't respond to this at all. She just asked him: "What are you going to do now?"

Palmer drew a hand along his stubbly jaw, as though he were considering her question. He came inside. There was a small wooden desk against one wall, a wooden chair in front of it. He grabbed the chair, turned it around backward, and straddled it. He gave Meredith a comical look, closing one eye and squinting up at her through the other.

"Who says I'm going to do anything?" he asked.

Meredith didn't answer and Palmer didn't seem to expect her to, because he just went on.

"I can't see my van from here," he told her. "It's old—it doesn't like coming up these hills—so I parked it down in the dirt at the bottom of the road. I can't see it—but I think I'd be able to see the smoke if they'd set it on fire, so I'm thinking it may still be there, may still be in one piece . . ."

"You're going to go get it," said Meredith.

"I'm going to try. If I can get out of here, if I can get to my plane, I might be able to fly across the border before the whole country goes up in smoke."

Meredith nodded slowly. "And what about the rest of us?" she asked.

Palmer gave another one of his ironic shrugs. "Well, I guess the rest of you will all be set free after the padre talks sweet reason to the freedom fighter for justice, right?"

"Stop it," said Meredith softly.

Palmer gave a half smile, but he dropped the sarcasm. "I'm not responsible for the rest of you, lady," he said. "You make your own decisions. Do what you want. I'm not waiting around for you to make up your minds."

I saw a tinge of red come into Meredith's cheeks. "What *can* we do? We can't come with you. We couldn't keep up. Nicki couldn't . . ." She didn't finish, only gestured toward where Nicki sat, limp and exhausted with her face buried in her hands.

Palmer gave Nicki a long, slow look before he turned back to Meredith. "Just as well," he said. "I'm a lot more likely to slip past these clowns on my own."

"Then what?" I asked. I was only beginning to comprehend what Palmer was saying. As I did, I felt another flash of anger in me. I stood up off the bed. "Then you—what?—just drive off and get in your airplane and fly for the border?"

"Something like that."

"And leave us here alone? Just leave us here?"

I felt something clutch in my stomach when Palmer's eyes met mine. I saw nothing but laughter in them.

"You're not my problem, kid," he said. "I'm just the pilot."

I tried to answer him, but I was so appalled, nothing would come out. I just stood there spluttering like an idiot. "I . . . I . . . I . . ." I looked to Meredith for help, but she went on watching Palmer, her lips pressed tightly together, her cheeks pink. "I can't believe this!" I finally managed to say.

I stalked out onto the balcony. I needed some air. I needed to get away from that room. It felt like a death trap. Because I guess that's exactly what it was.

I stood out there on the narrow platform, my hands on the railing. I was looking down at a broad alley between the hotel and the church. The sun was coming down on me from an angle as it sank toward the blue, misty mountains, which I could just make out at the alley's end to my left. I couldn't see the end of the alley to my right, but I knew it led into the coffee fields and the jungle beyond. Directly across from me was the white wall of the church, its narrow windows, its open Spanish-style bell tower with the cross on top. There were two men standing against the wall—two men in fatigues with machine guns strapped over their shoulders. They were passing a bottle of some kind of liquor back and forth between them.

I jerked back a little as another blast of gunfire went off on the street. From where I was standing, I could just see a small portion of the plaza. Now and again, someone would pass through my field of vision. Once I saw a woman clutching a child—she ran by in terror. Then there was a soldier, brandishing his weapon and stumbling along with a wide drunken strut.

When I looked in the other direction, I could see smoke—black smoke—rising into a sky that was already turning gray in preparation for the afternoon thunderstorms. I realized the smoke had to be coming from the nearby coffee plantation. I guessed Mendoza and his men had set the big house on fire. Probably killed the family that owned the land. Justice. Progress.

I looked down—down at the two men drinking in the alley below me—down and over at the turmoil that appeared to me in brief glimpses in the square. I didn't see how Palmer thought he was going to get down there, get past all the gunmen to his van. I knew I couldn't do it. And I knew he was right—he couldn't do it with us in tow. If he was going to have any chance of escape, he'd have to go alone.

But I didn't care if he was right or not. I was angry at him for talking about abandoning us. Just leaving us here to die at Mendoza's hands.

"If you're going," I heard Meredith say behind me, "I think you should go."

She was talking to Palmer—and now I heard his answer.

"No. It's too soon. They're not drunk enough yet. There must be thirty of them out there—thirty men with machine guns. One of me—and I'm unarmed. They're going to have to be awfully smashed for me to make any kind of a run for it at all."

Meredith answered. Her voice was still steady, but I could hear the urgency in it. "I think we both know that Pastor Ron doesn't have much time, Palmer."

"That doesn't change the facts. If I go out there now, I'll be killed."

"If you don't, you won't be in time to help him."

"Who said I was going to help him?"

There was a long silence between them. I stood on the balcony, my back to the room. I watched the two gunmen drinking, chatting, and laughing below me. One was leaning drunkenly against the church wall. The other wiped his mouth with his hand and staggered. He looked unsteady on his feet, like he might topple over any second.

"A moment ago," Meredith said behind me, "you asked me what sort of man I thought you were. Did you really want to know?"

"Sure," said Palmer ironically. "It'd pass the time."

"I think you're an exceptional man. I think you're a hero."

Palmer laughed—but Meredith went right on speaking over his laughter.

"Something's happened that made you bitter—I see that. And I see that you think you can get back at the world for whatever it is, that you're telling the world to go hang itself. And I can see it confuses you how that just makes your bitterness worse and worse."

I kept staring out over the balcony, but I wasn't seeing anything now. I was just listening—listening to Meredith's voice. The stuff she was saying to Palmer—it made me feel— I don't know—bad somehow. Maybe *jealous* is the word I want. I couldn't imagine her ever telling me that I was exceptional. A hero . . .

But Palmer only laughed at her again. "Wow," he said. "You sure have a lot to say on a lot of subjects. Are you gonna spit in my eye now too?"

"No," said Meredith. "But I am going to tell you one more thing."

"I'll bet you are."

"I'm going to tell you that you're about to do something very dangerous."

"Oh, I think I figured that out all by myself."

"I don't mean that," said Meredith. "I don't mean just getting shot."

"That sounds dangerous enough for me."

"I mean if you reach your van—if you reach your plane— if you get away from here, get out of this country—and if you leave us to die because you think the world has mistreated you and it can go hang—you're going to lose the man you were made to be. Not just misplace him, as you have now, Palmer. But I mean lose him, really, forever."

It was weird. I felt a real tightness in my throat as I listened to her. I'd never heard anyone talk like that before. So simple, so straightforward, so sure of herself like that, so sure of what she knew. And again, in a weird way, I sort of wished it was me she was talking to . . .

But Palmer answered in his sarcastic drawl, "Wow! Lady Liberty! What a piece of work you are. That's a lot of fancy talk just to get a man to risk his life for you."

"Not for me."

"Oh no! Sure. Not you. You don't care about yourself at all. You're not even afraid, right?"

"Look at me, Palmer," Meredith answered in her calm, quiet voice. "Do I look afraid?"

There was silence. I couldn't believe it: it sounded as if Palmer was finally lost for a smart reply. Out on the balcony, I found I had been holding my breath the last few seconds. I let it out now.

"Whatever," Palmer said then. "All I know is that those guys out there aren't drunk enough yet or distracted enough for me to make my move. And if you'll forgive me, I don't feel like getting riddled with machine-gun bullets for the sake of your high principles. And even if you won't forgive me."

I waited for Meredith to answer, but it seemed the conversation was over. I started to turn away from the railing, to head back into the room. But before I could, I saw something so horrible it froze me to the spot.

"Oh," I heard myself say. "Oh no."

A chair scraped in the hotel room. A second later Palmer was standing at my shoulder right behind me. Then

Meredith was at my other shoulder. Jim and Nicki were there too, pressing in to get a glimpse.

We all stood together and stared down into the alley. What we saw made me feel as if my heart had turned to ashes.

Two rebels, machine guns strapped over their shoulders, came marching into the alley. They were dragging Pastor Ron between them.

CHAPTER NINE

Pastor Ron had been beaten badly. His glasses were gone. His eyes were dull. His mouth hung open. His face was covered in blood and bruises. He couldn't walk on his own anymore—that's why the gunmen were dragging him. His feet went out behind him weakly as they hauled him down the alley. He wasn't even trying to move on his own steam. He was barely conscious.

Nicki screamed, "Oh no! Oh no! Oh no!"

At the sound of her voice, one of the two rebels glanced up at us on the balcony. He smiled. It was a grim, terrible smile. I knew in my heart that we were finished. All of us.

Her voice high and thin and filled with tears, Nicki cried, "They're not going to kill him, are they? Are they? They can't just kill him."

"No, no, they won't do that," said Jim.

||||||||||||||||||||||||||||||

Palmer looked around, looked at Meredith. I saw their eyes meet and I could almost hear the ideas passing silently between them. Of course they were going to kill him. That's exactly what they were going to do. And once Mendoza had shed blood, once he'd killed one of us—and a clergyman, no less—he would have to kill us all. He had nothing to gain by keeping the rest of us alive to bear witness to what he had done.

Desperately, without thinking, I shouted at Palmer, "Do something! You have to do something!"

Palmer only sneered at me as if that were the stupidest thing he'd ever heard. I wanted to slug him.

But Meredith said softly, "There's nothing he can do, Will. There's nothing any of us can do."

Whatever I was going to shout next died on my tongue. I knew if Meredith said this, it was true.

Nothing we can do. The idea was horrible to me.

I turned and looked down helplessly into the alley.

The soldiers dragged Pastor Ron directly under us. One of them barked orders to the two gunmen who were drinking against the wall. The drunken gunmen snapped to unsteady attention. The one with the bottle tossed it into the dust. Then both men fell in step with the other two rebels. All four of them continued to march Pastor Ron toward the alley's far end.

Nicki kept screaming and crying, "What are they going to do? What are they going to do?"

Jim kept saying, "They can't . . . They won't . . . They can't just . . ."

I didn't say anything. I couldn't say anything anymore. I felt as if there were a rock in the middle of my throat. Pastor Ron had come to our church about six years ago, when I was ten. I remembered him visiting the Sunday school to tell us Bible stories. He was always really nice and funny with little kids and we loved him. I remembered him shaking my hand on the receiving line after the service and telling me how much I'd grown. I remembered him saying the prayers at my grandfather's funeral . . .

And now—now there was nothing we could do for him.

We stood on the balcony and watched as the four rebel gunmen dragged him to the end of the alley. There, they turned the corner around the church and went out of sight.

I wanted to pray, but I didn't know what to pray. I just kept thinking the name of God over and over again. Finally, I just held my breath. I guess we all held our breaths. It felt to me as if the world itself had held its breath.

A long, silent second passed.

Then there was gunfire—and Nicki screaming.

CHAPTER TEN

I t was the worst moment of my life.

Nicki reeled back into the room, screaming and screaming. Babbling words through hysterical tears: "What's happening? Why won't anybody help us? Oh, they killed him! They killed him! What's going to happen to us?"

I turned and saw Meredith rush after her. She grabbed Nicki by the shoulders. Nicki struggled wildly in her grip, her head going back and forth, her hair flying.

"Let me go!" she screamed. "No! No! No! They killed him! I have to get out of here! I have to! I can't stand it!"

"Stop it! Stop it, Nicki!" Meredith said sharply. She shook her. "Have faith! Have courage! Stop!"

Nicki did stop—for a moment. She stared at Meredith through big eyes ringed with black mascara. Her mouth hung open. "Faith?" she asked, her voice breaking. "Courage?"

And then a light of understanding seemed to dawn in her. "Because they're going to kill us next, aren't they? That's why you're talking about faith and courage! They killed Pastor Ron and they're going to kill us next!"

Nicki was winding herself up to another fit. But Meredith took her face in her hands, held it hard, forcing Nicki to look at her.

"Nicki," Meredith commanded. "Look at me. Do what I tell you. Have faith. Have courage."

Trapped in her grip, Nicki could only go on staring at her. "Why?" she asked. "Why should I?"

"Because they're all we've got," Meredith told her.

Nicki stared at her another second, uncomprehending. Then she cried out, "I can't, Meredith! I can't! I can't!" And she collapsed, weeping, into Meredith's arms.

Jim, meanwhile, had wandered off the balcony into the room like a man in a trance. He was walking in aimless circles over the small open space of the floor, obviously in shock. He walked right past Meredith and Nicki as if they weren't there. He was muttering to himself in confusion.

"How . . . why did . . . they must've . . . they must've thought . . ."

For a moment, I stood watching him. I was also numb and dazed with shock and horror and grief. But then my anger came back—it came back with a vengeance. Before I could stop myself, I rushed into the room and planted myself in Jim's wandering path.

"You did this!" I shouted at him. "You told him to go! 'Go talk to him,' you said. 'They're not monsters.' You told him!"

Jim came to a standstill. He stood and gaped at me as if he couldn't comprehend what I was saying. That only made me angrier still. I don't know what I would've done next or what terrible thing I would have said next. My fists were clenched at my sides. Some awful words were about to explode out of me.

"Will!" said Meredith.

I turned to her. She had her arms around Nicki, who was sobbing against her.

"Don't," Meredith said. "It's not his fault."

"He told Pastor Ron . . . ," I began to protest.

"Pastor Ron was a grown man who had the courage to do what he thought was right. And what happened isn't his fault either. We're surrounded by bad men and they have guns and we don't and those are just the facts. This—this was coming from the start. There's nothing we can do but face it as well as we can."

I tried to take that in, tried to understand the magnitude of what she was saying. But I never had the chance.

Before I could think it through, before I could react at all, the door came flying open and Mendoza came in with four gunmen behind him.

Nicki screamed again and started up out of Meredith's embrace. She backed away from the intruders in fear. I found myself doing the same—backing away—my feet moving automatically, outside my will. Jim did the same thing. It was useless—there was nowhere to go—but we couldn't help ourselves.

Only Meredith stayed where she was. Still and erect in the center of the room. Looking at Mendoza, her expression as calm as ever.

Mendoza strode right to her. He stood before her, smiling—smiling cruelly—as if they had played a game to its end and he had won.

Then, all at once, the smile vanished. The rebel leader turned—toward me, I thought at first—but then I realized: no, he was looking at the balcony behind me—staring at the balcony, his mouth a grim line.

"Where is Palmer Dunn?" he asked.

Startled, I turned, looked over my shoulder.

The balcony was empty.

Palmer was gone.

CHAPTER ELEVEN

My heart was so full of fear at that point—I was so sure that Mendoza and his men had come here to execute us—that I seized on Palmer's escape as a ray of hope. *Surely,* I told myself, *surely he won't just leave us here like he said he would. Surely he's going to at least try to come to our rescue.* I don't know what I expected him to do—one man, unarmed, against an army of machine gun–toting rebels. But I guess I couldn't stand the thought of my own helplessness so I told myself there might yet be something . . . something . . .

Mendoza shoved me aside as he marched quickly to the balcony. He looked over the railing, down at the alley below. I heard him shouting orders to someone down there, some of his gunmen, I guess. A second later he was back in the room. Looking at Meredith again. Smiling at her again.

"Your friend Palmer is not a fool," he said to her.

"Desperate—but not a fool. He sees that your situation has become impossible."

"Impossible," said Meredith quietly. "Because, you mean, you've murdered a pastor, and now you have to murder the witnesses."

"Oh, please!" said Nicki. She was backed against the wall. Bent over, clutching her stomach with both hands. Sobbing and sobbing. "Oh, please! Don't murder us. I won't tell anyone, I swear. I just want to go home!"

Mendoza ignored her. He strolled back across the room toward Meredith—but before he got to her, Jim stepped up to him.

"Señor Mendoza, I don't think you understand . . ."

Barely glancing at him, Mendoza drove his elbow into Jim's belly. Jim gasped and doubled over, clutching himself. I caught hold of him by the shoulder, held him steady. I knew how he felt. The terror of the last few minutes had made me forget my pain, but my head and gut were still throbbing from the beatdown Mendoza had given me. I gave Jim's shoulder a reassuring squeeze before I let him go. I wasn't angry at him anymore somehow. There didn't seem to be any point. We were all in the same fix. And Meredith was right: blaming one another didn't change anything. The situation wasn't our fault. It was just our bad luck that we had gotten caught here, that's all.

Mendoza, meanwhile, confronted Meredith again, standing close to her, completely ignoring the sobbing Nicki over against the wall, who kept saying, "Oh, please! Oh, please! I just want to go home!"

"You had your chance to make friends," Mendoza said to Meredith.

Meredith's reaction amazed me. She rolled her eyes and shook her head at him—as if the murderous rebel were nothing more than some kind of annoying child who didn't know any better.

"Oh, señor," she said—really, as if he were a child. "You can have whatever . . . friendship you want from me—if you'll give my companions a car and let them leave this village unharmed."

"No, Meredith," I said. The words burst out of me. "Don't say that. What're you talking about?"

But Mendoza only sneered at her. "It is all too late," he told her. "You spit in my eye, señorita. I do not forgive this. Now you are going to die regretting it."

"I won't, you know," Meredith told him quietly. "Regret it, I mean."

Mendoza snorted—and I couldn't tell just then if what he felt for Meredith was hatred or some kind of twisted affection, some kind of twisted admiration. He seemed about to speak again, but he was interrupted by a shout from the alley outside.

The rebel leader pivoted away from Meredith and strode back out onto the balcony. I heard him shouting down to someone below. I heard someone shout back to him.

When Mendoza returned to the room, he said quietly, "Well, I suppose we must salute the United States Marines. Somehow, your Palmer has reached his van and left the village."

Whatever small hope I'd had that Palmer was coming to our rescue crashed inside me and went up in smoke. In the same way Jim had thought that the rebels *couldn't* kill Pastor Ron, that they would *have* to listen to reason, I had thought Palmer *couldn't* just abandon us to die, that he would *have* to try to help us. We were both wrong. People can do all sorts of terrible things. They do them, every day. And now Mendoza had murdered our pastor and Palmer had left us to the rebel guns. It was like Meredith said: we were unarmed and sur-rounded, and there was nothing left for us to do but to have courage and faith and face what came next as best we could.

"He will not get very far, I'm afraid," Mendoza went on. "Our armies have come out of the mountains in force and we are everywhere. But"—he gave a casual gesture—"however far he gets, it is not going to be of any help to you."

With that, he turned to the gunmen and gave them an order in Spanish—and then he translated the order into English, because I guess he wanted to make sure we under-stood—that Meredith especially understood.

"Take them to the wall and execute them," he said.

CHAPTER TWELVE

D o you want to know what it's like to die? What it's like, I mean, to know that you're about to die. To know for certain that the end of your life has come—not someday, but now, right now.

Well, let me tell you, because I know.

Once again, the soldiers started screaming at us, prodding us with their gun barrels, striking at us with their fists. Herding us, in other words, back the way we came, out of the hotel room, down the corridor, to the stairs—down to our place of execution.

It all happened very fast. It was all very violent, very confusing.

But here's the strange thing: inside my mind, it wasn't fast or confusing at all. Because something happened to me then—something weird. It was because I knew where we were headed; I knew that I was about to die. And somehow, knowing that made my mind feel detached from my body in some way. Even as the rebel gunmen shouted at us and hit us and forced us out the door of the room into the upstairs hall, I felt very quiet inside and all my thoughts were very clear.

Was I afraid? I guess so. Sure. But not as much as you might think—or, at least, not in the way you might think. You might think that going to be executed was the scariest thing that could ever happen, the real-life version of the last scene in a horror movie, the scene where the kid walks through the basement where the monster is hiding somewhere—you know, that kind of jangling, unbearable suspense as you get closer and closer to the place where it's going to happen.

But instead, I felt sad. Not just a little sad. I felt this huge, huge sadness. Sure, in church we talk about an eternal life and heaven and all that, but I wasn't in church now—and I was so, so sorry that *this* life was coming to an end. I didn't want to go. I didn't want to leave this world. I didn't want the new school year to begin without me. I didn't want to miss all the stupid ordinary things that happen in life: you know, just playing games or messaging your friends or going to the beach or whatever. I wanted to see my parents again. I wanted to grow up and go to college and get a job. I wanted to meet my wife and my children. I wanted to live—I wanted to live so badly. And it made my heart feel heavy as lead to know that I wouldn't, that everything in this world was over for me now, everything here was finished.

We stumbled down the hall, the gunmen shoving us and striking us and shouting. And my eyes turned hungrily in every direction. I wanted to see everything before it was done. I wanted to drink in every small second of life I still had left.

Everything looked different to me now. Everything looked clearer, much clearer, as if I had been watching the world streaming through a bad wireless connection and suddenly was watching it in hi-def or on Blu-ray. The incredible new clarity made even the littlest things seem kind of beautiful. The hall was just a shabby, dark corridor, the walls chipped, the paint peeling, but somehow it seemed like some kind of work of art. I wanted to slow down to appreciate it. I wanted it to last forever.

And the faces—people's faces—they all looked so amazing. So clear and beautiful. And everyone seemed different to me than they had before.

Like Nicki, for instance. There was Nicki, stumbling down the hall beside me, barely able to stand she was so afraid, barely able to walk. I saw her sobbing and heard her crying out pitifully again and again, "I want to go home! Please! I just want to go home!" And she wasn't pretty anymore or glamorous, the way she had been. But she just looked so wonderful, like such a wonderful person. I thought about how happy it always made her to dress up and wear jewelry and put on makeup and about the sweet way she would sit with the little girls in the village and teach them to do their hair. It was as if I realized for the first time how great she was, how perfect, really, the one and only perfect Nicki of the world.

And Jim—I saw Jim. The dazed look on his face as the gunmen shoved and jostled him. I could see what a smart guy he was, and how serious he was about wanting the world to be a better place. I was so, so sorry I had yelled at him back in the room because I could see now how good his heart was. The perfect Jim just like Nicki was the perfect Nicki.

I know it sounds weird, but this is what I saw. This is the way the world seemed to me, now that all the little stuff we think about and care about was over, now that there were only seconds left until I was shot to death.

We stumbled down the hall to the stairway. We stumbled down the steps. The stairwell was narrow, the walls chipped and scarred. I wanted to study it, to see every detail, to hold on to every second. My eyes went on moving everywhere, staring at everything.

✼

But it was over too soon. The rebels forced us down into the corridor below. As I came off the last step, I bumped against Meredith and I looked at her now, looked at her face.

Meredith always looked kind of wonderful to me. I guess the truth, I realized now, was that I sort of had a crush on her. Whenever I was around her, I wished I were older, wished I could get her to pay attention to me—pay attention to me as a guy, instead of just a kid. And now, at the end, she looked even better. She looked like one of those things you see that are too beautiful even to describe, like a sunset or a mountain or something. She had her arm around Nicki's shoulders. She was holding Nicki up, helping her walk to the place of execution, shielding her as best she could by taking the gunmen's blows on her own back and arms. As always, she was very straight, her eyes clear, her chin up, even as the rebels pushed and slapped and prodded at her. Her lips were moving and I knew she was praying—praying calmly, full of confidence. She had faith and courage even now.

The rebels shoved us out the cantina's back door. The next moment I was out in the alley, blinking and squinting in the bright daylight, still looking around me, still trying to take in every moment of life that I had left to live.

I looked up and saw the sky: big black majestic thunderstorms blowing across the last patches of blue. I saw the church bell tower rising nobly against those racing clouds. I saw the balconies of the hotel above, the dust of the alley swirling up below my feet, all of it clearer than anything I had ever seen before. All of it somehow beautiful.

Shouting, the rebel gunmen marched us toward the alley's end—to the same place where they had taken Pastor Ron.

My sadness grew heavier as the end came closer. It was like a great heavy weight inside me that I had to drag along. But even so, in my mind, there was still all that clarity and beauty and perfection, and the strange bright eagerness to live every second until all the seconds were gone.

I looked around me as we approached the end of the alley—and here is one last amazing thing I saw.

I saw the gunmen. I saw the faces of the gunmen. And I know this might sound like the weirdest thing of all—I know you might think they must have looked terrible or that I must have hated them because they were the ones who were about to shoot me. But they didn't look terrible and I didn't hate them. I felt sorry for them, kind of. I even *liked* them a little. I know: bizarre, right? It was as if I could see all their life stories in their eyes. How they had wanted to be heroes and men, real men, and how somehow they had become this instead, these killers, these murderers—like demons almost. It was like I could see that they were trapped forever inside their demon selves. Even now, even yards away from my execution, I was glad I was me and not them.

I faced forward—and my heart went cold inside me. There was the end of the alley. We were only a few more steps away. What had seemed like a long, slow journey inside my mind had in fact been less than a minute, a few seconds of rushing, confused stumbling from the hotel room to this final place.

The gunmen pushed us to the end of the alley and forced us to turn the corner.

"Please! Please! Please!" Nicki kept crying. "Just let me go home! I just want to go home!"

Jim was shouting now as well, his voice hoarse and weak. He was shouting, "Señores! If you would only listen to me for just a second . . . Señores, you don't understand . . . !"

My eyes moved over them—and past them—and I saw Meredith again, her face calm and luminous, her lips moving silently.

We had come around the corner of the church. We were in a back alley now, a stretch of dirt road bordered by the backs of the plaza buildings on one side and a line of old ragged sheds and piles of garbage on the other.

And something else. Something so terrible I can hardly bear to tell it. There were bodies. Just down the way. Three bullet-riddled bodies lying outside one of the sheds.

One of them, I realized at once, was Pastor Ron.

My heart cracked open with grief and fear, and I knew that within seconds my body would be lying there beside his.

The rebels shoved us toward the church wall. I could see that the wall was chipped and riddled with holes and I knew the holes had been made by gunfire. There were bloodstains too. And some of them, I knew, were from Pastor Ron's blood. And some of them would soon be from ours.

We stood with our backs against the wall while the rebels stepped away from us, ready to form themselves into a firing squad. And maybe you'll think now: *Well, why didn't you fight?* Or, *Why didn't you run away? After all, you had nothing to lose.* And the answer is: if we had tried to fight or tried to run away, they would have shot us dead right that second. And I didn't want to die that second. I wanted to live every possible second I could, every one. Anyway, there was no strength in my legs or arms. I had gone weak with fear. There was nothing I could do but live until life was over.

So I looked around one more time. At the sky, at the ragged tin sheds, at the garbage strewn in the gutter. At Nicki sobbing beside me, and Jim still trying to explain and Meredith praying—and the gunmen, lining up now, starting to lift their guns.

And it was all beautiful and it was all perfect and I wished I could stay forever and see it this way forever because I never would have complained about anything or hated anybody. I would have just been glad to be alive in God's perfect creation every second of every day.

That was the last thought I had.

Then the leader of the firing squad barked an order, and he and the three other gunmen lifted their weapons and pointed them at us. My mind stopped. My thoughts stopped. There was nothing left to see now or to think about besides the four black bores of the rifle barrels pointed at me, about to spit death.

There was a rumble of thunder. It was that time of day. There was always a thunderstorm here in the summer afternoons. The thunder rolled a long time and it seemed like all the sounds of the world—the thunder and Nicki's cries and Jim's voice and Meredith's barely audible whispers—the leader barking the order to take aim—even the breeze moving through the trees in the hills beyond the alley and the insects humming around us near the wall—all of it sort of blended together into a single buzz. In that last endless second before the gunmen pulled their triggers, the buzz grew louder. It became a roar. It seemed to fill my ears, to fill the world.

Time was up. There was no life left to live. I gasped and swallowed an acid terror and prayed for God to take care of me when it was over. I stared at the rifles and that last second went on and on and the roar of the world grew louder and louder in my ears.

Why didn't they fire? I shifted my gaze. I saw that the four gunmen of the firing squad were turning their heads—turning away from me.

It didn't make sense. All I could think was: *What? What?*

The gunmen continued to turn, to turn away. And that's when I realized that buzz, that roar—it was coming closer. It was getting louder.

I turned my head too—turned as the gunmen were turning in order to see what the gunmen saw, what they were staring at.

The growing roar was not the roar of the world. It was the roar of an engine.

Palmer Dunn's black van was rushing toward us down the alley.

CHAPTER THIRTEEN

I stared, my mouth hanging open. It was like I couldn't get my brain to work. I couldn't understand what was happening. My mind had been so far away, so immersed in the moment of my execution, that I just couldn't bring it back to what was happening now.

The gunmen looked baffled too. They seemed to hesitate, their guns still trained on us, as if they weren't sure whether to continue with the execution as planned or to turn around and face this big black vehicle that was roaring down on top of them.

Baffled, I glanced at the others beside me. Nicki was still screaming and crying, expecting to be shot. Jim was looking around, blinking, as shocked and confused as I was.

Only Meredith seemed to understand everything in a single second. She glanced in the direction of Palmer's oncoming van, and one corner of her mouth lifted in the smallest smile. So help me, it was as if she had been expecting this to happen all along.

The van sped toward the gunmen like a bullet. The confused gunmen hesitated another instant—but then they realized they had to do something, they had to turn and face this sudden threat, they had to shoot . . . not at us, but at the van.

And they started turning. But it was too late. Even as the firing squad pivoted to take aim, the van smashed into them. It struck the first two rebels full speed, sending them flying through the air. The second two gunmen tried to dodge out of the way as the van kept coming. One got clipped by the front fender. He went spinning through the air, his legs flying, and dropped hard to the ground. The other gunman—the last gunman standing—just managed to wheel out of the way. He staggered directly in front of me, unsteady on his feet. He struggled to regain control. Struggled to point his machine gun at the van's front window, the driver's window, where I could see Palmer sitting behind the wheel.

The gunman took aim at Palmer's head. Palmer stuck a pistol out the window with one hand and shot him. The gunman spun around. He grabbed hold of my shoulders. His face was inches from my face. I stared in terror as I saw the light of life go out of his eyes.

Then he fell at my feet, dead.

"Get his gun!" shouted Palmer.

He had brought the van screeching to a halt. He had jumped out of it even as it stopped moving.

"Get in!" he shouted at us—and then he shouted again at me, "Get his gun, kid!"

Jim stood still for a second, wide-eyed, stupefied. But Meredith was already hauling the stunned and sobbing Nicki toward the side of the van. She pulled back the van's sliding door, pushed Nicki in, and started climbing in behind her.

At the same time, quick as lightning, Palmer moved around the front of the van. The gunman who'd been thrown aside had already scrambled to his feet. He spun toward Palmer and loosed a wild series of shots at him—*rat-tat-tat*.

Palmer calmly leveled his pistol at him and shot the man dead.

The other two rebels—the ones who had been struck directly by the van—lay still in the dust. Palmer bent over and stripped their machine guns off them.

At that point, I started to come out of my daze.

Get the gun, I thought stupidly.

I looked down. The dead rebel lay inches from my sneakers, staring up at me with empty eyes. His machine gun was still strapped over his shoulder.

I swallowed. I didn't want to touch the corpse. But I had to. I took a deep breath and squatted down. I took hold of the machine gun. I tried not to touch the body underneath, but my knuckles brushed against his bloody shirtfront. I tried to pull the weapon free, but it was held in place by the shoulder strap.

"Let's go, go, go!" I heard Palmer shouting.

I knew what I had to do. I had just seen Palmer do it half a second before. Squinting so I wouldn't have to see the dead man's face so clearly, I took hold of the machine-gun strap and worked it quickly down over his arm until I could pull the gun away from him.

Then, with a gasp, I jumped out of my squat.

"Get in, kid, go!" shouted Palmer.

Still in a haze of confusion, I blinked and looked up. Palmer had grabbed Jim by the arm and was now shoving him toward the open side door of the van. I started to follow them.

But as Palmer pushed Jim into the van, he spun around and faced me.

"Listen," he said quickly. "Get in back, open the door. There's an army of these clowns on the streets and every drunken one of them is about to come after us. When they do, shoot them."

"What?" I asked.

"You heard me. You've got the guts. You can do it. So do it."

I nodded—but I didn't really grasp what he was saying. I mean, about five seconds ago—really, it could hardly have been more than five seconds—I was looking down the barrels of four machine guns, literally preparing to meet my Maker. And now I was still alive—which was so wildly incredible I could hardly believe it. And Palmer was telling me—what?—to shoot at people out the back of a van? I'd never even fired a gun before. I'd never even *held* a gun before. He didn't really expect me to kill anyone, did he?

But I nodded, all the same. Because there was no time to do anything else. And the next thing I knew, Palmer had me by the arm and was hoisting me up into the van with the others, the same as he had with Jim.

"And, kid," he said.

I looked back at him.

"Don't fall out."

I nodded again. What else was I going to do? And clutching the dead rebel's machine gun, I stepped up into the van as Palmer slid the door shut behind me.

It was dark inside. Dark and cramped: two bench seats filled most of the space in the van's narrow interior. My friends were sitting on the benches, Jim in front, Meredith and Nicki in back. Jim was leaning forward, his hands clasped between his knees. He was rocking himself and staring at nothing and muttering. Nicki was leaning against Meredith. She was staring too, and trembling so hard I thought she was having some kind of spasm. Meredith held on to her. Meredith's face was almost expressionless, but she was breathing quickly, nearly gasping, and I could tell that she, like the others, was trying to get over the shock of *not* being shot, of still being alive.

I was shocked too, but it didn't matter. I didn't have time

to be shocked. I had to get to the back of the van and do . . . something—I wasn't sure what.

Carrying the machine gun, I edged along the side of the benches. I reached the van's back doors. They were double doors. *"Open the door,"* Palmer had said. So, okay, I grabbed a handle and pushed one of the doors open.

At that exact moment, Palmer jumped back into the van, back behind the wheel. He put the van into gear and jammed his foot down on the gas.

The van spurted forward, and I nearly went flying out through the open door onto the dirt street. I just barely managed to grab hold of the edge of the door that was still closed and keep my footing and stay inside.

Don't fall out of the van. I reminded myself of Palmer's orders. Not *"fall out of the van."* *Don't fall out.*

Well, it was a good thought, anyway. But by this time, the van was bouncing and rollicking over the rutted dirt of the back alley, careening toward the far corner of the church. The back door kept slamming shut in my face. I kept pushing it open again. And every time I pushed it open, the van would hit another bump and nearly hurl me out into the road where I would have been left behind.

I tried to think. It wasn't easy. My mind felt like a jigsaw puzzle with all the pieces scrambled. The bright clarity of those moments before I'd been put up against the church wall—that was totally gone. I had left the bright moment of my death behind and was back in life, back in the world. And the world, let me tell you, was a mess, absolute confusion. I couldn't even get the van door to stay open so I could do what Palmer had told me to do.

I looked around for something that would help. I found it in a pile of tools and other junk lying on the van's floor. There was a coil of thick rope there. I picked it up. I pushed the door open one more time. I wedged a coil of the rope in the hinges, really jammed it in there. That did it. The rope kept the door from snapping shut as the van continued jouncing and rattling over the road. Now if I could just take care of that "don't fall out" part.

"Get ready!" I heard Palmer shout from the driver's seat. "It's time to rock and roll!"

Well, I had no idea what that meant, but somehow I didn't think it was going to be good.

I couldn't get steady on my feet, and there was no way to use the gun while I was being thrown here and there by the bouncing of the van. So I sat down—it was the only solution I could think of. I sat cross-legged—you know, like you do when you're sitting on the ground around a campfire, ready to cook some s'mores. Only instead of a box of graham crackers on my lap, there was this machine gun. So I sat like that, cross-legged, and held the gun and looked out the open door, not really sure what I was going to see but telling myself that I should get ready because we were going to . . . you know, rock and roll.

I was looking out at the back alley, the sheds and the

garbage and the back of the church. I saw the bloody wall against which we'd just been standing, and I saw the gunmen who'd been about to kill us and were now lying dead or unconscious in the dust.

Then the van swerved, hard, to the left. We turned a corner, with me leaning so far over to one side that, even sitting down, I nearly flew across the floor.

The execution wall disappeared. I wasn't sorry to see it go. Now, for a moment, anyway, I was looking out at a pile of garbage, and a hill of trees, and a patch of sky covered with black clouds in the background.

Then, almost at once, I heard Palmer let out a roar, and the van swerved again. We were barreling through the plaza, the center of Santiago. I looked out—and I could not believe how much everything had changed in such a short time.

The place where the people had celebrated their new school was completely transformed. It had been a nice little place. Kind of jolly. The church, the cantina, the market stalls. Christmas lights strung up for decorations.

Now the square was decorated with dead people. Men and women lying on the pavement, shot, bleeding on the stones. The Christmas lights were gone—I saw where a string of them had been trampled into the ground. The market stalls were all broken and turned over, their pillars splintered. The windows of some of the other buildings were broken and their shattered glass lay sparkling beneath the walls. A rebel with a gun staggered into view. He tipped a bottle of whiskey up to his lips and took a long swig. Then he fired a few bursts into the air and gave a shout of triumph.

I watched all this through the open door, sitting there cross-legged, holding the machine gun in my lap as the van raced through the plaza. Like my friends, recovering from our near-death experience, I had gone into a sort of stunned, distant daze. I wasn't really thinking about anything. I was just looking out at the scene as if it were some kind of television show, something that had nothing to do with me. I had almost forgotten what Palmer had told me to do.

"There's an army of these clowns on the streets, and every drunken one of them is about to come after us. When they do, shoot them."

Then it happened. Just like he said it would.

Even over the roar of the van's engines—even over a fresh roll of thunder from the sky above—I heard the gruff, angry shouts of the rebels. As I sat dazed, staring out the open back door of the van, I saw five or six men with rifles charging into the town's main street. One of them, I saw, was Mendoza himself.

The rebels staggered around for a second, confused, looking as if they were drunk—which I guess they were. But Mendoza was steady as a rock. And he had already spotted us—spotted the van rocketing out of town.

Mendoza pointed after us. I saw the whites of his eyes flaring in his rage. I saw his mouth open as he shouted orders.

At his barked commands, the rebels started rushing

around in different directions. Some ran out of my sight. But two of them charged into the center of the street, bringing their guns up as they came. They planted themselves, lifted their weapons, and took aim at the back of the van—at me.

For another half second or so, I continued to sit there in my stunned stupidity. Everything had changed so quickly, I was still having a hard time taking it in. I mean, one second you're standing against the wall in front of a firing squad, suddenly realizing that life is beautiful and that you should've appreciated everything more and been kinder to everyone—and the next second you're rattling around in the back of a van, racing to get out of town. And suddenly life isn't beautiful at all! It's nuts! Everything's wild and confusing all around you . . . not to mention the fact that there are guys pointing guns at you again . . .

But then, with a sort of flash, I came back to my senses. I remembered where I was, what was happening, what I was supposed to do. There were the two rebels in the middle of the street with their machine guns aimed at the van.

And I thought: *Oh, I get it! I get it now!*
It's time to rock and roll!

CHAPTER FOURTEEN

Before I could react, the rebels started shooting at us. I saw the flame spit from their rifle barrels. I saw pebbles kick up out of the road as the bullets hit the pavement just behind us. The van continued to race away from them, swaying and bouncing as Palmer kept his foot jammed down on the gas.

My sluggish mind finally came to life. *What do I do?* I thought.

And I heard Palmer answer: *Shoot them.*

Shoot them? I thought.

The rebels were getting smaller behind us as we pulled away. But once again, they raised their weapons, steadied their aim, got ready to fire again.

And I thought: *Yes! Shoot them!*

I lifted the machine gun from my lap, pointed it in their general direction, and pulled the trigger.

The gun leapt and jerked in my hand like a living creature as it rattled bullets out the open back door of the van. Of course, I had no chance of hitting anybody. We were too far away and I'd hardly even taken aim. But I saw the rebels duck to the side at the sound of fire, trying to get out of the way. And by the time they recovered, we were pulling around a bend in the road. They had lost their opportunity to take another shot at us.

I blinked. *Hey!* I thought. *Hey!* I had done it. Okay, I hadn't shot anybody. I didn't *want* to shoot anybody. But I had stopped them from shooting us. That was pretty good right there, wasn't it?

I smiled, feeling pretty proud of myself.

And just at that second, another rebel stepped into view. He seemed to come out of nowhere, but suddenly he was just off to my left, raising his machine gun, ready to blow out our tires.

Without hesitating this time, I turned the machine gun on him and let off another round of shots. I didn't hit him either. I wasn't really trying to. I just wanted to scare him— and I sure did. The moment the machine gun leapt in my hand, the rebel let out a scream and dived for the dirt. The van raced out of his range before he ever got a shot off at us.

I laughed out loud. This was cool!

It happened again. Two more rebels—they staggered out

of a house by the side of the road. They stared at us bleary-eyed as we rocketed past. Then they stepped into our dusty wake and aimed their machine guns at us.

I fired again—now I was purposely aiming my machine gun above their heads so I wouldn't really hurt them. And it worked: I didn't have to hurt them. Just the fact that I was shooting at them was enough to make the drunken rebels dodge for cover—one leaping one way, the other leaping the other.

I laughed again—in fact, I couldn't stop laughing. I mean, you know what this was like? It was almost exactly like a video game. There are all these levels in *Gears of War*—in a lot of games—where you're in some tank or some vehicle or other and you're racing along a road and every now and then some monster jumps out at you and you have to shoot him with your plasma gun or something. This was just like that. Except the monsters were people and they didn't explode into gobs of gore because I didn't have to really shoot them. All I had to do was fire in their general direction and watch them jump for cover.

And to make things even cooler, we were actually getting away! We were already leaving the village now. We were on the road that wound down out of the hills. The van was rocking and bouncing violently over the broken pavement. There were just a few more cottages here and there to either side of us. Soon we would be racing through the jungle to the airfield where Palmer's plane would be waiting for us.

I let out a shout: *"Whoo-hoo!"* Just like a video game: *Escape Trophy Unlocked!*

And then I raised my eyes and I stopped shouting, stopped laughing. Because I saw what was coming after us.

A truck had appeared on the road coming out of Santiago, the road behind us. It was a battered old pickup—but it was coming on like wildfire. There were two rebels in the cab and four in the open bed behind. And all of them had machine guns.

The truck quickly got larger and larger as it closed the distance between us.

I shouted over my shoulder into the van. "Palmer! There's a truck coming after us! They're catching up!"

He shouted back, "Well, stop 'em, boy, that's what the gun is for!"

My breath went short. I swallowed hard. I looked out the back of the van with wide, frightened eyes. I felt clueless. How was I supposed to stop a truck?

Then I thought: *the tires. What if I could shoot out the tires . . . ?*

I had no idea whether I could actually shoot *at* something—and whether I would hit it if I did. But I figured it was worth a try at least.

So I sort of raised the machine gun to my face and looked down the barrel. My finger tightened on the trigger as I lined the gun up with the oncoming truck's front right tire.

But I never got the chance to shoot.

Before I could, a man—another rebel—ran out of one
of the houses we were passing. He stepped up to the side of
the road. He lifted his hand—and I saw he was holding a
grenade.

The truck full of rebels sped after us on the road behind.
To the side, the rebel with the hand grenade grasped the grenade's ring and pulled it free. That meant the grenade was
going to explode a couple of seconds after he released it. And
of course, when he released it, it would be because he was
throwing it at us.

I lifted my machine gun again. I did what I had done
before: I fired over his head. He flinched a little, but he was
braver than the others. He didn't dive for cover. He didn't
stop at all. He drew his arm back, ready to throw the hand
grenade at us.

Panicking, I let off another round of bullets at him. It
had no effect—none. He just stepped forward and started to
throw the grenade at us. Down the road, the truck kept racing our way. One of the gunmen in the truck bed was trying
to steady his machine gun on the roof of the cab so he could
take a shot at us.

I didn't know what to do—that is, I did know. I knew
what I had to do. And I had less than a second—a micro-
second—to make up my mind and do it.

I lowered the machine gun. I aimed directly at the man
with the grenade. He had just begun to bring his hand forward in a throwing motion. He was just about to hurl the

grenade at the van. If he threw well, the thing would go off and blow us to smithereens.

I pulled the trigger of my machine gun.

As I looked on in fascinated horror, the bullets from my gun struck the man with the grenade in the chest. I could see his shirt ripple and see the black spots where the bullets hit.

The man's mouth opened wide in shock and pain. He stopped in his tracks. He clutched his chest with his free hand and toppled over backward. He lay still in the dust. I was pretty sure he was dead.

The grenade dropped weakly out of his other hand and rolled into the middle of the road.

I sat there cross-legged in the back of the van and stared at the fallen man—almost as if I were surprised to see him there, as if I didn't even understand that I was the one who had shot him, that my pulling the trigger was what had sent the bullets into him and killed him.

I shifted my eyes and saw the pickup truck with its cargo of rebels racing toward us. Gaining on us. Getting closer and closer.

Then, just as the truck ran past the fallen rebel, just as its front fender rolled over the grenade—the grenade exploded.

It made a sound like *whump*—not a great big blast but a surprisingly dull thud. A black cloud of smoke and shrapnel flew up under the pickup—and the force of it actually lifted the front of the truck right off the road into the air.

The truck went up quickly and came down hard. And

when it came down, it swerved sharply and started to tip over. Even from a distance, I heard the rebels in the truck bed screaming. I saw two of them leaping out of the bed, jumping clear. The other rebels were still holding on for dear life as the truck bounded off the road out of control and dropped onto its side. Flames shot out from the undercarriage and smoke poured from the windows. More of the rebels were jumping off it, and the ones inside the cab were quickly scrambling out.

Then our van turned a corner and the truck went out of sight.

"Nice shooting, kid!"

I looked back over my shoulder at the shout. It was Palmer. He had seen what had happened in his big side-view mirror. He pumped his fist at me once even as he guided the truck forward at high speed with his other hand.

I nodded to him. I smiled. But it was a sickly smile. Holding the machine gun weakly in my lap, I looked out the back of the van and stared at the winding jungle road spinning out behind us.

I didn't feel like laughing anymore. I didn't feel like shouting *whoo-hoo*. This didn't seem like a video game now. It didn't seem like any kind of game at all. This was happening, really happening, happening to me.

And I—Will Peterson—sixteen years old—from the quiet little town of Spencer's Grove, California . . . I had just killed a man.

CHAPTER FIFTEEN

A jagged bolt of lightning lanced the darkening sky. The thunder rolled again. The rain started slanting down, pelting the road behind us, turning up dust and beginning to transform it into mud. The van went on bouncing and shuddering along at top speed. I sat where I was and stared out into the storm.

We were clear of the village. For the moment, there were no more soldiers left to attack us. That was a good thing too. I don't think I would've been able to shoot anyone else. What I had done, I had done in a moment of danger and panic—a moment when it was kill or be killed. And I know, I know—I had to do it. I had to protect myself. I had to protect my friends. But now that it was over, I felt sick in my heart. I had ended a human life. And it felt lousy. Really bad.

The van turned off the road and started down a narrow

dirt path. If the ride had been rough before, it was really wild now. The van jumped and bucked and leaned this way and that. The jungle trees moved in close on either side of us. The leaves hung over us, so thick they actually held off the falling rain.

We were on the little side road now that led to the airstrip. I remembered the look of it from when we first arrived. Another few minutes and we would be at Palmer's plane. We would take off and fly north until we reached an airfield in the south of Texas. From there we would take another plane to Houston. From there, we would fly to Los Angeles and make our way home by bus.

It would all take only a few hours. In only a few hours we would be out of this nightmare and back in our homes, back with our families, back in the normal world.

All except Pastor Ron. He wasn't ever going back to his family again. And neither was the rebel I had shot in the chest.

I thought about that as the van bounced along. I thought about how we would go home and everything would be the same and everything would have changed too. I knew there was a lot of stuff I was going to have to think about and figure out once we got away. But all the same, I was desperate to go, desperate to leave this madness, desperate to get home.

The van came around a bend and began to slow. I looked over my shoulder and saw the airstrip through the front windshield. We had arrived.

The van came to a stop and I climbed to my feet.

"Thank you, God!" I heard Nicki say.

Palmer got out from behind the wheel. Jim slipped open the side door and climbed out too. Nicki scrambled quickly off her bench and jumped out. Meredith turned to me and offered me a sad smile, as if she understood all the stuff that was going through my mind. Then she slid off the bench too and got out of the van.

I set the rifle aside. I was glad to get rid of it. I climbed out through the open back door.

And because I was the last one to leave the van, I was the last one to see what had happened.

The airstrip wasn't much to look at. It was just a line of flattened dirt in the middle of a small clearing surrounded by jungle. The rain was falling fast now and the strip—that line of dirt—was quickly turning to mud. As I came out of the van, I felt the cold drops pelting me, pelting my hair, my face. I had to squint through the water to see—and I saw the others just ahead of me, standing in a cluster: Palmer in front, Jim at his left shoulder, Meredith and Nicki behind his right shoulder. They were all standing still, all looking out across the field, through the rain.

I joined them—and I saw what they were looking at: Palmer's plane, which was still sitting where he had parked it at the far end of the landing strip.

The plane had been totally destroyed. As in: totally. It had been set on fire. Even in the rain, it was still smoking—what was left of it—which wasn't much. Its landing gear was completely smashed, the tires flat, the struts bent out of shape. One of its wings was in fragments, almost gone. The windows were all broken. And the entire fuselage was burned charcoal black.

It wasn't going to fly us home. It wasn't going to fly anybody anywhere.

Looking at it, I felt something drop inside me, like an elevator falling out of control. It was an awful feeling. Our only way out of here, our only means of escape—ruined; gone. We had been so close—so close to getting out—only hours from getting back to our families—and now . . . it seemed like there was no way, no way home at all.

"What happened?" Jim murmured dully. "It looks like someone . . . blew it up."

Palmer nodded. "The rebels. Mendoza said they were everywhere . . . Maybe he even sent a few of his guys out here to make sure no one used it to escape."

"Well, what do we do now?" asked Nicki. I could hear the panic rising in her voice. She already sounded as if she was about to burst into tears again.

"Could we drive?" Meredith asked. "Could we get back in the van, drive to the border, try to break through to Belize or Mexico?"

Palmer turned to her. He seemed about to answer, but he didn't—he didn't say anything. Instead, he just stood there. His eyes were on her, but he seemed to be looking right through her into some unseen distance. And I realized: he was listening to something.

I listened too. Over the heavy pattering of the rain, I heard it clearly. Engines—cars or more trucks. Not far off—and coming closer, getting louder, quickly.

"They're coming," said Jim softly. "They're coming after us."

Nicki let out a noise, a little gasp. She brought her hands to her mouth as if to hold in her mounting hysteria.

"Mendoza knew we'd come here," I said. "Where else could we go? He knows right where to find us."

I looked at Palmer. We all looked at Palmer. With Pastor Ron gone, there was no question who our leader was now. Palmer might not be the nicest guy in the world, but he was a trained fighter, the only one we had, and we needed him.

But for another second, Palmer just stood there, silent. The noise of the engines kept growing louder. It sounded as if the trucks—and the rebels they were carrying—would be here in minutes.

"Shouldn't we get back in the van?" Jim asked nervously. "Make a run for it . . ."

Finally, Palmer responded. He gave a quick shake of his head.

"There's only one road and, by the sound of it, they're coming toward us from both directions," he said quietly, almost to himself. "There's no way to drive out of here."

I swallowed hard. In all honesty, I almost felt like crying. *So close*, I kept thinking. We had been so close to going home.

The lightning struck again and the thunder rolled again and the rain fell harder, washing my hair down onto my forehead. I had to brush it back out of my eyes.

Then Palmer started moving.

"Come on," he said to us.

"Where?" asked Jim. "Where can we go?"

Moving away quickly, Palmer answered over his shoulder, "Into the jungle."

CHAPTER SIXTEEN

L et's go! Move it!" Palmer barked at us—because the rest of us were just standing there watching him. We seemed frozen where we stood.

Palmer was now at the van. He was reaching inside. As I stood there watching, he brought out a machine gun and strapped it over his shoulder. Then he brought out a pistol and stuffed it into his belt. Then he brought out a knife—a great big dagger—which he put in his belt on the other side. It was almost comical: the guy was like a one-man army or something.

I was the first to come to my senses, the first to realize we had to move, we had to help him. I went to Palmer's side.

"That's a lot of guns," I said. "Where'd you find them?"

"A couple of rebels tried to stop me from reaching the van," he said.

I opened my mouth, but nothing came out. I understood what he meant.

"Get yours," he said to me.

"My . . . ?"

"The gun, the gun. Come on."

"Oh, right."

"And here." He handed me something—a curved metal container that I recognized as being part of the weapon. "Spare magazine," he said. And when I looked at him blankly, he added, "In case you run out of bullets."

"Right," I managed to murmur again.

The others had come up to join us now. Palmer pulled out a small backpack and tossed it to Jim. "Put that on. We'll need it." He turned to the girls. "Grab anything from the van that looks useful," he told them. "The jungle's not a fun place at night."

I left them there to go back around the van and get my gun. My mind was a jumble of thoughts and feelings. I couldn't sort them all out. I was thinking about the gun, I guess. *My gun.* And the spare magazine. Palmer was expecting more fighting, more shooting. And he was expecting me to be part of it. That meant I might have to kill someone else—maybe more than one person. The idea made something rise up into my throat, something that tasted ugly. But I swallowed it back down. I clenched my teeth. If that was the only way I could stay alive— if that was the only way I could keep my friends alive—then I was going to do it, I told myself. I had to.

I reached the back of the van. Took out the machine gun.

For a second, I just held it in my hand and stared at it. I wished I was home playing video games. Make-believe violence is a lot more fun than the real kind.

I went back to join the others.

The engines were coming closer by the second. I couldn't see the trucks yet, but they sounded really close and I thought they must already be heading down the side road. That meant they would be here any minute.

Palmer must have thought so too, because as soon as I stepped up to him, he said, "All right. Follow me."

He started off across the airfield.

Meredith took Nicki by the arm. Nicki cried out as the thunder struck again—louder this time.

"Come on, Nicks," Meredith said.

She struck off after Palmer, holding on to Nicki—and Nicki sort of stumbled along with her.

Jim followed them. I took a quick glance over my shoulder to see if I could spot the oncoming rebel trucks. There was still no sign of them. I hurried after the others.

The rain was falling harder now. The dirt of the field had turned to mud. It squelched up over my sneakers as I walked. I felt the cold and damp of it as it soaked into my socks. The sky was already nearly black with clouds and it seemed to grow blacker by the minute as the afternoon turned toward evening. The trees that bordered the airstrip were already growing dimmer in the fading light.

"The jungle's not a fun place at night."

Yeah, I was willing to bet that was true. As we neared the dense trees, I thought about all the stuff that might be hiding in there—all the creatures, I mean, ready to come out and start hunting as soon as darkness fell. As a rule, I'm not too fond of creatures. I mean, I like dogs a lot. We have a Labrador at home—Feller—getting old now, but generally a great guy. But the sort of creatures you are likely to find in a jungle— man-devouring snakes, crocodiles, and tigers immediately came to mind—don't exactly make good pets. As I walked on, my imagination playing over the possibilities, I felt a sort of bubbling acid of fear in my stomach. Rebels who wanted to shoot me at my back, animals who wanted to eat me up ahead. But what was I going to do? What was there I could do? Nothing. So I kept walking.

Palmer reached the trees. He never hesitated. He just charged on and quickly disappeared from view into the heavy foliage. Meredith and Nicki went in next, then Jim. And finally, I reached the edge of the jungle.

From the outside—from the airstrip—it didn't look like there was any path, but when I got close, I saw that there was. Brushing a humongous frond out of the way, I saw a narrow dirt trail that twisted between more humongous leaves and low bushes and the humped roots and outstretched branches of the surrounding trees. Palmer must've known the trail was there because he headed right for it and was now walking along quickly and surely. The others stumbled after him. I stumbled after them.

The thunder rolled again as we walked, and the rain hammered hard and loud against the roof of the jungle, rattling the thick covering of leaves. The water dribbled down from above in steady streams. It poured through my already dripping hair and soaked through my already soaking clothes. It was all pretty miserable.

We didn't go far, though. Not far at all. After a few moments, I glanced back over my shoulder and saw the airfield just disappearing from sight—and as soon as I looked forward again, I saw the others had stopped and were gathered right in front of me. When I reached them, I saw Palmer, holding up his hand to bring us to a halt.

He spoke softly, quickly. "Get low," he said.

He gestured for us to get down. We all squatted. I felt the damp earth squeeze up around my ankles.

"Ew," said Nicki.

"Ssh," said Meredith, and Nicki was quiet.

Palmer listened—and so we all listened, crouched there, dripping and shivering in the rain.

The downpour was really loud here, thudding relentlessly on the leaf covering above us. At first, I thought it had drowned out the sounds of the engines, but then I realized, no, the engines had stopped. The next moment I made out a series of clunking noises. It was the trucks, I realized: the doors of the trucks opening and closing.

The rebels had reached the airstrip.

I heard a voice barking orders in Spanish.

Mendoza. My mouth formed the word, but I didn't dare say it out loud.

Palmer was suddenly up and pushing past me. He didn't say a word, just headed quickly back down the path, toward the airstrip, keeping his back bent, his head low. I hesitated for a second, uncertain. He hadn't told me what to do. He hadn't told anyone. But then it occurred to me, you know, that I was the only other one of us who had a gun. If Palmer got into trouble, if he had to fight, I might be able to help. That's what I thought, anyway, so I decided to follow him.

I hurried down the path—imitating Palmer, bending over and keeping my head as low as I could. I retraced my steps until I found Palmer down on one knee, close to the edge of the jungle.

Weirdly, he seemed to be expecting me because without turning around, he held up his hand, gesturing me to stop, and then waved me down. So I went down, knelt down as he had. Instantly, the cold mud seeped through my jeans. Nicki was right: *Ew.*

Palmer peered through the trees and the falling rain so I did too. We were very close to the airfield. I could see it clearly through the gaps in the leaves. I could see two green trucks parked there now, one on either side of our black van. And I could see the crowd of armed rebels milling around in the storm. I counted a dozen of them and I noticed right away that one of them, just as I had thought, was Mendoza.

Unlike the others, the rebel leader was standing very still. Only his head moved as he turned it slowly to scan the edge of the jungle. He was looking off to our right but panning his eyes relentlessly in our direction.

Then he stopped—and he seemed to be looking right at us.

I caught my breath.

"Stay cool," Palmer whispered.

Good advice. I wished I could take it. But my heart was pounding so hard I was afraid Mendoza might be able to hear it.

The rebel went on staring at us—that's what it felt like he was doing, anyway. Then he started barking orders again.

"What's he saying?" I whispered.

"He's remembered this path. He knows we must've taken it."

"Will they come searching for us?"

Palmer shook his head. "I don't know. It's gonna be dark soon. He doesn't want to be out here in the jungle at night."

Yeah, I know how he feels, I thought.

In answer to Mendoza's shouts, two rebels had now gone running up to Palmer's black van. One leaned inside the driver's seat. A moment later the van's hood popped open. The second rebel approached the hood. He unhooked a hand grenade from his belt.

I heard Palmer whisper a curse. "I'm still paying for that van," he muttered.

Then Mendoza shouted something, which I'm pretty sure translated into, "Run!"

The second rebel pulled the pin of the grenade and tossed it under the van's hood.

The rebels scattered, running off across the airfield in all directions. Mendoza, meanwhile, calmly walked away from the van, casually getting out of range just as the grenade exploded.

The noise of the blast was huge in the open field. An enormous fireball engulfed the van—a huge blossoming dome of orange flame rising into the gray rain and the black sky. If the van hadn't been our last means of escape, it would've actually been kind of awesome to see. Even as it was, I knelt there mesmerized by the strange beauty of the vehicle's fiery destruction.

It took a couple of seconds for the sound of the explosion to subside. Then Mendoza shouted again and waved his hand to get his gunmen to follow him. Toting their machine guns, they all gathered at once and started walking across the airfield. They were walking straight toward us.

Palmer was up in the next second. He pointed down the path.

"Here they come, kid," he whispered sharply. "Time to go."

CHAPTER SEVENTEEN

I moved as quickly as I could in that crouching run. I felt Palmer rushing along just behind me. Up ahead, I saw the others—Meredith, Nicki, Jim—still squatting miserably in the rain, waiting for us, watching for us, their eyes large, their mouths open.

As we reached them, Palmer brushed past me. I heard him whisper to the others, "They're coming after us. Move fast and low. Follow me."

He took the lead and the others were up and after him at once.

We rushed down the trail, brushing past the jungle leaves, squelching through the mud, gasping through the rain. The thunder rolled and the rain was loud, but when I listened, I could hear the rebels right behind us. I could hear them crashing through the branches. I could hear Mendoza calling to them, "Vamanos." *Let's go.*

I glanced back over my shoulder. Their fatigues were hard to see amid the green leaves, but I caught glimpses of them. I wondered if they could see us too, but it didn't seem that they had yet.

They would soon, though. We were moving fast, but they were moving faster. Of course they were. They didn't have to keep their knees bent and their heads down like we did. If they spotted us, they would open fire and almost surely wipe us out in an instant, so we kind of had to run and hide at the same time. There was no way to do that and outstrip them as they just came marching on, relentless.

In my growing fear, I thought of calling up to Palmer: *They're gaining on us!* But how could I? If Mendoza heard us, it would all be over. Anyway, I had faith that Palmer knew the rebels were catching up. It was the sort of thing he *would* know. And I told myself he must have some kind of plan. He must have.

Funny. A few hours ago I'd really disliked this guy. His arrogant attitude. His mocking glances. His ironic drawl. He really rubbed me the wrong way. Now my life was in his hands and I was glad—glad, I mean, that *he* was the one who was leading us. As jealous as it made me feel, I understood now what Meredith had meant when she said he was exceptional—a hero. She was obviously right. That's obviously exactly what he was—or, at least, what he was meant to be.

Fearless, tough, decisive, and ready to risk his life for us—a bunch of kids he hardly knew. I guess you don't always have to be a nice guy to be a good man.

Anyway, like I said, I figured he must have a plan—and sure enough, he did.

Rushing down the trail, I glanced back over my shoulder again. What I saw made my heart clutch in my chest. The rebels were close. Really close. Any minute now they were going to spot us and riddle the jungle—and us—with bullets.

I turned back, feeling I really had to say something now, to warn the others—and the others were gone!

I had a second of real panic. Where were they? Then I saw them. They had followed Palmer off the trail to the left. They had plunged into the depths of the jungle and were now disappearing and reappearing into view as they pushed their way through the heavy leaf covering.

I went after them. I felt the roots and bushes close over my legs. I felt wet fronds slapping at my already soaking face and clothes. I felt the uneven ground under my feet and when I looked down, I couldn't see where I was stepping. And, yes, that made me worry about snakes—about stepping on some gigantic jungle snake I'd never heard of that could take off a man's entire leg with a single bite. Or something.

But Palmer was moving so quickly—and the others were keeping pace. There was no time to think about it. So I didn't think about it. I just charged on.

This time when Palmer vanished, he vanished right

before my eyes. I could see him up ahead through the jungle foliage, moving fast, bent low. Then he seemed to stoop even lower. Then he was gone.

The others went after him—down, down, and gone. And as I caught up I saw what was happening.

There was a ravine here: a steep-sided groove running along the ground, with a stream burbling along rapidly at the bottom of it. Palmer had dropped over the ravine's side. He was leaning against the dirt wall, his feet and ankles braced against rocks in the running water. He gestured to us and we got down too, leaning in a line against the wall. Down there, I realized, we would be hidden from the sight of anyone above us standing more than a yard or two away.

I looked along the line. Palmer was down at the other end. Then Jim next to him. Then Nicki, then Meredith, then me. Each of us was pressed against the mud of the wall. Each of us had our feet down in the stream at the bottom of the ravine. We all had dirt splattering our faces. Our clothes and hair were soaked. The cold water of the stream was running through our shoes.

We waited. It was noisy here—really noisy. The rain on the forest roof and the sound of the rushing water covered up every other noise. The air was getting darker by the second. Colder too, it felt like.

I shivered. My teeth chattered. I clamped my jaw tight to get them to stop. I glanced down the line and saw Meredith with her arm around Nicki, holding her close, keeping her warm. But Meredith herself, always pale-skinned, was incredibly white under the mud that splotched her cheeks. She always reminded me a little of a statue and now, in the freezing cold, she really did look like she was turning to white marble.

After a while, Palmer moved. He edged up the wall of the ravine until he could just peek over the top. I watched him as he watched the jungle. Then he turned to me. Pointed at me. Pointed at his eyes. Pointed at the wall.

I got it. He wanted me to look too. He wanted me to be ready for whatever happened, because I had the other gun.

I did what he did. I edged up the side of the wall. It was slippery and cold, the mud scraping against me. I got my eyes up over the side of the ravine and looked into the jungle.

I caught my breath. There they were, the rebels. I could make them out through the jungle foliage. They were marching over the trail. They were right alongside us, going steadily by. They thought we must be still on the trail up ahead of them. Another minute and they would go right past us.

I smiled grimly. I began to have some hope again. I began to think, *Hey, maybe we could get around behind these guys, sneak back to the airstrip and steal one of their trucks and make a run for it . . .*

The rebels went marching by on the trail—and then they were past.

All except one of them.

All except Mendoza.

Wouldn't you know it? Just as I was about to breathe

a sigh of relief, I saw that the rebel leader had not joined the others as they marched on. He had stopped. I peered through the trees, trying to see exactly what he was up to. After a moment, I understood: he was looking around him. He was studying the ground and the leaves to either side of him.

He knows we've left the trail! I thought.

Mendoza had been paying more attention to his surroundings than his rebels had. *Sure,* I thought. *He's their Palmer.* He's the one they counted on to think and plan and keep them alive—and to track us down and kill us.

Even over the pounding rain and the rushing stream, I heard him shout an order to his gunmen—who were still marching forward on the trail.

"Alto!"

I guessed it meant stop, because they all stopped. Then Mendoza said something else—and the rebels started coming back toward him.

I lay against the mud wall, peeking over the top. My teeth had started chattering again and I couldn't stop them now. I was just too cold. I watched as the rebels gathered around their leader. I heard the low murmur of Mendoza's voice but couldn't make out the words. I could pretty well guess what they meant, though.

I glanced over at Palmer. He was already looking my way, as if he'd been waiting for me to turn to him. He gestured to me with his open hand: *Stay cool.*

Good advice.

I looked out over the top of the ravine again. What I saw made my heart sink.

Mendoza was coming our way, pushing off the trail into the jungle just as we had, following the path we had taken through the trees. The other rebels followed him, pushing the big leaves and branches aside with the butts of their rifles.

There was a loud crash of thunder. That made the rebels pause a moment. Even Mendoza. They all looked up into the rain.

The darkness seemed to be gathering around us quickly. I couldn't tell if it was nightfall or simply the storm. The rain fell more heavily, the leaves around us bending and dripping. The mud of the jungle floor churned up and spattered as the water struck.

Still, Mendoza came on, came closer, studying the ground, waving the rebels to follow. They followed. Closer.

"Sst!"

That was Palmer, hissing to me. I glanced his way. He gestured for me to get down, to hide. Mendoza was almost close enough to see us.

I slid back down the side of the wall.

I saw Palmer slide down too. He leaned close to Jim and whispered in his ear. I got it. I leaned close to Meredith and she leaned close to me so she could hear.

"They're coming," I whispered to her in the quietest voice I could. "Keep down, keep quiet."

Meredith nodded. She leaned away from me and leaned close to Nicki and passed the message on.

We lay pressed tight against the mud wall as the rebels kept coming toward us. I knew they were getting close because I could hear their footsteps over the sound of the rainfall and the running stream. I could hear Mendoza speaking to the others in a low, gruff voice. He was close enough now so I could make out the words, but I didn't understand them.

Meredith caught my eye, motioned to me. I leaned close to her. She whispered in my ear: "He's cursing the rain because it's washed out our tracks."

I nodded. Well, that was something, anyway. But the rebels were still coming. I could still hear their footsteps in the mud, the wet sounds getting closer. Mendoza's voice grew steadily louder. *They must be right above us,* I thought. I figured it would be a matter of seconds before they took the fatal step and saw the ravine and looked down into it and found us.

A flash of lightning—the brightness muted by the leaf cover. A guttural roll of thunder like a great beast growling for its food.

A tremor went through my entire body. I was so cold I could no longer keep myself still. I lay there shivering and listened.

The rebels' footsteps had stopped. Had they seen us? No, it couldn't have been that. There would have been shouting—and shooting—if they had. They must be standing still, looking around, taking stock. They must be right above us, a step or two away.

Mendoza started talking again. I could tell he was just above me. I couldn't understand his low, swift Spanish, but the tone of his voice had changed. He sounded discouraged now—even disgusted—as if he couldn't believe he had been foiled in his hunt by the rain and the gathering darkness.

That's what I hoped his tone meant, anyway. I thought—I hoped—I prayed with all my might—that they were about to give up, about to turn around, about to go.

And I think they were planning to do just that—right up until the moment Nicki gasped.

It was a short sound but sharp and clear. Meredith moved fast and clamped her hand over Nicki's mouth, holding her tight. Nicki's eyes stared over Meredith's hand and they looked about as large and bright as two of those big spotlights they use to announce a new movie.

I followed her terrified gaze and felt my belly fill with a blackness of terror and disgust.

A snake. Slithering up out of the stream. Twisting up over the mud. Coming right toward us. Right toward Nicki.

It wasn't huge, but it was big enough, maybe four feet long and as thick around as a hot dog. It wasn't the size that bothered me, though. It was the colors on its scaly skin. Bands of black and yellow and red. I didn't know much about snakes, but I knew a little because there are some in California and you just hear about them from hikers and so on. And what I remembered was that there were two kinds of snakes with those sorts of colors: a harmless milk snake and a coral snake, one of the most deadly snakes alive. I remembered a little rhyme a science teacher, Mr. Larue, taught us once so we could tell the difference:

Red touches yellow kills a fellow. Red touches black, you're all right, Jack.

I peered down narrow-eyed through the rain and saw that the bands of red on the twining creature's scales touched the bands of yellow. It was a coral snake, all right. One bite from one of those and you were history. A lousy way to die.

In a panic now, Nicki was trying to draw her feet up away from the oncoming thing, but that just made her lose her footing so that her body slid down the mud wall toward it. I could hear her whimpering under Meredith's hand as she realized she had to let her feet down into the mud to stop her fall. She planted her feet right next to the snake—and the snake didn't like that. He lifted his head as if he were ready to strike, his tongue darting out of his mouth as his cold, blank, unfeeling eyes stared at Nicki's sneakers.

Nicki, wide-eyed with terror, somehow managed to keep still. Finally, I guess the snake decided the danger had passed. He lowered his head to the ground again and went on slithering toward her.

Meanwhile, above us, I heard Mendoza speak again. I wasn't sure what he was saying, but his tone of voice had definitely changed. He sounded discouraged before. Now he whispered harshly. *An order,* I thought. Then silence. Of course. Mendoza thought he had heard something—Nicki's gasp. But he couldn't be sure in all this hammering rain. And he still couldn't see us, still didn't know we were right beneath him. He was telling his men to listen. They were listening—in case the sound came again.

Shivering, I held my breath. I looked at Nicki. Meredith still had her hand clamped over Nicki's mouth and Nicki's eyes still beamed out over it, their brightness dimming as they filled with tears. I looked down and saw the coral snake. It was slithering now right over Nicki's sneaker. I saw Nicki's whole body give a huge, disgusted shudder. I saw the tears spill from her eyes. But somehow she managed to stay quiet, stay still.

There was quiet above me too as the rebels listened, waiting for us to make another noise so they could find us, kill us.

The snake slid slowly over Nicki's sneaker, slanting upward toward Meredith's leg. It paused to explore Meredith's muddy slacks and then slid on over them at the shin. I looked up at Meredith. The sight of her shocked me. Up until now, even facing death before the firing squad, I don't think I had seen the slightest trace of fear in her. Her courage, her steadiness were almost uncanny. But everyone's afraid of something— that's the truth. Everyone has something that they fear. And clearly, Meredith was terrified of snakes.

If she had seemed pale before—and, like I said, the cold and damp had turned her as white as marble—she now seemed gray and colorless as a corpse. A tinge of horrible zombie green had even entered her cheeks. And her eyes—they were red-rimmed and seemed almost lifeless with disgust.

But for all that, like Nicki, she didn't move, she didn't budge, as the snake made its slow, slithering way across her shin. She simply stared down at it with her dead eyes and her deathly pallor, giving one enormous shudder as the thing passed over first one of her legs and then the other.

Then it moved toward me.

A knot of disgust and fear rose in my throat—but before the snake got to me, it turned and headed back down the muddy slope toward the running water below.

At the same moment I heard Mendoza speak decisively.

"Vamanos." *Let's go.*

As I watched the coral snake nose its way back down into the stream, I heard the footsteps start up again above my head—the sharp, determined footsteps of the rebels moving away from us, moving back through the jungle toward the trail. Quickly, the sound of them faded. I heard Mendoza shout one more string of orders, his voice growing farther away with every word. I could tell the rebels were already back on the trail, already marching back toward the airstrip.

Cautiously, Palmer rose up again to peek over the top of the ravine. I watched him, waiting for him to give the signal that it was clear.

I saw him nod to himself and let out a breath, the tension flowing out of him.

He lowered himself until he was in the stream and came walking toward us along the ravine wall.

"They're gone," he said, still keeping his voice low.

With that, Meredith let Nicki go. Nicki immediately rolled away from her, sobbing violently. And for once, Meredith didn't comfort her. She just bent forward and covered her own face with her hands. I heard her make a noise and I knew that she was crying too.

I reached out to her. I wanted to touch her shoulder, to comfort her, but somehow I didn't have the nerve. I hated to see her so upset—but I couldn't work up the courage to put my hand on her. I glanced up at Palmer. I saw him look down toward the water. He saw the coral snake moving away on the opposite bank of the stream. He nodded once, as he understood what had happened.

"Hey. You. Girl." He nudged Nicki's shoulder with his knuckle.

She gasped out of her sobs and stared up at him as if he were some fresh danger.

"What's your name?" he asked her.

"Nicki," she managed to say in a trembling voice.

"Good job keeping quiet, Nicki. Saved our lives. Personally, those snakes always make me shriek like a banshee."

Nicki went on staring up at him as if she couldn't comprehend what he was saying. Then she did comprehend. Almost at once, her sobs subsided to a series of smaller sniffles. She nodded her thanks. She was proud of herself.

Then Palmer looked up at me—and with one swift smooth motion, he pulled that giant hunting knife of his out of his belt.

"Hold still a second, kid," he said.

Before I could even react—before I even understood what he was saying—his hand flicked like a bullwhip and the knife came flying toward me, flying straight at my face.

I didn't have time to flinch. I didn't have time for anything. The knife struck—plunged into the mud of the ravine wall—right next to me, right next to my head, maybe an inch or two away, no more.

I turned to look at it. And—I couldn't help myself—I let out a sharp cry and scrambled away from the spot, slipping and splashing in the mud.

There on the mud wall, pinioned by Palmer's knife, thrashing in its hideous death throes, was a spider the size of a loaf of bread. Really. I'm not exaggerating. The size of one of those big, round loaves of sourdough bread.

I gagged as I watched it die. I had to fight the urge to throw up. I guess my reaction must have looked pretty amusing because Nicki said, "Ew, gross!" and then covered her mouth to hide a laugh. Even Meredith, the tears still on her cheeks, smiled quietly.

"Ha ha," I said as I tried to recover a little dignity. "Laugh riot."

Palmer gave one of his wry, sardonic smiles. "Those things'll kill ya, kid," he drawled. Then, all business again, he tilted his head toward the ravine wall. "Vamanos," he said.

CHAPTER EIGHTEEN

We made our way back to the trail and followed Palmer along its narrow, winding way. He walked ahead of us at a quick, steady clip.

The storm was passing now. The thundershowers always came on hard and fast in the afternoon and dwindled away again just as suddenly. As we walked, we caught glimpses of the sky through the dense leaves above us. And as the black clouds dissipated, we saw there was still some light left. The sky behind the storm was gray-blue, and the sun, low in the west, came to us through the forest in slanting rays.

We trudged on. As the storm faded, and as the noise of the storm faded with it, the jungle seemed to come alive with new sounds—a lot of them. Birds made weirdly human whistles and laughing calls to one another—and sometimes they burst out of the leaves with a fluttering explosion as we walked by. A rattling commotion made me raise my eyes—and I saw monkeys climbing among the lacework of vines and branches over our heads. Kind of an eerie sight— like furry little human beings crawling along over us. And sometimes they let out a scream—*wa-a-a-a-a-a-a!*—that sounded like something from a totally other planet.

But I didn't look up at them for too long. I had to keep my eyes on the ground. I had to keep watching for spiders and snakes. Not to mention leopards and crocodiles. Or maybe I've already mentioned them.

I became aware of something else too. I was hungry. As in: way hungry. And crazy thirsty. Palmer had told us not to drink from the ravine or it would make us sick. I had caught some rain in my mouth awhile back, but other than that I don't think I'd had anything to eat or drink since Mendoza had walked into the cantina. I hadn't noticed it before, what with all the danger and excitement, but now, with every step, I was conscious of the rumbling pangs in my belly and of the dry crust coating the inside of my mouth. Back home, when it was getting to be dinnertime, sometimes I would say to my mom, "I'm starving," or sometimes, coming indoors after some touch football game or something I might say, "I'm dying of thirst." But I had never been hungry like this before. I had never been this thirsty ever. Yet, somehow, I had to keep going on—and because I had to, I did.

The sun sank lower. The air grew somewhat cooler, less dense. The last raindrops dripped down off the leaves and fell on us. My clothes were still damp and uncomfortable, squishing and chafing my skin with every step, but it was better than getting rained on. And anyway, I was too hungry to care very much.

We walked a long time. The jungle began to grow dark again—not as dark yet as during the storm because the low sun still cut through the foliage and sent its beams in to us, but the trees around us were beginning to sink into shadow and the sky, when we could see it, was less blue, more gray. I wasn't happy about this. Not at all. I wasn't happy about the idea of walking through this place in the nighttime, unable to see where I was stepping—or what I might be stepping on—unable to see what might be following us, what might be watching us hungrily through the darkness . . . As the dark grew deeper, my fear started to grow worse and worse. I watched the others ahead of me, marching on. I wondered if they were as scared as I was—or was I just a coward?

I remembered once in English class we read some of the works of Ernest Hemingway. I remembered Hemingway said that cowardice was "a lack of ability to suspend the functioning of the imagination." To be honest, I didn't really understand that when I read it. But I sort of got it now. The more I *imagined* the bad things that *might* happen to us out here, the more scared I got; and the more scared I got, the more nervous and weak I felt. If something bad *did* happen, well, I was beginning to think I wouldn't have the courage to deal with it, that I might run away and leave my friends to face it alone. That was no good. If I was going to stay strong, I had to somehow stop thinking about it all—about the snakes and spiders and leopards and crocodiles and so on. I had to find some way to force it all out of my mind. "Suspend the functioning of the imagination." Easy to say, Mr. Hemingway. Not so easy to do.

A monkey chattered and screamed. I tensed and gasped so loudly that Meredith, who was just ahead of me, actually glanced back to see if I was okay. I had clutched my machine gun and was pointing it in the direction of the noise as if I were going to blow some monkey away or something. I felt like an idiot. I had to find a way to calm down.

I thought of something. I thought of Pastor Ron. Not the way I'd seen him last, his body lying in the alley after the rebels had murdered him. I thought of the way he used to be. Back in our church. I thought of him the way he was when he would preach sometimes when Pastor Francis took a Sunday off. I could almost see him in my mind's eye, standing above us up in the pulpit. I could picture him so clearly, in fact, that I could almost hear his voice, as if he were walking along beside me right that second. I remembered once he said to us:

"Don't worry about anything—pray about everything instead."

That was a quote from the Bible, I knew, though I didn't know what book or anything. But it sounded like good advice. Practical too—you know? I mean, it wasn't just like saying,

"Don't worry." It was something you could actually do with your mind *instead* of worrying. A *way* you could "suspend the functioning of the imagination," like Hemingway said.

So I tried it out as we marched on through the darkening jungle. I focused on praying. I prayed that everything would be okay. Not just for me but for my parents too. They were probably getting pretty worried by now as news of the revolution in Costa Verdes reached them. All of our parents were probably getting worried. It was hard to imagine Palmer having parents, but he must have had them at some point, and even they were probably getting worried. So I prayed for all of our parents.

It worked. It distracted me, anyway. It made me stop thinking about the snakes and whatnot. And it made me feel that we hadn't lost Pastor Ron—not totally. It made me feel that he was still right there with us, at least in some way. So I forgot about all my fears for a while. And before I knew it, Palmer was lifting his hand at the front of the line and we were all slowing to a stop.

I came up alongside Palmer and the others. And I looked past them at an absolutely amazing sight.

We were standing at the edge of a clearing. It wasn't a full clearing like the airstrip, not flat and grassy like that. There were still some trees here and there and the grass and bushes were overgrown. But it was obvious that someone had cut away part of the forest here not so long ago. Without the thick jungle roof, the space was a little brighter. The sun was just visible through the western trees and the last of its rays were turning pale and dying. A sort of shroud of darkness seemed to be slowly settling down over the open field.

And in the center of this clearing, there was, so help me, a building. A stone pyramid of some sort. An ancient temple, I guess.

It was tall—really tall—taller than the surrounding trees. It rose up in layers of stone with a flight of stairs rising up the middle of it to an open door just beneath the peak. It stood there in the dying light, dark and mysterious, like something the hero might stumble onto in a jungle adventure movie. *Will Peterson and the Temple of Outrageous Weirdness*. Here and there throughout the clearing there were other stones, single stones, standing and lying on the grass. Looked like some kind of ancient cemetery or something.

"Whoa!" I said.

I stared through the deepening dusk. I remembered the ceremony we had watched in Santiago. The cave and the torches and the candles—and the painted idol who smoked a cigar while the people sang his praises. I wondered if some painted, cigar-smoking idol had ruled this temple long ago, commanding the villagers to carry out all kinds of bizarre ceremonies and human sacrifices and other cool stuff like that. Anyway, the idea gave the place a sort of spooky feeling, as if the ghosts of all those sacrificed people might still be floating around the graveyard stones, watching us, haunting us.

"There's a room up top," Palmer said, gesturing to that open door. "We can sleep in there tonight. It'll keep us off the ground away from the animals."

What a great idea! I felt a flood of relief that nearly made me laugh out loud. I had been worrying about that, you know, wondering what we would do when we couldn't walk anymore, when we had to go to sleep. I had been trying not to worry, trying to pray instead, but all the same, I hadn't been looking forward to lying on the forest floor in the darkness with coral snakes and spiders the size of bread loaves. I could just picture myself, everyone else sleeping soundly around me, and me lying awake waiting for something to slither over my face.

"There's a freshwater spring on the far side of the clearing," Palmer went on.

"Oh!" sighed Nicki. "Water!"

Palmer said, "Let's get a drink and then we'll try to gather some kindling before nightfall, start a fire, warm our clothes."

I wondered how Palmer knew so much about all this. The hidden trail off the airstrip. The temple. The spring. But I didn't wonder too much. I was just glad he did know, glad he had shown us the way.

I remembered again how much I'd disliked this guy a few hours ago. But boy oh boy, he was a great guy to know in a crisis.

We headed into the clearing.

CHAPTER NINETEEN

Forty-five minutes later we were sitting inside a little chamber at the top of the temple. We found enough dry wood in the surrounding trees to get a fire going. Palmer set it up just at the chamber door so that the smoke blew outside but there was enough room for us all to sit around the flames and catch some of their warmth. It was so expertly done, I got the feeling he had done all this before.

It was full dark now in the jungle. Over the crackling of the fire, I could hear the noises of life out there. Kind of like the noise you'd hear in any forest or swamp, only on amplifiers, you know, with the crickets and frogs and whatever else so loud and busy, it was just incredible. Now and then too, there'd be something else. Like a big boom of some kind, or a rough grunt or a growl—I had no clue what any of it was and to tell you the truth, I didn't really want to find out.

Better not to think about it. Suspend the imagination. For now at least I was feeling pretty good, pretty safe in here in this temple with the fire going and my friends around me and the darkness way out there beyond the fire.

Better yet, I wasn't thirsty anymore. I had drunk so much from that freshwater spring, I could still feel the water sloshing around in my stomach. And even better still, after we got the fire going, Palmer revealed that he had some food with him. He opened the backpack he'd given Jim and took out a plastic bag—and there were sandwiches inside! There were only two of them—Palmer had brought them along for himself—but they were big old submarines and we broke them into sections and shared them around. It was enough to kill the hunger that had been gnawing at me so painfully during our march.

After we'd eaten, we all just sat there awhile, staring into the fire, trying to get warm, trying to get our clothes dry. I stole glances at my friends, their faces lit in the orange glow. They stared into the flames, expressionless. They all looked as exhausted as I felt.

I stared into the flames too. So much had happened in so short a time that I could hardly think about it. Was it only hours ago we had been gathered in the cantina ready to go home? Only hours ago I had faced the rifles of a firing squad, trying to come to terms with death? Only hours ago I had shot a man as he tried to hurl a grenade at us? And was it only hours ago . . . ?

"I keep thinking about Pastor Ron," said Nicki quietly.

"So do I," said Meredith.

"Me too," said Jim.

"Me too," I said.

We were quiet then, thinking about him.

"He was going to get married soon," I said after a minute.

"He was," said Meredith. "I met his fiancée at coffee hour once. She's studying psychology. In Nevada somewhere, I think."

Frowning deeply, Jim picked up a twig and threw it into the flames. "Stinks." His voice sounded heavy and dead.

I remembered how I'd shouted at him back in the hotel after the soldiers had dragged Pastor Ron away.

"You did this! You told him to go!"

"Hey, Jim," I said now. "Back in the hotel . . . back in Santiago . . . I didn't mean that stuff I said. Wasn't your fault what happened, dude."

Meredith put her hand on Jim's shoulder. "It really wasn't, Jim."

He nodded, staring into the fire, frowning into the fire. "I just keep thinking . . . if we could get word to Fernandez Cobar in Santa Maria . . . You know? I read his book . . ."

Soldier of Justice, I thought. *Whoopee.*

"He's not like Mendoza and these others," Jim went on. "He's a man of . . . of culture, an intellectual . . . He only wants justice—justice for his people. If we could just explain our situation to him . . ." His voice trailed off.

I remembered what Palmer had said about Cobar, that

he was a "soulless psycho killer." So far, Palmer's assessments of human nature tended to be a lot more accurate than Jim's. Frankly, I was hoping that if we had to explain our situation to "Soldier of Justice" Cobar, we would do it by e-mail, from far, far away . . .

"What *are* we going to do?" I asked Palmer. "No plane. No van. How are we going to get out of here? Where are we headed?"

Palmer was leaning back on one hand, relaxed, one knee raised, his other arm resting on it. He watched the flames like the rest of us, but I could see he wasn't just staring, exhausted. He was thinking.

"We're going to make a run for Santa Maria," he said after a moment. "I know an airfield just outside the city. Plenty of planes. I figure we'll *borrow* one, so to speak. Fly to the border. We could reach Belize from there in no time."

"Santa Maria," said Jim. "That's over a hundred miles away. And we'd have to cross the mountains . . ."

Palmer gave one of those ironic smiles of his, lifting one corner of his mouth. "Well, I know a place where we might be able to get ourselves a lift, but I wouldn't worry about that yet."

"Why not?" asked Jim.

"Because the jungle'll probably kill us before we get there."

I laughed. Meredith smiled. Even Nicki smiled. After having some food and water—the warmth of the fire, a place to sleep above the jungle—I guess we were all feeling a lot better. More hopeful, more brave. Funny how little it takes to turn your emotions around.

I glanced over at Palmer—and a thought occurred to me—something I hadn't remembered to say before. I said it now: "Hey, Palmer. Thanks, you know? For coming back. Thanks for coming back to get us. You didn't have to do that. You had your van—you were outta there. You coulda kept driving, but you came back and saved our lives."

"Yeah," Jim added quickly, nodding.

"That's right," Nicki said. "They'd have killed us for sure."

"Yes," said Meredith. "Thank you." She was sitting across the fire from him, looking through the wavering light at him. She had washed herself down by the spring, as we all had, and she had untangled her hair, and her eyes were clear and full of warmth in her pale, cool features. I have to admit: it sent a pang through me to see her looking at Palmer that way.

But Palmer didn't seem to care. He didn't answer any of us. In fact, he acted like he hadn't heard us at all.

"We better get some sleep," he said. And with that, he stood up and moved away from the fire into the darker shadows of the chamber, muttering, "We're going to need it. We've got a long way ahead of us."

So we all left the fire to die on its own and moved off into our own corners of the chamber. I took my machine gun with me and lay down next to it on the floor in the dark. It was a small room and I could feel the others close by and even see the shapes of them by the fading firelight. I closed my eyes and listened to them breathing. It was a comforting sound.

"Oh," Nicki groaned. "I am *so* exhausted . . ."

A few seconds later I could tell by the way her breathing deepened that she had fallen asleep. Jim too—I could hear him snoring.

As for me—well, tired as I was, you would think I'd have fallen asleep too, just like that. But in fact I lay awake, my mind racing. After a while, I opened my eyes and stared into the flame-lit darkness.

I was still thinking about everything that had happened. Pastor Ron getting killed. And me shooting that guy who was going to throw the hand grenade. And that firing squad . . . I was remembering that feeling I had when I thought I was about to die myself—that feeling that life was incredibly beautiful, and that people were incredibly beautiful, or that they were meant to be beautiful, anyway, but that they did wrong things and messed themselves up somehow. I remembered how, in what I thought was going to be my last moments, I wished I'd enjoyed every minute of life more, even the hard parts, and I wished I'd been nicer to everyone, even people who got on my nerves. In those few seconds in front of the firing squad, I actually could understand for the first time how you might be able to do stuff like love your enemies or forgive people even when they'd really treated you badly.

But now—now that the immediate threat of death was past—those feelings were gone. Lying there in the dark, I tried to bring them back, but I couldn't. I could *remember* feeling them, but I couldn't actually *feel* them anymore, you know. I mean, for instance, I don't think I was enjoying this particular moment of life very much. My clothes were still damp and I was scared about tomorrow and I wished I were home instead of out here in the middle of this snake-infested nowhere—back home where—guess what?—my parents were probably still fighting with each other all the time, probably about to get a divorce. What was so enjoyable about that?

And as for loving my enemies—let me be honest here—no way. I didn't love Mendoza and his rebels. I *hated* them. I hated them for their cruelty and violence, for what they'd done to Pastor Ron and for how they'd tried to kill us and for chasing us into this awful jungle. As long as I'm being really truthful here, I should add that I didn't even love the people I was here with that much. I mean, I still knew that Nicki had a sweet heart and that Jim had a good soul, but . . . well, her sobbing and crying all the time kind of annoyed me . . . and Jim talking about what a great guy this Fernandez Cobar was . . . It just seemed stupid, that's all. And Meredith . . . the way she looked at Palmer across the fire . . .

It's too bad you can't always live as if it were the last moment of your life. Because, you know, it might be—it might really be. And if we could really see it that way, really live like that, I think we'd all feel a lot differently about everything; I think we'd all feel a lot more the way God wants us to feel.

I closed my eyes again and tried to sleep.

But then I heard something . . . a low whisper in the dark, very soft.

"Palmer."

It was Meredith. Even with her speaking so quietly, I recognized the calm, steady tone of her voice.

And Palmer answered her with a low noise: "Hm?"

"Why did you?" she whispered.

"Why did I what?"

"You know what I mean. Why did you come back for us? I thought you said you were going to get in your van and drive off. You said you'd have a better chance of getting away on your own . . ."

"Yeah, well . . . I would've."

"You would have. That's right, I know. But you came back for us."

"Actually, I just happened to be driving by."

Meredith laughed softly in the dark. They were both speaking in the quietest whispers, almost inaudible. I knew they thought all the rest of us were asleep.

"I knew you were going to, you know," she told him. "I didn't believe for a second you would leave us."

"Don't gloat, Lady Liberty," Palmer said. "It's an ugly habit."

"Was it because of me?" she asked him—and there was something in her voice I'd never heard before. Something—I don't know what you'd call it—girlish, I guess. All I know is the sound of it sent another pang through me. "Was it because of what I said to you?"

"You said something? I wasn't listening."

She laughed again—and it was a kind of laugh I'd never heard from her either, a sort of giggle, almost like one of Nicki's. The two of them were silent after that for a couple of seconds.

Then Meredith said: "What happened to you? Would you tell me?"

"Go to sleep, Liberty. We've got a long trek in the morning."

"What happened to make you so angry?"

He didn't answer.

"Was it the Marines? Was it something that happened in the war?"

And still, Palmer said nothing.

"Because when Mendoza mentioned your fellow Marines, you said, 'They're not my fellow Marines,'" Meredith went on. "My uncle was in the Marines. He told me that once you're a Marine, you're a Marine forever."

"That's true," Palmer said. "Unless they toss you out."

"Is that what happened?"

He was silent so long I thought he wasn't ever going to answer her. But then I heard him move. I stole a glance at him through my half-closed eyes and saw he had rolled over on his side to face her so that she could hear him more clearly. In that same low voice, nearly inaudible beneath Jim's snoring, he said, "We were outside the wire, up in Nuristan, deep in Bad Guy country. We were stationed at a local police base—just a bunch of tin shacks on a hillside. I got word that one of the local cops had arranged to lead us into a Taliban ambush. I asked him about it. I guess I wasn't very polite. It's possible I even stuck a pistol under his chin by way of a conversation starter."

It was a moment or two before Meredith responded. Then she said, "And did he tell you what you wanted to know—about the ambush?"

"Well, he did, in fact," said Palmer. "So we were ready for it when it came. Turned out to be kind of a disappointing ambush from the bad guys' point of view. We took out a couple dozen of them, chased the rest back into the hills."

"But you got in trouble for interrogating the policeman."

"Somehow a reporter back home got word of it, started asking questions. The brass were afraid of being embarrassed by some headline like 'Marine Tortures Sad-Eyed Shepherd.' You know how the headlines work. So they gave me a choice: leave the service quietly or face court-martial, maybe even prison . . ." There was a pause and then he added, "I don't think I would have liked prison."

Palmer lay down again and they were both quiet. I lay where I was with my eyes fully closed now. It was a strange feeling, eavesdropping on the two of them like that. Not a good feeling. I mean, I was sixteen—not all that much younger than Meredith and Palmer. But just then, I felt so much younger than they were that it was almost embarrassing. I mean, I felt like I was about four years old, lying upstairs in bed listening to the grown-ups talking at a dinner party downstairs. I felt like a child, while Meredith and Palmer were adults.

"I'm sorry that happened to you," Meredith whispered.

"You're not going to say something inspirational, are you?" he asked.

"What do you mean?"

"You're not gonna say something like: 'Everything happens for a reason,' or 'When God closes a door, he opens a window.'"

"No," said Meredith. "I wasn't going to say anything like that."

"Good. I didn't want to have to shoot you."

She laughed. "Well, I do want to say something," she told him.

"Hold on, let me get my gun."

"I want to tell you I've changed my mind about you. I said I thought you were in danger of losing the man you were meant to be. I don't think that anymore."

"Well, Liberty, that is a great relief to me," said Palmer. "I was seriously planning to lose sleep over it."

"Oh, shut up," said Meredith gently.

I heard Palmer shifting on the floor in the dark. "So what about you?" he asked. "What happened to you?"

"Me? What do you mean?"

"I mean: What made you the way you are?"

"I don't know. What way am I?"

Palmer paused only a second. Then he answered her with a single word: "Fearless."

She gave a little huff. "That's silly. Nobody's fearless. That snake almost made me scream like Nicki."

"Yeah. But the way you spit in Mendoza's eye. The way you looked when they put you up against the wall. I saw your face as I came driving down the alley. I've known a lot of really tough guys in my life. I've never seen anything like it. I want to know what happened that made you that way."

In the silence that followed, Nicki whimpered softly in her sleep. Jim snored loudly. I'm embarrassed to admit it, but I strained to listen—to listen in—because I wanted to hear Meredith's answer.

But all she said was, "Go to sleep, Mr. Dunn. We have a long trip in the morning."

Palmer chuckled softly. Then neither of them spoke again. After a while, I heard Meredith's breathing grow deeper and more steady. Palmer's too.

But I lay awake for a long time in the darkness.

CHAPTER TWENTY

I woke up stiff and sore. My legs ached from so much walking. And every time I touched the bruise on my face where Mendoza's gunman had slugged me, the pain shot through my whole body. Plus I was hungry. Plus the idea we had to travel a hundred miles made me tired before we even got started.

We were all in pain, all complaining, groaning, as we tromped down the stairs of the temple back to the stone-dotted plain below. We got some water from the spring. Meredith had salvaged a plastic bottle from the truck. Palmer filled it with water and put it in Jim's backpack for later. He found some coconuts too—which didn't taste all that great but at least stopped my stomach from grumbling. Palmer put some pieces of them in Jim's backpack as well.

So anyway, by the time I slung my machine gun over

my shoulder and took a last glance at the ancient temple and marched off with the others into the jungle, I was feeling okay—as okay as could be expected, anyway, under the circumstances.

The good feeling didn't last long, though. The trail out of the temple clearing was narrow, and it got narrower with every mile we walked. Soon we were pushing through thick underbrush. Palmer had to take the knife out of his belt and cut through some of the tangled branches. It was slow going.

As the day wore on, it got hot too. Really hot and really humid. The sweat poured off me and my clothes got damp again. I was panting hard—harder with every step. The air was so thick you could hardly breathe it. I was getting so tired I hardly had to work at suspending my imagination. I was too hot, too sticky, too wiped out to be afraid of what might happen next.

I started to look forward to the afternoon thunderstorm. It would drench us, but at least it would cool us off. As it turned out, I shouldn't have worried about it. Because very quickly, the heat became the least of our problems.

It got to be around noon. Palmer called a halt and said we should rest. He gave us a sip of water and some pieces of coconut. It wasn't much—it wasn't enough—but it was something and made me feel a little stronger.

We were sitting in a small open patch of ground. There were two big trees here. Jim and I had our backs against one. Palmer and the girls sat against the other. We were all dripping sweat in the steamy heat, all sitting with our heads thrown back, resting against the trees, our mouths open as we tried to catch our breath and gather our strength to keep on walking.

After a while, I lowered my head and I saw that Palmer was gone. I could just glimpse him up ahead through the trees. I decided to see if I could help him with anything.

I worked my way to my feet and headed off. Pushed through the thick branches until I found him. He was standing still, staring into the tangle of the jungle. As I came crashing up to him, he raised his hand to get me to stop. I stood beside him.

"You hear that?" he asked.

I listened. For a second, all I could make out was the usual sounds of the jungle: the birds laughing and calling, the monkeys screaming once in a while. But then I picked out something else. A sort of steady hissing whisper. It blended in with the other noises so it was tough to hear at first.

"Water," I said.

"The river," said Palmer. "About a half mile off. We're going to have to cross it."

"We have to swim?"

He shook his head. "It's not that deep here. But it's fast . . . and there are rocks a little way down . . . a falls after that. Get swept into the rocks and they'll cut you to pieces. And if they don't, the falls'll finish you."

"Great," I said. I hardly felt strong enough to walk at this point, let alone cross a raging river with my life at stake.

Palmer glanced at me with those mocking eyes of his. His face was rugged, and his stubble of beard had become a lot darker. He looked like a hard man, a tough man who had seen a lot of bad things. Which I guess is what he was.

But to my surprise, he reached over and slapped my shoulder—almost affectionately, I thought.

"Don't sweat it so much, kid," he said. "You got it in you."

I didn't understand him. "Got what?"

"Everything you need. You just don't know it yet. Come on, let's go round up the others. We gotta get moving."

He headed back toward the clearing. I stood for a moment, watching him go, trying to figure out what he'd just said, what it meant. I wasn't sure exactly, but it sounded like a compliment. Rotten with sweat and exhausted as I was, it made me feel a little better about things, anyway.

I followed him then. Even before I got back to the clearing, I heard the others groaning as Palmer urged them to their feet.

"I can't go another step," Nicki complained. "I'm serious. I need to rest. I *need* to. I'll *die* if we just keep marching like this."

"Well, we're heading on," Palmer answered. "You can wait here and catch up with us when you have the strength."

I didn't hear Nicki's answer, but a moment later she came down the narrow path with the others, so I guess she had gone another step and she didn't die—at least not just yet.

Palmer took the lead again. We followed him on through

the heavy underbrush. Now that I knew it was there, I heard the *whoosh* and burble of the river continually. It was growing louder every second.

Then I heard Nicki up ahead of me let out an astonished, "Oh. No."

A second later I was standing with her and the others, staring at the river stretched out before us.

The jungle broke off here and then there was a muddy strip of earth and then the water. Beneath a ribbon of open sky winding over the clustered trees, the current snaked down out of the mountains to our left, and snaked away into the forest to our right. I'm not much good at measuring distances, but I guess the river was about as wide at this point as a football field is long. And while the water seemed dark here, you could look at the reeds bending over in it and you could see the force of its flow.

I turned to look downriver and I saw where the white water began just at the next bend. Gray shadows of rocks jutted dangerously out of the swirling rushes and eddies. Palmer had said there was a falls after that, but it must've been around the curve, out of sight.

"How deep is it?" asked Nicki nervously.

"It'll be close to your waist at the deepest part," Palmer said, "but it's the shallowest spot we can reach."

"The current seems slower up there," said Jim, lifting his chin to point toward the mountains. "Less likely to knock us over."

"It's slower, but it's deeper in the middle," Palmer told him. "We'd be over our heads and off our feet and the current would carry us right back here before we got to the far shore."

"But what happens if we do get knocked over?" asked Nicki.

Palmer didn't answer her.

"What happens if we get knocked over or fall?" Nicki insisted.

"Just don't," Palmer told her—and he squelched down the muddy bank toward the river's edge.

He started calling instructions to us as we trudged after him. He had to raise his voice over the sound of the rushing water.

"Kid," he said.

I looked at him. He looped his rifle strap over his head so he wouldn't have to fight to hold on to the weapon in the current. I did the same. Then he turned to the others.

"All right, we're gonna lock arms. Boy-girl-boy-girl, with me on one end and the kid on the other, Jim in the middle. The guys are heavier and stronger and that'll keep us all anchored. Face upstream—that way, toward the mountains—but we're gonna slant our path slightly downstream as we move to absorb some of the pressure. Stay on your feet and keep moving. Let's go."

With a soft splash, Palmer stepped into the water. He offered Meredith his arm. She linked her arm in his and Jim linked up with her. Then Nicki. Then me. Nicki's arm felt very slender and fragile in mine.

"This is the worst thing that's ever happened," Nicki muttered forlornly.

"Yeah," I said. "Since the last thing that happened."

Palmer moved out deeper into the river, tugging the rest of us after him. For the first few steps, the water only swirled up around his feet. Then, very quickly, it was up to his knees. Meredith sank in after him and Jim, Nicki, and I followed.

I felt Nicki shudder beside me as the water came up over the cuffs of her khakis. "Do you think there'll be more of those snakes?" she asked in a small voice.

"Try not to think about it," I told her. That's what I was trying to do—and I really didn't appreciate her bringing it up.

"Oh, thanks," said Nicki. "How am I supposed to not think about getting killed by poisonous snakes?"

"Try praying instead."

"I haven't *stopped* praying! That just makes me think about it *more*."

"Maybe try some different prayers," I said. *Silent ones,* I added to myself.

The water climbed up my jeans as we were speaking. It wasn't too cold, but the force of it was pretty surprising— almost shocking. It was a steady trembling push, as if some invisible giant had braced himself against the earth and was trying to shove us over with all his might. The deeper it got, the harder it got to fight against it. It seemed about to carry us away—and the slippery rocks and pebbles that kept sliding around under my sneakers on the bottom didn't make it any easier.

"It's so strong," said Nicki.

"Just keep steady," I said—trying to sound more confident than I felt. "We're all locked together. We won't let you fall."

"What happens if we do fall? Will we die?"

"Just concentrate on staying steady, Nicki."

"Why won't Palmer just *tell* us what will happen?"

"I guess he wants you to suspend your imagination," I said.

"What is *that* supposed to mean?"

"It means try not to think about it."

"Oh, great, that's what you said be—"

Then she slipped. She gave a little cry and I felt her weight on my arm as one of her feet went out from under her. Our human line stopped as Jim and I both bent our arms harder, fighting to hold on to her. I could feel the weight of her dragging us downstream. But she quickly worked her feet back under her. Then she was standing and Jim and I kept her steady. We started edging across again.

Now maybe you'll pay attention to what you're doing, I thought, annoyed. Somehow I managed to keep from saying it out loud.

We came out toward the middle of the river. As we got farther from the banks, farther from the trees, we had a wider view upstream. It was a pretty amazing sight, I have to say. The deep-green jungle rose into soft-green jungle hills. The hills rose into steel-blue mountains, their jagged peaks hazy in the rising mist. The first clouds of the day were coming in over the high horizon. Their majestic white shapes decorated the pale-blue sky and cast running shadows over the jungle below. A bird cried out and a huge blue heron suddenly winged out of the trees and passed overhead—it looked like a living airplane, something out of a fantasy.

"It's all so beautiful," I heard myself say.

"Beautiful?" said Nicki at once. "Yeah, if the snakes don't bite you or some animal doesn't eat you or you don't fall into the water and die."

"It *is* beautiful," said Jim on the other side of her, as we edged even deeper into the water. "It's a beautiful country. It's the people who make everything stink."

The water rose up my legs. I felt the push of the current grow stronger against me and had to focus on keeping steady on my feet. Still, I lifted my eyes to take in the incredible view one more time. I guess, in one way, Jim was right. There was a lot of poverty and violence and cruelty in this country. So without the people, I guess it would all just be beautiful scenery like this. But then, without people, what difference would any of it make? Who would even appreciate how beautiful it was—besides God, I mean.

The water was high now, high on my thighs—higher on the shorter Nicki. She was up to her waist in it. And suddenly, she made a noise—not a scream or anything, just a little trembling gasp of fear—and she stopped moving.

My shoulder bumped into her and a rock went out from under my sneaker. I staggered and nearly fell but managed to sort of squat down and steady myself, fighting back against the water that was pushing against my chest. I straightened, the water splashing down around me. I tried to continue edging along, but Nicki had stopped completely. Our little line came to a standstill.

"Let's go," Palmer called harshly. "Keep moving."

He tried to start off again. Meredith, then Jim went with him. I felt the pull of them. But Nicki just stood there, a dead weight. I couldn't get around her and she held us all.

"Nicki," I said. "Let's go."

She didn't even turn to me. She was staring upriver. Her mouth was open. Her face was white. I turned to follow her gaze.

I felt the blood drain out of my face too.

"Oh, please don't tell me," I said.

"Come on," Palmer shouted. "Move it!"

For a second I was frozen, as frozen as Nicki. I was staring, just as she was. Jim too—I think he saw us staring and followed our gaze as well and saw what we saw.

As we watched, terrified, a massive lizard rose from the banks about fifty yards upstream where the slower water was. It looked once our way. Then it lumbered toward the water.

It was such a frightening sight, it took me a moment to find my voice. But then I called up the line to Palmer. "Alligator!"

"Probably a crocodile!" Jim called, his voice sounding as unsteady as mine. "Maybe a caiman, although it's kind of big for one of those."

"Well, thank you, National Geographic," I said. "But the thing is: I think it saw us."

"It did, it did, it did," said Nicki, her voice filling with frightened tears.

"Keep moving," said Palmer. "It probably won't come down into the faster current. But the sooner we get to shore, the better. It'll have the advantage over us in the water."

Well, I have to say, I was looking at this creature as it moved down the bank to the river. It was maybe, I don't know, ten feet long—as long as two short people end to end. It had thick, stumpy legs like living tree trunks. It had a snout the size of a teacher's desk and it was a sure bet its mouth was filled with teeth the size of daggers.

With all due respect for Palmer, my guess was it would have the advantage over us pretty much anywhere.

Still, hurrying along seemed like a good idea. Palmer started moving again, tugging the rest of us after him. And now Jim used some force to pull Nicki along and I pushed in on her without giving her a chance to resist. She staggered sideways reluctantly and our line started moving again. We continued to cross.

But all the while, of course, we also continued to watch the crocodile, or whatever it was, as it tromped with a weird slow grace over the mud toward the water's edge. Another moment and its huge body knifed into the river without so much as a splash. A flick of its gigantic tail and the dark shape of it curled around and turned in our direction.

Then it vanished from sight under the dark water.

I glanced toward the opposite shore. Still fifty yards away at least—about as far from us as the crocodile. I didn't know how fast crocs were when they came after something, but I was guessing it was pretty fast. I hoped Palmer was right about it staying in the slower water above us because if it came this way, it would be moving downstream, with the current carrying it along.

My heart plunged inside me. If you've never been in this particular situation, let me tell you: when it's a real possibility, the prospect of being eaten alive is very, very hard to stop thinking about.

And I guess Nicki felt the same way. Because when the croc submarined out of sight like that, she just panicked.

"No. No. No," she said, shaking her head—as if she could somehow argue the situation out of existence. She shook her head some more and started to back away from the spot where the crocodile had last appeared.

"Nicki, what are you doing? Stay on course," I started to say—but I never finished the sentence.

Because Nicki, stepping back, gave a sudden shriek as she slipped on something in the riverbed—and she lost her footing completely. She fell backward, straightening her arms. In an instant, she slipped out of my grasp.

She splashed down into the water, her other arm still in the crook of Jim's elbow—but only just. Jim clamped his arm tight to try to hold her, but the water was dragging her away from him too.

"Don't let her go!" I shouted to Jim—and I went after her.

Nicki was off her feet completely, on her back in the water, being pulled downstream hard. One of her hands was up over her head, the other was pincered by the wrist in the crook of Jim's arm. The water was flowing rapidly over her face so that she had to fight to come up for air.

I slogged unsteadily toward her, my movement downstream adding to the force of the river behind me. I felt like I was going to be hurled forward at any moment. The gun strap over my shoulder and head restricted the use of my left arm, but I reached out for Nicki with my right.

"Nicki, grab hold!" I shouted to her.

I heard her sputter as the water rushed over her face again. She gasped up out of it and saw me. She brought her hand down from above her head and reached for mine desperately. I stretched. I touched her fingers. I forced my legs forward another step and another. I wrapped my fingers around her wrist.

And then Jim lost hold of her.

Nicki's hand slipped out of the crook of Jim's elbow. The force of the current carried her downstream quickly—and Nicki carried me. I flew forward, tripped off my feet, and splashed face-first into the river.

I went under, the water burbling up around me. I had no chance to fight the current now. It forced me along like the wind carrying a feather. I burst up into the air, catching a breath. I heard Nicki start to scream and then choke as the water rushed into her mouth. I still had hold of her wrist. Trying to keep my head up, I craned my neck around and saw her. She was downstream, turning helplessly in the current—and just below her I saw the rapids and the rocks.

The rush of the river filled my ears but I heard shouting.

"Keep moving across!" Palmer barked at the others.

"Palmer!" shouted Meredith. "You can't just leave them behind."

"Do what I tell you!" he shouted back—and I hoped she would, because I knew there was nothing Palmer and the others could do to help us now. Nicki and I were caught in the current. We were on our own.

The river spun us round. I caught glimpses of the first rapids coming close, coming fast, the jagged edges of the rocks jutting out of them. There was nothing I could grab hold of, nothing I could do to stop us.

Nicki went under and came up again, spitting water. The current was tossing her around like a rag doll. Scared I might lose my grip on her, I pulled her to me. Wrapped my arm around her waist. Held her fast against me. This way, at least, we'd hit the rocks together and maybe I could take the worst of it on my shoulder or back.

She tried to scream again in my arms, but again the

water overwhelmed her—overwhelmed us both. We went under. I held on to her with my left arm and fought toward the surface with the other. The water was dark—just swirling green and dirt all around me. I wasn't even sure I was heading toward the surface. Then I broke out and saw the light and gulped the air. And I looked downstream.

I realized at once that I had no chance of protecting Nicki—any more than I could protect myself.

We had come around a small bend. I could see the rapids clearly now. They stretched out before us: boiling white water swirling, rising, spitting over the tops of boulders. As a wave of water lifted me up, I caught a glimpse of the river beyond them—and I saw the falls. It was a gauntlet of roaring, seething, frothing foam with sharp rocks rising from the chaos like a dragon's teeth—and then a sharp drop out of sight.

Once we hit that, we'd be battered to death, the two of us. There was no doubt in my mind.

But frankly, I didn't think we were going to live long enough to die that way. Because just then we sank down into the first swirling whirlpool of white water. I clasped Nicki as securely as I could as I was spun full around sharply and then flung up to the surface. Gasping for breath, I looked downstream. I saw we had entered a smooth black, rapid flow that was pulling us inexorably toward another sucking drop of white foam from which two sharp rocks jabbed up into the air. The rocks were close together, no more than two feet apart—they stood like a sort of gateway. And I could see exactly what was going to happen when we hit them. First, we'd suffer the impact—the shock of the blow—then we'd be pulled quickly into that gap between them into the length of foaming, speeding waves beyond. After that, it was all a tumbling rush of white water. There'd be no stopping our progress until we went over the falls.

I had maybe five seconds before we hit—time enough for the full situation to flash through my mind. Five seconds—and then four . . .

And then I had an idea.

There was no time to think it through, no time even to wonder if it would really work. I just acted in the little time I had left. I shifted Nicki and clamped her tight against me with my right arm. With my left hand, I grabbed hold of my rifle. I stripped the strap up over my head as we rushed and spun through the black water toward the two rocks.

Already, the rocks were on us, a second away. I turned in the water, turned upstream with Nicki held in front of me so that my body would hit the rocks first, taking the worst of the impact for her. I stretched out my left hand, holding the rifle in front of us.

We hit the rock. It was a blow, all right. It caught me right in the soft spot on the side of my back. I made a noise like "*oof!*" and the breath was forced out of me. The shock stopped our progress for an instant—and in the next instant we were sucked into the little gap between the rocks—sucked down toward the last stretch of rapids.

The water turned us. I was helpless to stop it. It sucked Nicki through the gap first.

"Will!" she shrieked.

I went through right after her, still clasping her tight.

And still holding that rifle out in my left hand—holding it out to my side now, upstream, making sure it was the last thing to come through the rocks, making sure it was stretched out lengthwise across that narrow gap.

The rifle struck the rocks. And stuck—it was wedged across the small space, unable to pass through.

The AK-47 machine gun was close to three feet long—longer than the gap between the rocks was wide by nearly a foot. I think if we had hit any harder, it would have rattled through—the weapon might even have just shattered, just come apart in my hands. But that first impact of my body on the rocks had slowed us. The gun didn't hit all that hard. It stayed together, and I had time to maneuver it so it was securely braced against the rocks on both ends. I held the rifle with one hand and kept my other arm wrapped around Nicki—and the rifle held us both in place.

It all happened so fast, it took me a moment before I realized—realized with amazement—that my idea had actually worked. We were held there, just above those final rapids, just above the falls.

Breathless, I looked around to get a sense of our situation.

The water continued to rush over us, to pull at us and sometimes drag us under, but we had stopped moving downstream. In fact, we were in a place where the rocks gave us some shelter from the pounding of the current. As long as I kept hold of the rifle—and Nicki—and as long as the rifle stayed wedged in the rocks, we would be safe.

At least that's what I thought. Until I saw the crocodile.

It surfaced upstream where the white water began. As I gasped up out of the current, I caught the black flash of its head peeking out above the water. So much for it staying upstream. It was looking straight at us, coming right toward us. There was no question about what it was going to do.

It was an awful moment—awful. Even standing before the firing squad hadn't felt as bad as this. The firing squad—that was just death, you know. A few seconds of fear, maybe an instant of pain and it would have been over. But to have this creature tear us apart, to have it devour us: to me, that was a nightmare of horror.

The croc took one look at us and disappeared again under the water. It was heading toward the rapid black flow that had just carried us into the rocks. Now the same flow would carry the crocodile to the place where we were trapped.

The beast was now gone from sight—but unfortunately, before it went under, Nicki caught a glimpse of it too.

I had seen her hysterical before. I had heard her crying and pleading as the firing squad forced us to the wall. But this was beyond that. She just went crazy now. She just started screaming. Like the girls in the horror movies, you know: just one deafening, high-pitched shriek after another—wordless shrieks and then my name. She'd get cut off as the river doused her and dragged her under and then she'd bob to the surface again, screaming and screaming.

"Will! Will! Will!"

I held tight to the rifle to stay in place, to stay above water. I swallowed hard. My spit tasted like copper. That was the taste of fear, I realized. I was sick with fear.

But I knew what I had to do.

Nicki was flailing in my arms, twisting and thrashing, trying to escape my grip, trying to get away from the invisible onrushing crocodile. But that was no good. If she'd broken out of my grip, she would have been swept immediately into the rapids and over the falls to her death. I had to use all my strength to hold on to her. But I did. And I forced her around me, forced her up to the rifle.

"Will! No! No!" she screamed as I pressed her up against the wedged rifle.

"Nicki!" I shouted—shouted as loud and forcefully as I could over the rushing noise of the water. I sank under. I pulled myself up. Gasped for air. "Grab hold of it! Grab hold of the gun! Grab hold!"

She wouldn't stop shrieking. She wouldn't stop flailing.

"Let go of me! Let go of me! It's coming! Let go!"

"Take hold of the rifle! I'll protect you!" I shouted.

Her scream became babbling words interrupted by gulps and gasps.

"You can't . . . You can't . . ."

"Grab hold, Nicki!"

Confused—terrified beyond rational thought—she did what I said. She put her hands on the rifle between the rocks. She gripped it.

And I, still holding the rifle myself, let go of her and ducked under the water.

It was hard to fight the current, but my grip on the rifle gave me a little leverage, and I only had to maneuver myself a few inches upstream. Then I splashed to the surface—and now I was in front of the rifle, held in place by it, while Nicki held on to it behind me.

"Will!" she sobbed. "Will!"

The water drove into my face. Gripping the rifle, I fought my way out of it. "Just hold on," I gasped. "You'll be all right."

I wasn't shouting anymore. I didn't have the strength—I was too scared. I didn't even know if she could hear me over the white water. I was staring in the direction I'd last seen the crocodile. I couldn't see it now, but I knew it was still coming—I knew it was almost there, almost on top of me.

I just hoped it wouldn't take both of us. I just hoped that one of us would be enough.

I wondered if I would see it before it struck or if it would hit below the surface and just cut me in half before I realized it was there. I wondered how long I would have to live with the agony of being eaten alive before I mercifully died.

Then I stopped wondering. *Suspend the imagination,* I thought. *Don't worry about anything. Pray about everything instead*. It was the only way I could stay in place, the only way I could keep up my courage—what there was of it. Which wasn't much.

As it turned out, the creature did surface. I saw the enormous bulk of it rise up out of the black flow of water. I saw its huge tail lashing as it propelled itself toward me. I saw the length of its great snout and death in its small, cold, indifferent eyes.

Nicki coughed and gasped and screamed my name one last time.

"Will!"

And I screamed. I couldn't help it. Tears of terror flying from my eyes, I let out a ragged scream into the face of the crocodile.

"Come on, then!" I told it. "Come on! Come on!"

The river washed over me. I broke out of it and its wash of sound surrounded me. Nicki was screaming. And I was screaming. I couldn't hear anything else but the river and the screams. I couldn't think of anything else but the onrushing crocodile.

I never heard the gunshots at all.

All I saw was that something hit the croc's head and something black and red flew off the place above its right eye and up into the air. I hardly understood what was happening as the beast thrashed enormously only a few yards away from me. The screams stuck in my throat and my heart seized in my chest as the creature's great tail flew up out of the water.

The crocodile rolled over sideways and struck the rock to my left—only about six inches from my arm. The great length and weight of its body was flung away from me, and the river carried it wide of the rocks so that it went rushing past us and down into the rapids. Turning my body full around against the rifle, I saw its limp, massive form carried into the seething turmoil of the falls and out of sight. It was only then I realized that it was already dead.

Nicki went on screaming and gasping, her eyes shut tight, her hands gripping the rifle with all her strength.

Dazed, I held myself above the surface and looked around me. I saw Palmer standing on the shore. He was just now lowering his machine gun from his shoulder. Meredith and Jim were running up to join him.

Of course, I thought.

Of course he had not left us behind. He had known he couldn't help us while he was in the water. He had crossed over first, saving the others, and then rushed down the bank to take his shot at the crocodile, to kill it before it killed me.

I ducked under my rifle and wrapped my arm around Nicki again. I held on to her and held us both in place.

"It's all right," I said into her ear between gulps and gasps. "It's all right, Nicki. It's gone now. It's over."

But it was a long time before she managed to stop screaming.

CHAPTER TWENTY-ONE

It wasn't easy to get us out of the water. It was a dangerous business in itself. Palmer and Meredith and Jim had to make a human chain to reach us. The river was narrow here—we weren't that far from shore—but the current was so strong that it was hard for them to bridge the gap without being swept away themselves.

Nicki was part of the problem. I had my arm wrapped securely around her again, holding her in place, but she was so crazy upset, sobbing and weeping and twisting around, that she nearly slipped out of my hold about fifteen times before the others got to us.

Whenever I could get my head above water, I watched, shivering in the rush of the current, as Palmer and Jim and Meredith dragged a fallen tree along the riverbank until it was as close to us as they could get it. Palmer braced himself against the trunk and then he held Meredith by the wrist and Meredith took hold of Jim.

The first time they tried to stretch their way out to us, Jim was taken by surprise by the force of the rapids. It nearly swept him off his feet and carried him away. Luckily, not only was Meredith holding on to his wrist, but he was holding on to hers, and the link between them held. He tried again and got close—but not close enough. Neither Nicki nor I could reach his outstretched hand.

All the while, the river coursed over us, trying its best to knock us free from our precarious perch and carry us off toward the falls.

Jim and Meredith retreated toward shore and tried again, but this time Palmer took the strap off his rifle and Jim brought it with him. When he got out as far as he could, he tossed the strap out to us. He had to do it several times, but the third time I got hold of it. I brought it to Nicki and worked her hand through the loop, then wrapped it around her wrist and told her to hang on.

To be honest, I wasn't sure she would do it. I wasn't sure she *could* do it. She was so shaken, so upset, trembling so badly. But finally, I managed to make myself understood above the noise and through the haze of shock that seemed to have clouded her eyes. She gripped the strap in her hand and Jim pulled her in.

My heart lifted as I held the rifle and watched the others bring Nicki to shore.

They came back for me. Now that they had the system down, it went more quickly. A few minutes and I had hold of the strap myself. I was reluctant to pull my rifle from the gap in the rocks—it had been my only security all this time. But I did it. The river started to carry me off, but Jim pulled me in before it could get me.

Jim and I held on to each other as we slogged the last few feet through the current back to the shore.

The moment I hit dry land, I collapsed down into the mud. I was surprised how weak I was, how exhausted. The fight with the river and with my own fear seemed to have drained every ounce of strength out of me. I couldn't even get myself to drier land. I just sat in the mud with my knees lifted, my arms draped weakly over them, my head hung down.

Somewhere in the distance I heard Nicki crying and Meredith, as always, murmuring words of comfort to her.

"Oh, it was so awful!" Nicki kept saying. "I want to go home so much!"

"I know," Meredith kept answering gently. "I know. We all want to."

After a while, I managed to gather just enough strength to lift my head and look out at the water. From where I was— the blessed safety of dry land—the frothing rapids didn't look quite as threatening. The rocks didn't look quite as sharp.

I thought: *Did that really just happen? Is any of this really happening?*

How was it possible? How was it possible this was happening to *me*? Didn't all these gunmen and snakes and rapids and crocodiles understand that I was just sixteen-year-old Will Peterson from Spencer's Grove, California? I was not supposed to be in situations like this. They were supposed to happen to other people . . . like adventurers . . . or characters in movies maybe . . . people who were used to danger, who were ready for it. Maybe all these killers and beasts and rapids had mistaken me for some more dramatic type of guy!

I heard a footstep near me and turned and saw Meredith coming my way. She had left Nicki sitting farther up the bank, on drier land. Nicki stayed there, sitting in the dirt, her shoulders slumped, her head bowed. Now and then, her body sort of gave a little heave and I could hear her sobbing even above the sound of the water.

Meredith came to me and stood over me. Her shirt and khakis were dark with water and mud, and there were streaks of mud on her cheeks and forehead. She looked tired—I guess we all looked tired—but her pale brown eyes still had that clear, steady gaze.

I raised my head to her. I watched her as she slowly crouched down in front of me until we were eye to eye. Suddenly I wasn't thinking about the crocodile anymore or the rapids or anything. I was just looking at Meredith as she looked at me. I thought she was going to say something—she looked like she wanted to—but she didn't. She just reached out and put her hands on my face, one hand on each of my cheeks. I could feel her river-damp and chilly skin through the gritty mud all over me. I could feel my heart beating as she leaned in close to me. Then, very softly, very gently she placed her lips against my dirty forehead. She kissed me there and then drew away. She stood up.

"Come up to the dry land out of the mud," she said.

And she walked back to Nicki.

For a moment or two, I just went on sitting there. I was trying to hold on to the moment, I guess, to hold on to the feel of her lips on me, her kiss. It wasn't the kiss I would have had from her, I'll admit, but it was still a good one. I thought I would've faced any number of crocodiles for another.

I looked around in a kind of daze and saw Palmer. Grimy, soaking, unshaven, he was kneeling in the dirt, working his strap back onto his rifle. He winked at me. I smiled.

Slowly, groaning with the effort, I worked my way up out of the mud. I stood and turned my back on the river and looked up the bank into the surrounding trees.

The jungle, I saw, was filled with gunmen.

CHAPTER TWENTY-TWO

I don't know how many there were: maybe a dozen. They were stationed just within the trees, nearly hidden by the giant fronds and dense leaves all around them. They looked like villagers, like the folks back in Santiago. They had flat, dark brown Indian features. They wore jeans and cotton shirts and some of them had baseball hats. A few wore kerchiefs tied around their necks or foreheads, like the rebels did, only their kerchiefs were blue instead of red. Each of them was holding a rifle in his hand, low by his side.

"Uh . . . ," I said.

Kneeling over his AK, Palmer glanced up at me questioningly. I gestured with my head toward the jungle.

He looked that way—and he practically jumped to his feet. At first I thought he was going to raise his gun and open fire. Instead, he grinned. The gunman standing closest to us—a very large, very broad-shouldered man—also grinned, his smile white in his red-brown features. He came forward out of the trees. The other men followed him onto the river-bank, toting their rifles with them.

Until that moment Nicki, Meredith, and Jim hadn't seen the gunmen. They all started in surprise when they did and Nicki moaned, "Oh no!" as if this were the last straw, as if she just couldn't take any more excitement.

But Palmer and the large gunman were already grasping each other's hands and slapping each other's shoulders in a friendly greeting.

"Paolo," Palmer said.

"Amigo," said the gunman.

The two of them started talking to each other in rapid Spanish. Palmer laughed. He turned to us, his features unusually bright.

"He says they got word of what happened to us back in Santiago. They've been expecting us."

"You mean they're not rebels?" asked Jim.

"Not hardly," said Palmer with another laugh. "They're Achil—one of the oldest and purest tribes in the country. I was heading toward their village. It isn't far. They'll take us there and give us a ride to Santa Maria."

Palmer and Paolo talked some more in rapid Spanish. Palmer pointed at the river, then at Nicki, then at me. I guessed he was telling him what had just happened with the rapids and the crocodile and all. Paolo nodded judiciously, looking my way. Then he moved away from Palmer and stepped up to me.

He was even bigger up close. I'd bet he was six-five or so. He towered over me. He looked down at me from his great height and nodded. He spoke in Spanish very quickly. He pointed out at the river—to the place in the rocks where I'd just been stuck. Then he pointed over at Nicki. Finally, he reached out with one enormous fist and pounded me lightly on the heart. It was just a tap, but he was so large it knocked me back half a step. Then he tapped his own heart as well.

"What's he saying?" I asked Palmer.

"He says you're the single ugliest little punk of an American he's ever seen," Palmer said. "He says they're thinking of shooting you just to save the women from the misery of having to look at you."

Meredith gave that laugh—that girlish giggle I'd heard in the temple chamber the night before. "Palmer, stop," she said.

The big villager gave me a playful slap to the side of the head—which nearly knocked me unconscious—and walked away. He headed into the jungle with the other villagers behind him. Palmer gathered his weapons and Jim got his pack and they followed. Meredith helped Nicki to her feet.

"That isn't really what he said, Will," Meredith told me. "He said . . ."

"I get it, I get it," I said—and, embarrassed, I hurried off into the jungle before she could tell me anything else.

We moved through the trees quickly now. I couldn't see any trail, to be honest, but the natives seemed to see one well enough. They moved through the branches and leaves as if on some invisible path of least resistance. Simply by staying in their wake, we were able to move along far easier than we had before.

The land started to rise. We were climbing a hill. It was still hot, and soon we were all panting and sweating as we trudged along. After about half an hour, the villagers stopped. They had canteens strapped to their belts and they shared the water with us. That made us all feel stronger and we continued up the slope.

Palmer and Paolo walked together and as they walked, they kept up a steady dialogue in Spanish. I couldn't understand what they were saying, of course, so after a while I stopped listening. Their talk just became another of the jungle noises.

After another half hour or so, the jungle seemed to grow a little thinner around us. We broke out of the trees as we reached the top of the hill. There was a village there. Not much. Just a bunch of little cinder-block-and-plaster houses with red-shingled roofs arranged around small gardens and fields. There was a central stone plaza that had a large round well. And lots of laundry lines strung up between one house and the next with clothes hanging from them. The place occupied a small clearing at the top of the hill and spilled down the opposite slope. There was more jungle surrounding it, but I could also see a dirt road winding off into the distance and several ancient green pickups parked nearby.

Most of the men of the village seemed to have come down to find us and walk with us, but the women and children were here in the village and they poured out of their houses and climbed up from their fields to meet us. They seemed especially glad to see Palmer. Several of the women kissed his cheeks and the children danced around him and plucked at his jeans for attention. The women made a fuss over Meredith and Nicki too—which Nicki seemed really grateful for.

I moved up beside Jim. He was standing off to one side by himself. His skinny, stoop-shouldered figure seemed sort of pulled into itself as if for protection. Those buggy eyes of his were scanning the village scene intensely, his thin lips pressed together.

I stood next to him and gestured at the sky. Now that we were out of the thick trees, I could see that the clouds had covered the blue completely while we walked. The clouds were still a light gray, but they were darkening by the minute.

"Guess the thunderstorms are on their way," I said, by way of making conversation.

"They murdered these people," Jim answered. "They wiped out whole villages."

Well, it wasn't the usual answer to a remark about the weather. So I said, "What? Who did?"

"The soldiers—the government. To try and suppress the

rebel movement, the government sent soldiers into the native villages to terrorize them. They slaughtered men, women, and children." He looked at me with his intense, intelligent eyes. "That's what men like Fernandez Cobar and Mendoza are fighting. That's what they're rebelling against."

I looked around at the villagers—all of them seemed to be out in the open, greeting Palmer, fussing over Nicki and Meredith.

"These folks all seem okay."

"The soldiers were here, though," said Jim. "I heard Paolo and Palmer talking about it. Apparently Palmer brought the villagers guns."

"Really?"

"Yeah. When the soldiers came, they were surprised because the villagers fought them off. Paolo says they haven't been back. So I guess Palmer must've known."

"Known what?"

"Palmer must've known what the government was doing."

The way he said this—that Palmer knew about the soldiers—was almost accusatory. It made me feel like I should say something, you know—defend Palmer. He had saved all our lives, after all. He'd saved mine more than once.

"So what?" I said. "So he knew about it. You knew about it . . ."

"I read about it in Cobar's book and his op-eds in the newspapers."

"So then anyone could know about it. And Palmer

brought the people guns so they could defend themselves, so that's a good thing, right?"

Jim didn't answer. He just looked off in Palmer's direction with a sort of sullen glare.

I was about to ask him what he was angry at Palmer for, but before I could, I saw Meredith coming toward us. She had left the crowd of villagers, but several of the little children had apparently adopted her. They were dancing around her the way they'd danced around Palmer.

"They say the storm is coming," she told us. "The road won't be usable again until the morning. We'll have to stay the night."

Well, that was fine with me. I was tired of walking. Hungry, thirsty. Wet, sweaty, smelly, generally disgusting. Spending the coming storm indoors—and getting a night's sleep before moving on—these seemed like good ideas to me.

In fact, that night was pretty much the first non-horrible thing that had happened to us since Mendoza walked into the cantina and shot Carlos. The villagers gave us some fresh clothes to wear while our clothes dried out. I can't tell you how good that felt—or how pretty the girls looked in the long, colorful native skirts. Then all the women rushed around bringing in the laundry before the rains came. And then they rushed around making dinner.

Paolo and Palmer, Jim and I, meanwhile, walked along the ridge to a small open field. The mountains fell away into flatlands below us, giving us a nice view for a pretty good distance. We could even make out a sort of blue haze near the horizon line that Palmer told us was Santa Maria, the capital. Paolo gestured out over the expanse, moving his hand back and forth and speaking quietly but with what seemed to me great seriousness.

"Can you tell what he's saying?" I murmured to Jim.

"He says the rebels have control of everything from here to the capital. They're patrolling the area with helicopters to make sure the government soldiers don't try to regroup and make another attack. He says trying to get to the capital will be dangerous. If we're spotted by one of the choppers, they'll come after us, especially if they think Palmer's with us."

That surprised me. "The rebels are after Palmer?"

We were talking in low voices so as not to interrupt Paolo and Palmer, but I guess they heard us because Paolo turned to us and started speaking very quickly.

The afternoon had gotten very dark and now the black clouds let out a rumble of thunder. Paolo glanced up and spoke again and started moving back toward the center of town. He walked with Palmer while Jim and I trailed after.

"What'd he say?" I asked Jim.

"He was talking too fast," Jim said. "I only got parts of it. Something about the guns Palmer was bringing people . . . but I'm not sure."

The storm came just as we reached the house. It was nice to sit inside with a fire going in the fireplace and listen to the rain on the red tiles of the roof. I dozed off sitting by a wall, and when I woke up, the storm was subsiding and it was dinnertime. We sat around a wooden table and had a great meal of tortillas and rice and beans. Nicki and Meredith had helped Paolo's wife and daughter prepare it.

"Boy, the guys get a good deal in this place," said Nicki, sounding a little bit more normal than she had for a while. "The women cook and clean and the guys sit around and talk and sleep."

"Sounds like a good system to me," I said.

"Don't get used to it," Meredith said with a laugh. "We're bound to get home sometime."

All the while we were eating, Palmer and Paolo went on talking to each other. And Jim sat silently. Now and then, I'd glance his way and I'd see him watching Palmer with that same dark glare. What was his problem now, I wondered.

Finally, Paolo's wife—Corinna, her name was—started to clear the dishes from the table. When she came to Palmer, she stopped. Then, sort of impulsively, she grabbed his head in her hands and gave him a great big smooch on the top of his head. This made both Palmer and Paolo laugh.

But somehow it seemed to really get on Jim's nerves. "I don't get it," he said suddenly. He was talking directly to Palmer—and the words seemed to burst out of him before he could stop them.

Palmer glanced at him—and raised one eyebrow in a sort of comical, questioning look. "Something troubling you, Professor?" he drawled.

"I . . . I just . . . I don't understand what you're doing here."

"I'm providing transportation to tourists like yourself," Palmer said.

"You're running guns," said Jim. "Aren't you?"

Until that moment, there had been a sort of general chatter at the table. Nicki and Meredith and I talking, and Corinna and her daughter, and Paolo and Palmer. But now everyone fell silent. Everyone looked at Jim and at Palmer and then down at the table.

The silence went on a long time—at least it felt that way to me. All the while Palmer kept looking at Jim, one eyebrow cocked in that mocking way of his.

Finally he said, "Now and then, I may have supplied a weapon or two to people who needed them."

"*These* people, you mean," Jim insisted. "*These* villagers. You brought guns to natives like these all over the country. You brought them weapons so they could defend themselves against the government."

"I seem to remember something like that happening from time to time."

"Because the government soldiers were murdering them, right? Their own citizens. The government was murdering the natives in order to terrorize them so they wouldn't join Cobar and the rebellion."

"I believe that was the general idea."

"You fought the government . . . this murdering

government that Fernandez Cobar has just overthrown. The same government that the United States—our country—us—supported and helped keep in power during the last revolution."

Jim seemed to feel he had made some kind of important point here, because he sort of sat back in his chair and gave Palmer a triumphant glare.

But Palmer just shrugged. "You don't like it, write your local congressman and complain," he said. "From my point of view, if you're interested, the US supported these government clowns back in the day when the Communists in the Soviet Union were trying to take the continent over—the continent and the world. The murderous Costa Verdes government stood against the Soviets—who murdered and enslaved a nice little chunk of humanity, if you remember—so the US stood with the Costa Verdes government. I'm sure if we could have found someone a bit more like Abraham Lincoln down here, we'd've supported him instead."

"That's why Mendoza didn't kill you right off the bat," said Jim bitterly. "He didn't like you, but he thought you were a friend to the rebels. That's why he didn't kill you, isn't it?"

"You'd have to ask him," Palmer said. "I thought it was because of my sunny personality."

"And that's why the government wants to find you now, because they realize you're not on their side at all. That you're against them. Or maybe you just don't care. Maybe you were just running guns for the money."

Palmer answered with another shrug.

"But . . . I don't understand. How can you be against the rebels?" Jim sputtered as the fervor of his beliefs overwhelmed him. "Fernandez Cobar has risked his life, has risked everything, to bring this horrible government down. Even Mendoza . . ."

"Mendoza, who gave the order for you to be lined up against a wall and shot," Palmer reminded him mildly.

"I know. I know," Jim said. "But don't you think Mendoza has a good reason to be angry? You know he does."

Again, it was a long time before Palmer answered, and during that time no one said anything. Nicki and Paolo and Corinna and her daughter went on studying the table, as if the whole conversation just embarrassed them. But Meredith—she kept her eyes on Palmer, watching him, listening to every word he said. Trying to get some idea of who he really was, I thought.

Jim, meanwhile, waited for an answer, glaring at Palmer across the table, his eyes practically leaping out of his head. Palmer casually looked down at his own hands, fiddling with his spoon and smiling with one corner of his mouth.

"What I know about Mendoza," he said slowly after a while, "is that he's a petty gangster who enjoys pushing people around. I've already told you what I think of Cobar: a psycho killer."

"But in his book—"

"I know," said Palmer, lifting a hand. "But a killer who

writes a book is still a killer—even if it's a book about peace and justice. A thug with a lot of high-blown political ideas is still just a thug in the end."

"But he's at war with a brutal government . . ."

"Gangsters get in wars with each other all the time," said Palmer. "That doesn't make one side good and the other bad. And it doesn't mean I have to care which bunch of bullies and thugs wins the day. You think the people in this village will be any better off when it's Cobar's government murdering them instead of the government they had before? The only one who'll feel any better about it is you, because you'll think it's all for some higher cause—*fairness* or *justice* or whatever they're calling it nowadays. Whatever they do call it, it always translates to the same thing in the end: obey the man with the gun or he'll kill you. The truth is, Professor, there's only one higher cause I know of. That's the right of every man to go his own way and spend his own money and speak his own mind and find his own salvation. You show me the side that stands for that and I'll fight for them. I was a United States Marine, friend. I *have* fought for them."

Palmer made a face then, as if he was annoyed with himself for saying so much. "I'm going to sleep," he said. "I suggest you all do the same. We leave before dawn."

CHAPTER TWENTY-THREE

A hand shook my shoulder. I woke out of a sound sleep to hear Palmer's whisper in the dark: "Move it, kid, let's go."

I was still only half awake when Corinna put a tortilla in my hand and kissed me on the cheek and sent me out the door.

We piled into the back of a pickup jalopy: Nicki and Meredith and Jim and I. Paolo drove and Palmer sat beside him in the cab. We bounced down out of the village on the rough dirt road. Even though I could feel the first fresh breezes of dawn coming down to us over the tops of the jungle trees, the open sky above us was still night black, splashed with bright, white, twinkling stars.

We rode in silence mostly. Nicki was sleeping. Jim, I could see, was staring gloomily down into the truck. Meredith—I stole a glance at Meredith now and then and she was leaning back against the side of the truck bed, gazing up at the stars. She looked as if her mind was far, far away. I wanted to ask her what she was thinking, but I wasn't really sure I wanted to know the answer.

So I sat quietly too and thought about all the things that had happened. I thought about the stuff Palmer had said last night. About how the government were bad guys and the rebels were bad guys too, and no matter who won, the regular people, the natives in their villages, were going to get hurt. The more I thought about it, the sadder it seemed. Costa Verdes was a beautiful country. The people we'd met had mostly been nice people, just like anyone you'd meet back home. The children especially were just like children anywhere. I remembered how excited they were when we came to rebuild their school and how they'd watch us shyly from a distance and how happy the girls were when Nicki did their hair for them and so on. And no matter who wound up running the country, nothing was going to get better for them. Because everyone was fighting to make them be what they wanted them to be, but no one was fighting for their right to be whomever they chose.

I was thinking about that—and then my mind flashed back to the man I had shot. I saw him again, the bullets from my weapon ripping into him as he tried to throw the hand grenade at our escaping van. The image of it made something go sour in my stomach. I found myself wondering

about the guy. I wondered if he'd had a family: a wife . . .
kids . . . He had a mom and dad somewhere, for sure, just
like I did. I wondered if he had really wanted to be standing
there, throwing a hand grenade at a group of people he never
met, who never did him any harm. I wondered if he would
have been different if his government had left him alone to
live whatever life he chose . . .

I must have drifted off a bit while I was thinking about
it, because the next thing I knew my head sort of jerked up
off my chest and when I looked around, it was lighter than
it was before. I lifted my eyes to the sky and saw that a faint
touch of gray had seeped into the deep pool of blackness up
there. There were fewer stars than there were before, and
with every second that went by there were fewer still.

Dawn was coming.

And, as it did, the helicopters came as well.

There were two of them. I heard the beat of their rotors
first, and when I looked around I saw one and then the other
come swiftly into view over the trees to our right. Black,
insect-like shapes against the lightening sky, they got closer
and closer, larger and larger, until they swept right over us,
pounding the air, the noise deafening. They didn't pause or
hover. They just kept going, the noise fading swiftly as they
disappeared over the trees to our left.

Whew, I thought. *That was close.* But it seemed they
hadn't seen us.

The next thing I knew, the truck—already bouncing hard

in the deep ruts of the dirt road—stopped short, jerking me and the others forward toward the cab, then flinging us back to the rear of the bed. The truck started moving again right away, but now the sound of voices reached us from inside the cab—Paolo's and Palmer's voices, raised in anger.

Meredith and Jim and I exchanged looks. Then we peered forward through the dusty rear window of the pickup's cab.

We could see Palmer and Paolo in there, Paolo behind the wheel, Palmer sitting to his right in the passenger seat. We could see Palmer gesturing angrily with his hand, his face dark, his voice harsh. And Paolo was shouting back at him, also gesturing with one hand while steering the truck unsteadily with his other. Their voices, muffled by the cab, were still loud enough to reach us where we were sitting.

"What's going on?" I asked Meredith.

She shook her head. "Not sure. I can't hear it all. But it seems Palmer wants Paolo to stop the truck and let us out."

"Let us out? Why?"

"Something about the helicopters," she said.

"I don't think they saw us . . ."

"That's what Paolo's saying," said Meredith, "but Palmer seems to disagree." She shuffled herself a little closer to the front of the pickup. Listened through the dusty glass. "Palmer says it's too dangerous for Paolo to stay with us now."

"But what will we do without the truck?" asked Nicki. I thought she was still asleep, but all at once she seemed to be totally awake.

The truck continued moving—but the front passenger door—Palmer's door—suddenly came open. We heard Paolo shout and the pickup bucked again, stopping and starting. It was still moving forward when Palmer jumped out.

Palmer hit the ground and stumbled a few steps before he could bring himself to a halt. The truck slowed, then jerked forward with a squeal, then bucked again, then stopped.

The passenger door was still ajar and Paolo was leaning over in the front seat shouting at Palmer in Spanish. Palmer ignored him. He came back to the bed where we were and said sharply:

"Get down. We're going on foot from here."

We didn't hesitate. I pushed open the tailgate and climbed down, my rifle strapped over my shoulder. Meredith and Jim and Nicki tumbled out right behind me.

Paolo was still shouting at Palmer through the truck's open door. Palmer rudely slapped the door shut, making Paolo's words difficult to hear.

"What's happening?" I asked.

"Crazy Indian wants to get himself killed," said Palmer. "But too bad, we're not gonna let him."

"Is this about the helicopters?" asked Meredith.

"If they spotted us, there'll be rebel gunmen here any minute. We gotta make a run for it, see if we can reach the airport before they find us."

Paolo hammered with his fist on the truck window.

"Get out of here!" Palmer shouted at him. Then he

muttered to himself, "If the rebels find him here, they'll kill him. Then they'll go up to his village and kill his wife and daughter and anyone else they don't like the look of. Just like they did in Santiago."

"Well, what'll they do if they find us?" Nicki asked.

"Pretty much the same thing," said Palmer. "So let's get moving. The airfield's only about a mile and a half from here. With luck, we might just get there before the rebels show up."

Paolo was sticking his whole torso out of the driver's window now, half standing up and yelling at us across the top of the truck—or yelling at Palmer, anyway. Palmer just started walking down the road, the Spanish tirade bouncing off his back.

After a couple of steps, Palmer turned as he walked and shouted at Paolo, "I said get outta here, you crazy Indian! Or, so help me, I'll shoot you myself."

Throwing up his hand in frustration, Paolo angrily dropped back into the pickup. The truck backed up quickly, spewing dust from under its tires. Then it turned around and bounded back along the road the way we had come.

I shrugged and was about to follow after Palmer. But I saw Meredith was standing still in the road, watching Paolo go. Palmer, glancing over his shoulder, saw her too.

"Hurry it up," he said gruffly. "The rebels could be here soon."

"We didn't even thank him," said Meredith.

Palmer gave an angry laugh and kept walking.

Jim and Nicki went after him, but I stayed with Meredith another moment.

"You know that whole thing about Paolo being a crazy Indian and if he didn't get out of here, Palmer would shoot him?" I said to her.

"Yes," she murmured, still looking with concern after the receding pickup.

"I think that *was* Palmer's way of thanking him. It's a guy thing."

Meredith blinked. "Oh," she said after a moment. "Right. Right."

And finally, reluctantly, she started down the road, and I went after her.

It was easier walking on a road in the open than through the jungle, so Palmer kept us moving at a fast pace. The sky grew lighter as we walked. The sun rose. The cloudless blue stretched wide around us. The heat grew more intense and the air grew thicker. Pretty soon we were almost as sweaty and breathless as we had been when we were fighting our way through the trees.

But the jungle had fallen away behind us completely. In its place there were green valleys and a horizon ringed with hills on every side.

After a short while trudging uphill, we came to the top of a rise. Palmer, in the lead, waited there for the rest of us to catch up.

I crested the hill and saw the city. Santa Maria. The

capital of the country. Its buildings rose blue-white out of the green scenery: impressive skyscrapers, churches, office buildings and open parks and playing fields. We had passed through the city when we first arrived, and I knew it looked a lot better from this distance than it did up close. When you were actually there, you could see that most of the buildings were old and worn and dirty, the streets full of litter, a lot of people homeless and poor.

But to me, from up here, it looked great: the end of our journey, maybe a way home. Everything seemed to lift up inside me at the sight of it.

"There's the airfield," said Palmer.

He pointed and I strained my eyes. But all I saw were stretches of empty green and then houses gathering and growing more dense until they blended with the rising capital.

"If we can make that, I'll have us out of here in an hour," Palmer said.

Nicki let out a little exclamation of joy. "That would be so, so, and did I mention *so* awesome."

Palmer made a little *come on* gesture with his head and started down the hill.

This time, instead of bringing up the rear, I walked alongside him. He didn't seem to notice me. He just kept his eyes moving, scanning the empty skies and the open road.

"No sign of them yet," I said, trying to make conversation. "Maybe the choppers didn't see us."

"Don't get your hopes up."

"What do we do if they *do* show up?" I asked. "Will we have to fight again?"

Palmer seemed to consider it. He tilted his head back and forth a little. "Depends on the setup."

I walked another few steps in silence, unsure if I should say anything more. Then the words just sort of came out of me on their own.

"I sure hope I don't have to shoot anybody else," I said.

Palmer sent me a mocking glance—just a quick one before he went back to scanning the skies and the road and our surroundings.

"You didn't like that, huh?" he asked.

"Shooting someone? Let's just say it isn't as much fun in real life as it is in video games."

He laughed once. "No. I guess not."

I didn't want to look at him so I just sort of did what he was doing: scanned the hills and fields ahead. "It kind of keeps bothering me, you know," I told him. Palmer didn't say anything, but somehow I felt I had to keep talking anyway. "I keep thinking about . . . I don't know. Maybe the guy I shot had kids or something. Or maybe he had, like, a mom who loved him."

"Well," said Palmer, "most people do have a mom, it turns out."

"Yeah. Yeah, that's what I was thinking. I mean, maybe he didn't even want to be in this stupid revolution."

"I wouldn't be surprised."

We continued to move quickly down the road to the

valley below. I kept my eyes on the blue-and-silver city growing more and more clear on the horizon. "I was thinking about Pastor Ron, you know," I said. "He gave a sermon once about how you shouldn't answer evil with evil, you should answer it with good."

"Mm," murmured Palmer, squinting up into the bright sky. "Turn the other cheek, you mean."

"Yeah, I guess. Like that."

"Except it wasn't your cheek to turn, was it?"

"What do you mean?"

"I mean, if you hadn't shot that guy—with his wife and his kids and his mom who loved him—he'd have thrown that grenade and killed every single one of us. Nicki. Jim. And your girlfriend Lady Liberty too."

I looked away from him so he wouldn't see me blushing. "Yeah," I said. "I know."

"I bet if you asked them, you'd find out they have moms too. Nicki and Jim. Meredith. They maybe all have moms."

"Maybe even you," I said.

"Well, let's not jump to conclusions," Palmer drawled.

I walked another moment in silence. It was a pretty miserable choice, you know. You either kill a guy or he kills your friends. Either the murderous rebels win or the murderous government. It was like the whole country was just one big series of bad choices.

"Back at the river," Palmer said. "Back when the croc was coming at you, remember?"

"No," I said. "I forgot. I always have so many crocodiles attacking me, they just sort of slip my mind."

Palmer gave another laugh. But then he stopped laughing. He said, "You were ready to die there, weren't you?"

"Not very."

"Ready enough. You were ready to die so someone else could live."

I shrugged. "Yeah. I guess. So?"

"So sometimes, in a war, you have to be willing to do even worse things than die—and to live with the consequences afterward."

"But that stinks!" I burst out. "That just stinks!"

He sighed. "It does. That's the truth. It stinks."

"I just came here to build a wall! To build a school!"

"I know you did, kid."

I was about to say more—to complain some more, basically—but just then, we heard the choppers again.

Palmer stopped, holding up his hand to bring the others to a stop behind us. I looked up, panning my eyes across the cloudless blue, looking for the source of the noise. At first I didn't see a thing. There was just that stuttering thunder filling the air, seeming to come from everywhere at once, growing louder and louder. But when I saw Palmer looking off in the direction of the airfield, I picked out the black dots hovering against the morning sky.

Jim and Nicki and Meredith had joined us now.

"Do you think they're coming for us?" asked Jim.

Palmer nodded vaguely as if he was only half listening. His eyes were scanning the territory and I knew he was looking for a way out. Meanwhile, the chopper noise got louder and the black machines got larger and more distinct as they flew our way.

"Shouldn't we run? Shouldn't we get away?" asked Nicki.

Palmer still didn't answer for a moment as he looked around. But then he said, "Dump the guns."

"What?" I asked.

"They've got us," said Palmer. "Those choppers are just for backup. There must be trucks on the way too. Dump the guns and we'll keep walking and tell them we're just innocent tourists trying to get home."

"But Mendoza must have been in contact with Santa Maria by now," said Meredith. "They'll know who we are."

Palmer nodded. "Probably. But this is our only chance. If we try to run or fight here, they'll just shoot us down."

"And if they don't believe we're innocent tourists . . . ?" Jim asked.

"They'll arrest us first—and then shoot us."

"Great."

"If you've got another option, let me know, 'cause I can't think of one."

Right, I thought. *That's Costa Verdes for you. Nothing but bad options.*

I looked around. I spotted a small field of tall grass just to the left of the road.

"There?" I asked.

Palmer looked at it—nodded. He and I jogged quickly off the road to where the high grass grew. Palmer slung his machine gun and pistol and knife in there. I threw in my machine gun after it. Funny—after talking about how I didn't like shooting people, I was sorry to let the weapon go. It had saved my life more than once—in the van and in the river too. I hadn't realized it before, but just having it with me sort of made me feel safe. Without it, I felt sort of undressed, sort of vulnerable.

Unarmed, Palmer and I jogged back to the road. We all started walking again, just like before.

The choppers were already plainly visible in the near distance. They were coming on fast. Half a minute later the machines were right over us, making the air shudder with their rotors.

They didn't fly by this time. They just hung up there above us. In each of them, there was a man with a machine gun sitting in the open door, looking down at us through dark sunglasses.

We stopped. Palmer shouted to make himself heard above the chopper noise. "Here come the rest of them," he said.

I looked and sure enough, there was a cloud of dust on the road ahead.

My mouth went dry and my heart started beating faster. Trouble again. Danger again. Would there ever be an end to it? Would we ever get free from this nightmare country?

Jim must've been thinking the same thing. His pale features turned even paler. Nicki clutched Meredith's arm and her lip trembled, but she didn't cry or scream or anything like that. In fact, she seemed to be working hard to keep herself under control. Meredith put her hand on Nicki's hand.

We watched the road as the trucks burst out of the cloud and rolled on toward us. We could see now that the truck beds were filled with men. And all the men had guns. And all the guns were pointing straight at us.

CHAPTER TWENTY-FOUR

You say you are tourists trying to get back to America?"

The choppers still hovered directly over us. The man had to shout to make himself heard.

He told us his name was Lieutenant Franco. He was a slick piece of work. A rotund man around thirty-five or so. He was wearing fatigues topped with a jaunty green beret pulled to one side on his pitch-black hair. He had a round face with small eyes—looked sort of like a mean elementary-school teacher. His attitude was arrogant and distant, as if he were looking down at us from a great height.

He was wearing a pistol on his hip, but he didn't pull it on us. Well, he didn't have to. He had ten men surrounding us, their machine guns leveled.

"We've got no quarrel with anyone," Palmer said to him. "We just want to go home."

Lieutenant Franco drew his thumb slowly across his lower lip. He studied each one of us, his eyes lingering a little on the girls. I held my breath. I couldn't even hope he would believe us—just give us a lift to the airport and let us go back to the US. Nothing could ever be that easy in this country.

After a few moments, the lieutenant straightened. "I am under orders from President Cobar and the revolutionary council to bring all foreigners in for questioning," he said. Even over the chopper noise, I could hear he spoke excellent English with only a slight accent. "You will be taken to the Central Prison until the council has decided what is to be done with you."

Suddenly Jim spoke up, raising his voice boldly. "I would like to see President Cobar. If I could just speak to him for a moment, I believe I could make him understand . . ."

But Lieutenant Franco was no longer listening. He turned his back on Jim and shouted orders to his soldiers in Spanish, gesturing our way.

I felt a hand on my arm and glanced down to see Palmer gripping me. At first I didn't know why, but in the next moment I understood.

Because in the next moment Nicki cried out. The soldiers had surrounded her and grabbed her by both arms. They grabbed Meredith too and started hauling the two girls toward one of the trucks. I realized with dread: they were going to separate us, girls from boys. My whole body tensed with the instinct to try to stop them, but Palmer's hand on my arm kept me from reacting . . . which probably also kept me from getting shot on the spot.

They hoisted the girls into the back of one pickup. Three soldiers got in with them as two more got into the cab. The soldiers in back with the girls were leering and grinning and making remarks to the other soldiers, the ones who were left behind with us. The looks on their faces made my heart turn black with fear and anger.

But now Jim and Palmer and I were shoved toward the other truck and forced to climb up into the bed. Three soldiers got in with us as well, two in the cab. We were shoved down to the truck bed and sat with our backs against the wall.

"Will the girls be all right?" I asked Palmer.

He didn't say anything. He didn't have to. I saw the answer in his eyes. It was a look I hadn't seen there before—or maybe I just hadn't noticed it. A cold, faraway look. The look of a killer. No, not a killer. A warrior. He wasn't angry. He wasn't vengeful. He was just willing—willing to do whatever he had to do . . .

But that didn't make me feel any better about the girls.

The girls' truck started off and ours started right after it, bounding down the slope over the rough dirt road.

I sat in silence. The green valleys fell away. The road turned and became smoother: it wasn't dirt anymore, I guess. We had joined the highway into the city. The trucks sped up. We traveled quickly.

Houses began to appear. Small huts on the edge of fields,

then clusters of shabby, dilapidated homes, then even more dilapidated apartment towers with lines of laundry hanging from their balconies. The city sort of grew up around us.

Soon we were going down dark, narrow streets lined with four-story apartment buildings. The buildings were painted bright colors—yellow and pink and light blue—as if they had been built to be cheerful places. But the paint was so scarred and the structures themselves were so broken and slanted that some of them looked like they might tip over and crumble to dust at any minute.

Now and then, in the distance, I heard machine-gun fire. Not far away either. Maybe the rebels were still fighting the soldiers in some parts of the city, I thought. Or maybe they were executing people they didn't like. I didn't ask. I didn't really want to know.

Now we turned a corner onto a broad avenue. It was a part of the city I'd never seen before. *The worst part,* I thought. There were pine trees growing up on either side of the road, but under the trees, there were piles of garbage. Amid the garbage, I saw rows of sheds—shanties with walls of wood and roofs of corrugated tin. On some of them, the fourth side was open to the weather—no wall but a blanket that could be pulled off the roof and used for a curtain. I could see women with their children sitting inside the sheds, sometimes men too. It seemed unbelievable that anyone was actually living in this sort of poverty in the middle of the capital, but there were a lot of them, one shed after another, one family after another.

I had risen to my knees in the truck bed by this time in order to get a better view. Holding on to the bed wall, I leaned out and looked up ahead down the road.

At the end of the avenue stood the prison.

Two large gates rose, framed by guard towers on either side. At the top of the towers were enclosures with glass walls, men with guns standing watch inside. As our trucks approached, the gates swung open. We passed beneath the towers—beneath the guns—into an open courtyard surrounded by white walls with barbed wire on top. On the other side of the courtyard was a large stone building, grimy tan. The sight of it sent a fresh spurt of fear through me. It might have been any government building, an office building or something. But I took one look at the place and knew somehow that horrible things happened in there and that a lot of the people who entered never came out.

The girls' truck reached the front of the building first, then ours pulled up behind it. I watched as the rebel gunmen hustled Meredith and Nicki off the truck bed and marched them inside. I caught a glimpse of Nicki's face. She was pale and there were tears glistening on her cheeks. But she was quiet, her lips pressed tight together now as if she were trying to keep herself from losing control and screaming. As for Meredith—well, as always, her back was very straight, her face very still, her eyes very clear. *Fearless*, Palmer had called her—and that's how she looked: fearless.

Palmer had asked her what had happened to make her

like that, to make her fearless. In that moment, I wondered the same thing myself, because I was definitely *not* fearless. I was *full* of fear—for myself, yes, but especially for the girls.

The girls were taken inside, and the soldiers brought me and Jim and Palmer off the trucks and marched us into the building after them.

Everything moved very quickly then. They rushed us through a security checkpoint crowded with guards. Past gates, down empty halls. I tried to keep track of where the girls were being taken. But I also kept seeing things that claimed my attention and inflamed my terror. I saw men with brutal faces toting guns and clubs. I saw people lying on hallway floors, unconscious—one in a pool of blood. I saw a woman with two children clinging to her skirts. The woman was screaming and crying and holding out her hands in supplication to one of the gunmen—who ignored her. I felt like scenes from a horror movie were flashing in front of me. Only it wasn't a movie. It was real.

We were taken down a flight of stairs into a cellar with rough stone walls. There were bare lightbulbs hanging from the ceiling. There were small patches of glare beneath the bulbs, then long passages of darkness. The girls went down a corridor to the left, and I had to bite my lip to keep from shouting out as I lost sight of them. Palmer and Jim and I were hustled along—under another bulb, through more darkness. Then I saw a thick metal door with a sliding steel panel in it.

The door opened and we were shoved through. We were in a stone cell lit by the glare of a single bare bulb.

Jim staggered against the wall as he was thrown in. "I demand to see President Cobar," he shouted. "He'll want to hear what I have to tell him."

The guard slammed the heavy door shut. We heard the bolt shoot home.

Did I say I was full of fear before? I guess that wasn't quite true—I couldn't have been totally *full* because when I saw this place, my fear rose.

It was a dungeon. I mean, really. Like something out of a movie about knights in armor. All that was missing was a bearded prisoner chained to the wall. It was just an empty room of rough stone. Just stone walls and the iron door and the bare bulb. Nothing else. Oh, wait—there were also two buckets in a corner. One of the buckets was filled with water.

My eyes passed over the place. Came to rest on the two buckets. I stood there staring at them stupidly.

"One's the sink, one's the toilet," Palmer told me.

"Uch," I said.

"I asked for the room with cable TV, but they were booked up."

I tried to laugh, but I was too heavy inside to work up the energy.

"This is madness," Jim said, pacing angrily. "It's insanity. We tell them we're innocent tourists and they put us in here?

If they would just let me talk to President Cobar for five minutes . . . If they would just let me talk to *somebody*."

Yeah, that's sure to help, I thought. But I turned to Palmer.
He had moved to one wall—the wall across from the door.
He put his back against it and slid down and sat on the floor,
one knee lifted, one arm draped over his knee. He looked
relaxed. Or, that is, his body looked relaxed. And he was still
wearing that small, mocking half smile.

But the warrior look in his eyes hadn't changed at all. He
kept those eyes trained on the door.

"What do you think they're gonna do now?" I asked him.

He glanced up at me as if he had forgotten I was there.
He shook his head—he didn't know the answer. He looked
at the door again.

"They took over the city fast," he said. "Very fast. They
have the prison. Helicopters. The army must've run for it—
or joined them. Cobar must've had this well planned. He
must have had a lot of support from within the government."

"I heard shooting in the city as we were coming in," I
said. "I thought maybe there was still some resistance."

But Palmer shook his head again. "That wasn't battle.
Those were executions. It's a different sound."

"That's not good," I said, licking my dry lips. "Executions."

"No," said Palmer. "It's not."

"They're not just going to execute us," said Jim, pacing
back and forth. "Why would they execute us? It's like we told
them: we're tourists. We just want to go home."

Anger flared in me. "They don't need a reason!" I nearly shouted at him. He was really starting to get on my nerves. How could somebody be so blind to what was right in front of him? "They almost executed us once already, Jim. We were just as innocent then."

"Ach." Jim waved off the idea. "That was Mendoza—a provincial idiot. Fernandez Cobar's a sophisticated man . . ."

"Right," I said bitterly. "He wrote a book. Maybe he'll beat us to death with it and save bullets!"

Jim went on pacing. I turned my back on him.

"You think they believe us about being tourists?" I asked Palmer nervously. "You think they'll eventually let us go or . . . ?"

Palmer lifted his eyes to mine, and if my heart could have sunk any lower, it would have.

"They've got the city, they've got the army, they've got the country," Palmer said. "There's nothing to stand in their way. They can pretty much do what they want now. And there are a lot of people who'll cheer them for executing Americans."

"Well, yeah," Jim muttered—as if he thought executing Americans sounded like a great idea, as if he thought they could execute Americans without bothering him at all.

I shook my head. "I don't see how this can get any worse," I said.

And the moment I said that, we heard the bolt slide back. The dungeon door swung open.

And Mendoza walked in.

CHAPTER TWENTY-FIVE

So much for our story about being tourists. Mendoza knew exactly who we were. He had ordered our executions once, and I saw no reason he wouldn't do it again.

I thought about that—and then I thought about Meredith. Meredith, who had spit in Mendoza's eye; Meredith, who had defied him. She was somewhere in this dungeon now, the same as us, helpless like us. And I knew Mendoza would not have forgotten how she'd insulted and humiliated him in front of his men.

As the rebel stepped into the little cell, I saw that he had changed since we had seen him in Santiago only a few days before. His lean, broad-shouldered body had a new easy swagger to it. His rough features were relaxed, and the cruelty in his black eyes was almost gleeful. He was more sure of himself. More sure of his power. Well, of course, why not? The entire country belonged to Cobar now. Mendoza could do whatever he liked.

Two men with machine guns stepped into the cell behind him. The last one in shut the heavy cell door.

Jim stopped pacing. I stood still as well.

Palmer, sitting relaxed against the wall, looked up—and smiled broadly, as if some old buddy of his had dropped by for a visit.

"Well, well, well," said Palmer. "If it isn't Señor Mendoza." He gestured at the cell. "Welcome to my extremely humble abode."

Mendoza grinned back at him, just as friendly a grin as Palmer's. His hand rested lightly on the butt of the pistol strapped into the holster on his belt. "If you don't get on your feet in the next second and show respect for me, I will have you shot dead right here," he said.

Palmer laughed out loud—as if Mendoza had made some pleasant remark, the kind of joke you might make at a party or something. He got his feet under him and pushed himself up the wall, saying, "Well, then I will definitely stand up right away to show my deep respect for your power to kill me."

Mendoza, still smiling, looked at him. Then at Jim. Then at me—a look that made the strength go out of me. He came forward casually until he was standing in front of Palmer, up close. The two men were eye to eye, smiling, but not really smiling, if you know what I mean. I was barely breathing, just waiting for Mendoza to strike Palmer down. Who was there to stop him now?

Mendoza turned and looked over his shoulder at the rest of us—then at Palmer again. "By direct order of the president, I have been assigned to question you about your suspected counterrevolutionary activities. You—and your lady friends."

I had to swallow down the words that came up into my throat. I knew enough not to start making empty threats.

Jim said, "That's ridiculous. We're not counterrevolutionaries. If you'd just let us explain . . ."

One of Mendoza's two gunmen stepped toward Jim and lifted his rifle, ready to drive the butt into Jim's head. Jim shut up and, cowering, covered his face with his hands—as if that would have stopped the rifle.

Luckily, though, Mendoza made a small gesture and the gunman lowered the weapon. Sure. Mendoza didn't need to bully us now. He had all the power—and all the time in the world to do whatever he wanted. He could torture us at will and at his own chosen speed.

He turned away from Palmer. Looked at Jim.

"You tell me you are not counterrevolutionaries . . ."

Jim slowly lowered his arms. "No. We're not. I have great respect for President Cobar. I'm familiar with his work."

"Ah. Well. I am glad to hear this." He took a step across the little cell and stood in front of Jim as he'd stood in front of Palmer—too close—smiling too much—dangerous. "But then, if you have such respect for our president, perhaps you could explain to me . . ." He gestured toward Palmer. "What are you doing in the company of a man who supplies guns to our enemies?"

Jim's eyes went wide, his mouth came open. He stared from Mendoza to Palmer. He said, "I . . . I mean, we didn't . . . We never . . . We didn't know anything about that . . ."

"And this young man," said Mendoza, gesturing at me so that I stiffened, my heart thundering in my chest. "We have witnesses who saw him murder a revolutionary guard in cold blood."

I swallowed hard at that. And Jim licked his lips, still gaping. "But he didn't . . . They were . . . We were just trying to . . ."

"Well, well, well, never mind," said Mendoza in a friendly voice. He held up his hands as if all were forgiven. "We will straighten it all out in the interrogation room, no? In the interrogation room, all the confusion will end, all the lies will stop, and only the truth will remain."

"But you don't understand!" said Jim. "Really, if I could just explain . . ."

"Oh, believe me, you *will* explain. You will explain everything. There is not a single thing you will not tell me in the end."

Yeah, well, I was pretty sure that was true. By the time they were finished with us, we'd probably tell them the moon was made of marmalade if that's what they wanted to hear. For my part, if they wanted me to confess I'd shot that guy with the grenade just for the pleasure of it, I knew that's exactly what I would say eventually. I didn't think I was the sort who'd be able to stand up to torture like some kind of hero. Torture? Man, I don't even like going to the dentist.

"So," said Mendoza, "who will volunteer to go first?" He put his hands behind his back. Moved from one to the other of us as if he were a shopper looking at neckties, pondering the positives and negatives of each selection. Oh, he was having a good time now, Mendoza was. He considered Jim first. "Perhaps it will be you. Since you have so much respect for our president. Perhaps you are eager to explain your actions."

Jim's mouth opened and closed like he was a fish out of water. "I . . . I . . . ," he said very softly.

But Mendoza had already turned away from him, had already turned to me.

He stood over me, his black eyes boring into me, full of good humor and anticipation. My mind started to race over all the things they would do to me to cause me pain. *Suspend the imagination*, I thought desperately. *Don't worry about anything. Pray about everything instead.* But Mendoza's eyes seemed to empty me of everything but terror and I stood there, unable to think, unable to speak, unable to move.

"What about you, my young friend?" he asked. "You are the gallant gentleman, as I remember. You are the one who stands up for the ladies, yes?"

He paused for me to answer, but all I could do was lick my dry lips, my hands trembling at my sides.

"Well, since you like the ladies so much," Mendoza went on, "perhaps you would enjoy watching me question *them* first . . ."

"You thug!" I screamed—and my voice cracked so that I sounded about twelve years old. Tears filled my eyes. "You dirty gangster thug, I wish I could . . ."

"Shut up, kid!" Palmer barked at me.

But Mendoza only laughed. He waved Palmer quiet. "No, no," he said. "Let the gallant gentleman speak his mind. He will be speaking even more of his mind before long." He stopped smiling suddenly. "Before long, he will see things and experience things he has not even imagined."

I wiped angrily at my eyes with my hand. I wanted to wipe that arrogance off Mendoza's face with my fist. I wanted to knock him right through the dungeon wall. But I knew if I tried it, one of those gunmen would pound me senseless. So I just stood there, furious. I've never felt so helpless in my life.

And Mendoza, to rub the insult in, sneered with disdain and turned his back on me. He returned to stand in front of Palmer, as he had before. Smiling, just as he had before.

"But all in all, I think we should begin with you, Señor Dunn," he said. "These others—they are really only children, isn't it so?"

Palmer nodded. He still looked relaxed—he still wore his mocking half smile—and his eyes were still a warrior's eyes. "Yes," he said. "It's so."

"Spoiled American children who have lived their rich,

free, peaceful American lives and don't know what the real world is," said Mendoza casually, as if he were just making conversation. "They think a tragedy is when they can't afford the car they want or to buy a new telephone."

"That's right," Palmer said.

"*You* are their only strength. You are their real power. You are the one thing that has kept them alive in this country. Am I right?"

"Pretty close," Palmer said.

"Mm," Mendoza said. And grinning, he went on: "And when they see that you are broken, when they see you on your knees, weeping and begging me for mercy, then they will know that there is no hope for them."

And Palmer—so help me, I'm not making this up—Palmer grinned right back at him. As if he and Mendoza were just two old friends chatting. And he said, "That's right, Señor Mendoza. That's exactly right. When they see me on my knees begging you for mercy—or begging you for anything—that's when they'll know there's no hope left at all."

I think it took Mendoza a moment to understand what Palmer had just said. He started to laugh—and then abruptly he stopped laughing. Because, of course, Palmer was telling him that we would *never* see that, we would never see him broken, there would never come a time when our hope was gone.

And it was as if Palmer had slapped the rebel without moving a muscle. Mendoza's face convulsed, his lips twisting down, his eyes flashing with rage. As he had with me, he turned his back on Palmer. He walked away from him, back toward the cell door. And as he did, he snapped his fingers at the two gunmen.

"Bring him to the interrogation room," he said.

At once, the two gunmen charged forward and seized Palmer by the arms.

One second later they were both dead.

CHAPTER TWENTY-SIX

I never saw a human being move so fast. It was some sort of serious kung fu movie action, over so quickly my eye couldn't even record it in detail. I remember moments of it—like snapshots kind of, frozen in my brain. Palmer's open hand jabbing up like a knife. The same hand slicing like a sword. The one guard reeling backward, his mouth open, his tongue out, his eyes wide. The other guard folding at the knees and collapsing to the floor like a dropped rag doll. And Palmer's arms wheeling around—like he was doing some kind of magic act, you know, trying to distract your attention. But what he was doing was twisting the second guard's rifle off his shoulder even before the guard had time to drop.

Before I could comprehend what had happened—before my mind could even register what I'd just seen—the two guards lay lifeless on the floor and Palmer stood alone with a machine gun in his hand, the barrel leveled straight at Mendoza.

And there was one final snapshot captured by my brain—my favorite snapshot.

Mendoza, remember, had turned his back on Palmer. He was walking to the door. When the fight started behind him, he heard the noise and wheeled around—but it was all over so fast that by the time he was facing Palmer again, Palmer had the gun on him. So I caught this final image of the look on Mendoza's face, pure shock, the arrogance draining out of his eyes, the color draining out of his cheeks. His hand had gone automatically to the pistol on his belt . . . but it was already too late.

"Go on," Palmer said quietly—smiling, grinning just like before. "Go on. Pull it, Mendoza. I want you to."

But Mendoza took one look at Palmer—Palmer standing between the corpses of the two gunmen on the floor—and he knew the American would empty the machine gun into him before the pistol got halfway out of that holster. His hand moved away from it. Both his hands lifted from his sides.

I hate to remember what went through me then. Seeing Mendoza standing there at gunpoint, I felt a lightning flash of rage and hatred in me so terrible it seemed almost to take me over. I felt I had no control over myself—that the power of my rage was forcing me into motion. Because there was Mendoza—Mendoza who had threatened me when I was helpless—who had threatened Nicki and Meredith just seconds ago—threatened us all with terrible tortures. And now *he* was the helpless one, all his power gone. And my rage and hatred for him had taken me over and were telling me to launch myself at him, to wrap my fingers around his ugly throat and . . .

"Easy, kid," said Palmer. "We're the good guys. Remember?"

I don't know how he knew what was going on inside me. I hadn't moved from the spot. I hadn't said a word. But he did know somehow. And the moment he spoke, I *did* remember. I remembered who I was, what I was. And it turned out the electric rage and hatred could not control me after all.

The emotion drained out of me almost at once. My hands, which had curled into claws ready for the attack, relaxed. My arms fell to my sides.

It was a moment that would come back to me later. It was a moment that would come back to me a lot and for a long time.

"Put it on the floor, Mendoza," Palmer said now. He meant the pistol. "Slowly. Thumb and finger."

Mendoza had regained a bit of his composure. He was relaxed again—or, that is, he was pretending to be relaxed in spite of the fury in his eyes. His hand went back to his belt. Slowly, he followed Palmer's instructions.

"You are surrounded by guards and barbed wire," he said as, using only his thumb and finger, he unbuckled his holster and drew out his gun. "You really think you can escape from here?"

"I think I can kill you in a split second if you don't do what I tell you," Palmer said.

Mendoza tried to snort at that, but his eyes were full of helplessness and anger. I knew how he felt. He dropped the pistol to the floor in front of him.

"Kick it over to the kid," Palmer said, nodding at me.

Sneering with disdain, Mendoza kicked the pistol to me. I started to bend down to reach for it.

But Palmer said, "Not yet, kid. The fatigues. Put them on."

For a second, I didn't know what he was talking about. But then I realized: he wanted me to undress the dead guard and put on his uniform.

"You want me to dress up as a guard?" I asked. "But my face . . . my hair . . ."

"It's fine," Palmer said quickly. "It's not like in the hills. Plenty of Santa Marians are as pale-skinned as you are—especially now after the sun has been baking you for a week. Just cover as much of your hair as you can with the bandanna. Now do it. Fast."

I knelt down next to the body. I thought back to how I'd had to strip the rifle off the gunman from the firing squad. I hadn't wanted to touch a dead man then, and I didn't want to do it now. But I guess I'd gotten a little practice in suspending the imagination since then. This time I just decided not to think about it, and I didn't. I took the corpse's clothes off as quickly as I could. I stripped out of mine. And a minute or two later I was wearing the khaki uniform of the revolution.

Not a bad fit either. I tied the red bandanna around my forehead and pulled it up to hide my hair.

"Now pick up the pistol," Palmer said. "Click off the safety."

I didn't know much about guns, and it took me a second to find the little switch he was talking about. But I found it.

"Now point the gun at Mendoza and if he moves, pull that little trigger gizmo on the bottom," Palmer said.

I pointed the pistol at Mendoza, my finger on the trigger. Palmer leaned his rifle against the wall. He stooped down and started pulling the fatigues off the other dead guard.

Mendoza turned from him to me. He looked down at the pistol I had aimed at him. He smiled a condescending smile.

"You really think you have the courage to do it?" he asked.

I heard myself laugh—it was a crazy sound. But if he only knew how close I'd come to killing him with my bare hands, he wouldn't have asked the question.

I guess he got his answer in my laughter, because his condescending smile disappeared. He turned away from me. He turned to Jim instead.

Jim was standing against the opposite wall. He looked as if he couldn't comprehend what was happening. His lanky body had gone completely stiff. His face had gone completely blank. His bug-eyes were staring straight ahead—staring at nothing, as far as I could tell, just staring into space.

"And you," Mendoza said to him. "You who know better than these others."

Jim blinked. He shifted his stare from nothing to the rebel. "What?" he said in a distant voice.

"You are not a fool like they are. Not just some spoiled American. You understand the difficulties facing my country, my people."

"Yes . . . ," said Jim, still as if he were very far away.

"Do you still wish to speak to the new president?" Mendoza asked him.

"I . . . ," said Jim.

"Because this can be arranged, you know. It is not too late. Fernandez Cobar is a great man, a great spirit, but he is always ready to listen to even the humblest petitioner."

I heard Palmer chuckle at that as he stripped down, getting ready to change into the guard's fatigues. "What a guy!" he muttered.

I went on pointing the pistol at Mendoza, barely listening to what he said, just watching for any sudden movements— half hoping, if you want the truth, that he would give me an excuse to pull the trigger.

Jim just went on staring at him. His mouth opened and closed. And then he said, "Who are you? Who are you people?"

Mendoza straightened a little as if with pride. "We are soldiers of justice," he said. "You say you are familiar with President Cobar's work. You should know this. We are soldiers of justice."

Jim slowly shook his head, like a man coming out of a

dream. "You were going to torture us. You were going to tor-ture the girls. You said you were acting on direct orders of the president."

Mendoza answered with a little shrug. "Do you think justice is easy? Do you think you can make things fair with-out using force? People are not equal by nature—you must *compel* them to be equal. President Cobar understands that if you want to build a better world, you must destroy all of those who stand in your way."

"But . . . But . . . But . . . ," said Jim, slowly coming back to himself. "That's *not* a better world. That's *this* world. That's the world we have already."

Palmer chuckled again. "You can probably get some cash for those old Cobar books on e-Bay, Professor," he said with a grin. "You can throw in your Che Guevara T-shirts while you're at it."

He was just buttoning up the khaki shirt. It was too small for him—it looked like it would rip open if he moved too fast—but I guessed if nobody looked too closely, he would pass for a rebel, same as me.

When he'd finished tying the red bandanna around his forehead, he put his hand out to me. I gave him the pistol. He held it on Mendoza while, with his free hand, he took the machine gun off the wall and tossed it my way. I caught it. Then, while I trained the rifle on Mendoza, Palmer shucked the magazine out of the pistol and popped out the shell in the chamber. He handed the empty gun back to Mendoza.

"Holster it," he said.

Mendoza hesitated, glancing at me, at my gun. He didn't like taking orders. But he didn't have much choice. He slid the empty pistol back into its holster.

Palmer took a deep breath. He looked at Jim. He looked at me.

"All right, boys," he drawled in that ironic way of his. "I think we better go rescue Lady Liberty before she hurts someone."

CHAPTER TWENTY-SEVEN

Palmer's plan was so simple it was kind of brilliant. Mendoza had come into the dungeon cell with two guards. He had been going to bring one of us out—one prisoner—for interrogation. And in fact, he walked out with two guards and a prisoner, exactly as he was supposed to. Except the guards were Palmer and I, and the prisoner was Jim. And if Mendoza made one wrong move, we'd shoot him. So it was a little different.

Before we left the cell, Palmer told Mendoza exactly what to do and say, speaking in rapid Spanish. I couldn't understand the words, but I could guess the gist of it. He wanted Mendoza basically to play the part of himself, as if everything were going according to plan. Mendoza listened silently to Palmer's instructions and gave a single, stiff nod. He was going to obey for fear of getting shot—but you only had to look in his eyes to know that he would be waiting and watching, every second, for a chance to break free.

Well, I thought, *let him try.*

When he was done talking, Palmer nodded toward the cell door. Mendoza took a breath—to get control over his anger, I thought. Then he pounded on the door with his fist and shouted, *"Abran!"* Which I guessed meant open up.

There was a second's pause. During that second, I felt the nervousness coursing through me—a flood of adrenaline. If I had thought about it, I would've realized that Mendoza was probably right. We *were* surrounded by guards with guns, not to mention walls topped with barbed wire. We *didn't* really have much of a chance of getting away with this. But somehow, although I was tense—really tense—I wasn't as frightened as you might think I would be—or as I might think I would be. I guess I felt, like, at least we weren't just sitting there helplessly waiting to be tortured or killed. At least, if we went down, we would go down fighting. That was something. Actually, that was a lot.

My breath caught as I heard the bolt on the dungeon door slide open. A guard in the corridor outside started to open the door—and I suddenly thought: *He'll see the bodies of the two guards!* But before he could, Mendoza, as instructed by Palmer, barked an order at him. The guard moved away from the cell entrance and Mendoza stepped out into the corridor. Palmer and I quickly followed, pushing Jim ahead of us at gunpoint. And Jim marched out, looking just like a prisoner on his way to the torture cell. He looked depressed and defeated and afraid, I mean—and I'm not sure he was pretending.

The second we were in the corridor, Palmer shut the cell door behind us and threw the bolt. There were two more guards out here and Mendoza was giving them orders. One used his key to double lock the door. The others went running off, I don't know where, to whatever chore Mendoza had told them to do.

We moved quickly. My impressions of what was happening were fleeting and confused. I was so wired, so tense. My eyes were moving rapidly every which way, looking to see if anyone recognized us or realized what we were doing. Everything went by in a kind of hectic daze.

Mendoza took the lead, but Palmer was right at his shoulder. Palmer kept up a steady murmuring in the rebel's ear, telling him what to do, telling him what would happen to him if he didn't do it. Mendoza's expression remained frozen as we left the corridor of cells and entered another hall and pushed through another door into another corridor. Twice, armed guards appeared in front of us, making my hand tighten on my gun. But both times Mendoza barked orders at them and they scattered—and we marched quickly on.

Now, we were in another dark hall of cells. Naked lightbulbs burned above us and we moved through the pools of light beneath them into areas of darkness. I caught my breath as yet another armed guard approached us out of the shadows—I never saw him coming out of the dark before he was right there in front of us. Yet again, Mendoza gave him orders. But this time, the guard turned on his heel, a 180, and started marching ahead of us down the hall.

We stopped before another metal door. More orders from Mendoza as Palmer stood by watchfully. The guard unlocked the door. Threw the bolt. Stood back as the door opened.

We walked into a cell, another dungeon cell, no different than ours had been.

A huge jolt of excitement went through me as I saw Nicki and Meredith there.

The girls were huddled together against the far wall, sunk in shadow. Nicki seemed to be resting on Meredith's shoulder. Meredith had her head tilted back, resting against the rough stone.

The girls leapt to their feet as Mendoza came in. Meredith's face was already setting in a mask of defiance, her eyes blazing, her lips set. She looked as if she was getting ready to give Mendoza any kind of hard time she could think of.

And then her eyes flicked to the gunman at Mendoza's shoulder: Palmer. I saw her lips part in surprise. She glanced quickly at me. She understood. She seemed to go very still, her expression wary.

"What are you going to . . . ?" Nicki started to say.

But then she got it too. She gave a little gasp and then, very quickly, fell silent. She edged forward, out of the shadow, into the glaring light of the single bare bulb above us. That's when I got my first good look at her face. And I felt the anger boiling up inside me.

There was a massive red bruise on one of Nicki's cheeks. It was already beginning to swell and turn dark purple. Her eye was almost shut. Someone had hit her, really belted her. I wondered if it was the guard who had unlocked the door for us. I wondered how he would look with a bullet hole in the center of his forehead . . .

We're the good guys, remember, I told myself. Yeah, yeah, I remembered. But these guys who beat up women—they seriously tick me off.

"You are to come with us," said Mendoza gruffly. I could tell the words were just about sticking in his throat, but he said them—he had no choice. He stood aside and gestured to the door. "This way."

Meredith, back straight and chin lifted as always, walked majestically out the dungeon door. Nicki followed, passing close to me as she went. And as she did, she looked into my eyes. I expected to see terror there and pain, but instead there was something new—new for her, I mean. She looked . . . steady. More than that. Despite the ugly bruise marring her pretty features, her eyes were sort of sparkling. I almost thought she started to smile at me . . .

Then she went past, following Meredith out the door. Jim followed them. Then Mendoza, with Palmer and me right behind.

Now it began again: the swift march down the hall, out the door, down the next hall to the stairwell. Mendoza and Palmer went ahead with Nicki and Meredith and Jim right behind, and me in the rear as if I were guarding against the prisoners' escape. As before, I was looking every which way. As before, I was waiting every moment for someone to point at us and shout, "Wait! Stop them!" And so, as before, the trip to the stairwell went by in those quick, frightened flashes with my pounding heart keeping rhythm as we moved.

We reached the stairs. Marched up. Stepped out of the well into the main hallway. We pushed through a gate. Down another hall. Through another gate. It was the same path we had taken coming in. The front door—the exit into the prison courtyard—had to be getting close.

Again, as we walked quickly forward, I caught glimpses of men lying unconscious on the floor—of a pool of smeared blood where a body had recently been—of a woman, the same woman who had been begging for help when we came in, now sitting in despair against a wall with one child under each arm, her head tilting forward as she tried to fight off sleep.

This poor country, I thought. *This poor, sad country.*

Then I raised my eyes and looked ahead and every thought left me except for one: *escape*.

Because I saw the prison door. The checkpoint where we had first entered. The way out.

It was just a long table with a cluster of guards standing around it. There was a metal detector, but no one seemed to be walking through it. In fact, the guards didn't seem to be doing very much besides chatting with one another and smoking cigarettes. I guess since the rebels had only recently taken over the place, things were still a little disorganized. So the guards milled around, not knowing what to do—and just beyond them, just a few steps beyond, were the doors, the front doors out into the courtyard.

Escape.

There was a long way to go, I knew. Even once we were outside, we would somehow have to get a truck, get through the walls, get past the guard towers. I didn't know how we were going to manage it. I couldn't think about it yet. All I could think about was getting past that checkpoint, getting out those doors.

But something was wrong.

I saw Mendoza start to slow down ahead of us. I saw Palmer leaning in toward him, whispering something in his ear. Mendoza started to glance at him, as if in surprise. But Palmer whispered again, harshly this time, and Mendoza faced forward. He started moving again.

My mouth had gone dry. My pulse was beating so fast it was almost painful. We were so close. What was happening? What was wrong? I was weak with suspense as, step by swift step, we approached the guards standing around the checkpoint.

The guards saw us coming now. One of them—a guy who looked no older than I was—gestured at us with a cigarette.

He spoke a few words to another guard standing in front of him. This other guard was standing with his back toward us. He was clearly the leader here—I could tell by the stripes on the shoulder of his uniform and the bright green beret pulled sharply to one side on his dark black hair. The young guard was telling him we were coming . . .

The leader turned to look our way.

I heard someone make a noise: a small choked noise of fear. It was a second before I realized that the sound had come out of my own mouth.

Because I saw that the leader—the man in the beret—was Lieutenant Franco—the rebel who had arrested us outside the city.

And I was sure he was going to recognize us.

CHAPTER TWENTY-EIGHT

I figured Palmer would stop marching us toward the check-point. I figured he would turn us around, lead us another way. But there was no other way, no other exit. We had to get out to that courtyard if we were going to leave the prison. So we had no choice: we kept moving forward, Mendoza in the lead, Palmer at his shoulder, me in the rear with our "prisoners" up ahead.

Lieutenant Franco turned to face us. The pudgy little man in the jaunty green beret put his hands behind his back, waiting as we came toward him. He looked stern, suspicious, and threatening.

Palmer murmured in Mendoza's ear one last time. At once, Mendoza started giving orders, waving his hand in a very dismissive way. He was obviously telling Lieutenant

Franco to get out of the way and let us through, trying to bluff our way past him before Franco realized who exactly it was in those fatigues.

For a minute, I thought it actually might work. Mendoza was so convincing, I thought Franco might just jump at his orders and step aside. But no such luck. Franco, after all, was a "lieutenant." He wasn't going to be pushed around. He waited right where he was until we had almost reached him. Then quietly, with a great show of self-assurance, he lifted his open hand like a cop stopping traffic.

"Alto, por favor," he said quietly.

Mendoza stopped. He had no choice. There were no less than six gunmen standing behind Franco, ready to back him up. He couldn't just push through them to the door.

But he gave it a try. Well, of course he did. He knew if any shooting started, Palmer would make sure he took the first bullet. So he put on a very impatient sneer and unleashed a series of harsh commands into Lieutenant Franco's face, waving one hand this way and that as he did.

But Franco couldn't be budged. His arrogant superior expression remained in place and so did he. He sniffed at Mendoza's orders, his thin mustache twitching. And when Mendoza finished, he responded quietly but certainly. I didn't understand the words, but I was pretty sure I knew what they meant: *I am in charge of this checkpoint and no one gets through without my say-so.*

Mendoza threw up one hand, as if to say: *Look at the*

idiots I have to deal with. He gestured toward us: *Go on and look at them if you want.*

And that's exactly what Lieutenant Franco did.

I held my breath as he put his hands behind his back and walked around to get a better look at the "prisoners." He studied Jim first. Then he moved on to Meredith, gazing down at her along the line of his nose like a connoisseur examining a work of art. Finally he reached Nicki. My heart pounded as he paused in front of her. He took her chin in one of his hands. She tried to pull back, but he held her hard. He forced her face to the side so he could get a better look at the raging bruise on her cheek.

Then he chuckled. "Perhaps you have learned a lesson, eh?" he said, with a leering smile.

I expected Nicki to cry or tremble, at least. But she didn't say anything. In fact, she looked directly into Franco's eyes—so directly that, after a moment, the "lieutenant" seemed to feel uncomfortable. In any case, he let her go and turned away.

As he did, his eyes went over me.

Up till that moment, he hadn't looked at me—or at Palmer either. Why would he? He was there to check on the prisoners, not the guards. Even now, he didn't exactly examine me or anything. His gaze just happened to pass over my face as he was turning.

I saw something flash in his eyes and I thought, *He remembers me!* But he didn't—not exactly. I think something caught in his brain, something he couldn't quite pinpoint . . .

He didn't bother to take a second look and figure it out. He just gave a quick wave of his hand to Mendoza, as if to say, *Off you go.*

And off we went.

A sigh of relief flooded out of me as we started moving again. We went past the security check, under the watchful eyes of the guards. We kept moving to the front door.

Escape.

Mendoza pushed through the doors, Palmer following close behind him. Another second and we went out too—out of that hellhole of buried dungeons—into the open air of the courtyard.

Even surrounded by the walls, even surrounded by barbed wire, even watched by the gunmen in their high towers, I was glad to see the sky above me again, glad to feel the air and the heat of the sun. I wanted to lift my face and feel the touch of freedom . . .

But I couldn't. Not yet.

Mendoza had begun shouting orders again. Guards were running at his command. I looked and saw a row of trucks parked against one wall. Most of them were pickups. One or two were army troop carriers, their rear beds hidden under green canvas. We were moving toward them, and Mendoza was gesturing at the front gates.

I could hardly believe it: I saw the gates begin to open.

Escape.

We kept moving toward the trucks. A guard ran up

to Mendoza, handed him a set of keys. Palmer spoke in Mendoza's ear. Mendoza reluctantly handed the keys over to him. Palmer looked over his shoulder at me. He pointed to one of the pickups.

I nodded. I nudged Jim in the back with my rifle as if I were shoving a prisoner along. When he looked back at me, Nicki and Meredith looked back too. I gestured with my head toward the pickup. We started moving in the truck's direction. We were only a few steps away. I glanced over to the front gates. They were still swinging wide. They were almost open all the way.

Escape.

Somehow, I thought—*miraculously—we are actually going to pull this off. We are actually going to walk right out of here.*

I thought that—and the next moment, the shouting started.

I turned and saw Lieutenant Franco. He was rushing out the prison door. Screaming at the guards in the courtyard, pointing frantically at the gates, pointing frantically at us.

"Alto! Alto!"

Stop. Stop.

He had remembered us.

❦

|||||||||||||||||||||||||||||||

CHAPTER TWENTY-NINE

We had come so far, gotten so close—and all at once our chance of escape was gone. More guards came pushing past Franco out the door, guns lifted and at the ready. Guards who were already in the courtyard started to turn our way. In a moment, we were surrounded with no way out. We had no choice but to surrender.

Palmer opened fire.

I jumped at the noise. I thought it was the guards shooting at us. But no, I turned and saw Palmer. He had grabbed Mendoza by the collar. He was holding him in front of him like a shield with one hand. With his other hand, he was gripping his machine gun and letting loose short bursts of lead, first in one direction, then the next.

It did the trick. The guards scattered. They had recklessly come running out into the open to get us. Palmer had a clear shot at them—and they couldn't shoot back without hitting Mendoza.

So they ran. And Palmer kept firing. And I started firing. I kept Jim and Nicki and Meredith behind me, shielding them with my body. I imitated Palmer, loosing a burst in one direction, then a burst in another.

One of the running guards screamed and clutched his leg and fell. Another threw up his hands, dropped his gun, and pitched face-forward to the ground. The others were ducking for cover behind anything they could find—trash cans, old barrels, open doors, a couple of jeeps on the courtyard's far side.

I kept firing, trying to keep them all pinned down.

But Palmer shouted, "Kid!"

I turned. Palmer let go of Mendoza and tossed the truck keys at me.

I snatched the keys out of the air. But even as I did, Mendoza seized his chance. He started running toward where Franco stood in the prison doorway.

Palmer trained his gun on Mendoza but he never had the chance to take a shot. Because as soon as Mendoza was out of the way, the other guards started firing at us from behind their shelters.

The earth around me erupted as bullets flew into the dirt right in front of me. I caught sight of a guard peeking out from behind a barrel, aiming my way. I shot wildly in his direction and he disappeared, ducking down under cover.

"The truck!" Palmer shouted at us. "Get in the truck!"

I glanced over my shoulder and saw Jim and Nicki and Meredith already running as fast as they could toward the pickup.

But I kept myself turned toward the courtyard. I backed slowly toward the truck. I kept firing—first at one guard, then at another—trying to keep them pinned down, trying to keep them from getting off a good shot at us. The guards would pop out from behind their cover—a jeep, a trash can, a barrel . . . They would take a wild shot and I would force them down again. It flashed through my mind that they were like characters in a video shooting gallery. But I knew now that this was no game. I knew it was life or death, them or us.

A guard poked his head out from behind a door. Pointed his gun my way, pulled the trigger. I heard the *rat-tat-tat* and in the same instant, I heard bullets singing by my ear.

I fired back. The guard ducked away again. Another guard popped up from behind a barrel. I fired at him, forcing him down.

I kept firing—and Palmer kept firing beside me—as we both backed away toward the truck.

I caught a movement out of the corner of my eye. I turned. It was the two great gates of the prison. They were slowly swinging shut.

I knew what that meant: we had only seconds to get out of there. Once those doors closed, there would be no way out.

"Palmer! The doors!" I shouted.

He didn't look. He didn't have to. He already knew.

"Go!" he shouted back.

The guards kept popping up, kept firing. I swept my gun over them, pulled the trigger, forcing them down. And then the gun went still and silent in my hand. The magazine was empty. I was out of bullets.

I didn't hesitate. I turned and ran.

I was only steps from the truck now. I saw Nicki and Meredith and Jim in the bed, crouched down behind the metal walls. I leapt to the cab, pulled open the door. As I did, I heard a blast behind me and a hole appeared in the inside of the door about three inches away from me. With a shout of fear, I jumped into the cab.

My hand was shaking crazily, but somehow I managed to get the key in the ignition, managed to switch on the engine. It roared to life.

The passenger door flew open and Palmer jumped in.

"Drive!" he said.

I put the car in gear. But there was no one left outside to hold the guards off, and I heard Nicki scream in the truck bed as the gunmen in the courtyard broke cover and set off a fresh barrage. Palmer stuck his weapon out the window and fired back.

I hit the gas.

The pickup jerked backward. I swung the wheel. Slapped the gear stick. Hit the gas again—and the truck jolted forward. Again, I wrenched the wheel. Gunfire sounded over the engine's roar. The window by my ear cracked as a bullet shot through it, lanced past my face, and embedded itself in the dashboard. Palmer let off another long burst of fire out his window. Then he dropped back inside.

"Out of bullets!" he said.

Now I had the pickup's front fender pointed at the prison gates. The gates were still swinging toward each other, swinging closed. I wasn't sure I'd be able to fit the truck through the gap—and every second the gap was getting smaller.

I jammed my foot down on the gas, pressing it all the way to the floor, pinning it down.

The truck was already accelerating, but now it blasted forward, hurling me back against the seat. Outside, I heard the gunfire get heavier, faster. The guards must have realized we were out of bullets, realized we couldn't pin them down anymore. They must have raced out into the open after us, firing as they came. I heard a series of slugs pound into the pickup's body. I felt a stutter go through the truck's racing frame.

And now, even worse, the guards in the high towers started firing down at us too. Palmer gave an angry shout as a bullet came straight through the roof into the seat-well beside him. I prayed wildly for the lives of the girls and Jim in the open bed behind me.

All of this took no more than a few seconds. And up ahead I saw the gates, the closing gates, filling the windshield, growing larger and larger as the opening between them grew smaller and smaller. On the other side of the gates, outside the prison, I glimpsed the palm-lined avenue, the shacks of the slums. But already it seemed to me that the outside world was barred to us, that the truck couldn't possibly make the passage, that it was just going to slam into the edges of the closing gates.

A sort of wildfire of emotion gripped me. I understood that everything would be decided in the next several seconds: freedom or capture, escape or imprisonment, torture, and death. My life—my friends' lives—so much at stake—everything at stake on a single chance, our last chance. It was sort of like that moment before the firing squad, that moment when I thought I was going to die: in those final seconds before we reached the gates, everything seemed brighter, more precious, more real.

The world raced by the windows. The gunfire grew so steady it seemed like one long blast, answering the blast of the engine. The truck raced toward the closing gates. The gap between the gates grew narrower.

Palmer started shouting—no words, just the wild emotion coming out of him in a roar. I was shouting too. I couldn't help myself. The gap between the gates was all I could see out the windshield. And I could see it was far too narrow now. We were going to crash for sure.

And then: impact. The edges of the closing gates ripped into the sides of the truck. There was a brutal jolt and the sound of tearing metal as both side mirrors snapped off and flew away.

But while the truck shuddered, it never stopped. It burst through the narrow passage into the avenue beyond.

We were out of the prison.

At that moment, a deafening siren went off. A prison alarm. The whole city must have heard it. I knew at once that rebel gunmen from every section of town would soon be heading our way.

And over the siren: Gunfire. The engine. My own shouting. Palmer's shouts.

Then suddenly, a man . . .

There was a man—a hunched old man walking in the street in front of me! He froze, turning his head toward me, staring at me. I saw his eyes wide with terror, his mouth wide with surprise as the truck barreled toward him.

"Watch out!" Palmer yelled.

I swung the wheel. The truck's fender went wide of the old man—but now a palm tree loomed in front of me, yards from my face. I swung the wheel again. I saw bullets hitting the pavement, bursts of dust and gravel flying into the air.

Palmer shouted: "Turn! Turn!"

I didn't see any place to turn, but I did what he said, hauling the wheel over as far as I could. The tree was gone. A shed appeared in the windshield. A woman clutching her baby was huddled under the tin roof, staring at me, staring at the oncoming truck. She didn't even have time to cry out in fear.

But the truck kept wheeling round, wheeled past her—and

then I saw what Palmer saw: there was a narrow alley right beside her shed.

I muscled the wheel over even farther. The shed and the screaming woman went by the window as the truck bounced over a pile of garbage and charged into the passage between two buildings.

The alley wasn't wide. I felt the buildings pressing close on either side of me. I kept my eyes glued to the road, fighting to keep the truck centered so we wouldn't sideswipe the walls.

Palmer was shouting over the siren: "Left! Left! Left!"

We burst out the other side of the alley onto another street, a narrow street with crumbling apartment buildings crowding close. I swung the wheel left.

The truck came around the corner at unbelievable speed, two tires threatening to lift into the air so that I thought we might flip over and come crashing to the earth.

But the truck righted. I pointed it down the road. I had no idea where to go or what was happening. All I could do was drive and hope that Palmer had a plan.

But Palmer let loose a cry of fury and frustration.

And I looked up ahead, down the street, and saw the troop truck rushing toward us. The siren had brought reinforcements. They were racing to the prison. The street was too narrow to get around them.

There was no way past.

CHAPTER THIRTY

H it the brakes!" Palmer shouted.

I hit them—hard—without thinking.

The truck went into an insane sideways skid. Even over the siren, I heard someone scream behind me as the bed fishtailed and the wheels lifted and the tires let out a hoarse scream of their own as their rubber burned and smoked.

Even before the pickup came to a full stop, Palmer was out the passenger door, shouting, "Go, go, go!"

I looked out the window and saw the troop truck barreling toward us. It was still about a block away and coming on fast.

I grabbed the handle of the driver's door and threw my shoulder against it. It flew open and I tumbled out into the street.

I looked around—confused, disoriented, the siren blowing

the thoughts right out of me. Where were we? What were we doing? Were Meredith and Nicki and Jim all right? Had they been shot by the guards in the tower? Were they hurt? Had they been killed?

And where was Palmer?

I saw him. He was at the door of one of the old apartment buildings. Lifting his foot . . .

He kicked out and the door flew open. He charged through it—and, with a wave of relief, I saw Nicki and Meredith come out from behind the truck and charge in after him with Jim right behind them. They were alive. They were all right.

One last glance at the troop carrier racing toward us, and I dashed off after them. Into the building, out of the dim daylight of the narrow street, into the interior darkness.

I couldn't see a thing. My eyes hadn't adjusted. The prison siren was dimmer. I heard screeching tires outside. The rebel reinforcements. They were on our trail. They were right behind us.

Up ahead, I heard running footsteps. My friends. I stumbled toward the sound. Then there was a loud *bang* and another door flew open, sending in gray light. I saw we were in a shabby corridor. I saw Palmer and the others rushing out the door at the far end of it, into the gray light of the day outside.

I rushed down the dark hall—out the door—into a cramped courtyard: a square of dead grass with a broken stone fountain at the center. Litter—empty bottles, crumpled newspapers, old cans—was strewn everywhere. Out here, the siren was loud again—so loud I couldn't think. I didn't try. I just looked for Palmer.

There he was, racing toward the courtyard wall. He leapt at it. Grabbed it. Swung up until he was sitting on top.

He stopped there, straddling the wall. He reached down for Nicki. She took his hand and he hauled her quickly up, helped her over the side. Meredith had already started to climb. Palmer grabbed her arm and helped her over. Jim clawed his way up next.

I raced toward the wall and leapt as I'd seen Palmer do. In a moment, I was up and over.

Palmer dropped down beside me.

"This way."

I was breathing hard as we went down a very narrow passage between two buildings. There was barely room for us to move along it single file. I glanced behind me, knowing the rebels were only a few steps away, knowing they could appear at any moment—and that if they caught us here—or blocked the way out—we'd be trapped and helpless.

But we made it to the other end and came out into a cobblestoned plaza. A large church blocked out the sky and cast the square in shade. Its heavy wooden front doors were shut. Its stained-glass windows were dark. It looked completely empty.

All the same, Palmer raced across the plaza to the church

door. I looked left and right as we ran after him. There were no rebels in sight for the moment, but there were other people. An old woman, a hefty man in overalls, a young woman with a scarf over her head . . . They stood watching us, blank-faced, as the siren filled the air around us.

I saw Palmer bang on the church door—what sounded like a code—three pounds, then two. What was the point, though? The church was obviously closed, obviously empty. The rebels were right behind us. There was no time for this. No time.

I glanced back anxiously over my shoulder, expecting to see the rebels come racing down the little alley while we dawdled here.

When I turned around again, the church door was open. Palmer and the others were ducking through it into the darkness beyond.

I followed after them. The shadows of the church closed around us. The smell of old incense filled the air, along with the hollow chill of stone. I peered into the dark and saw Palmer and my friends following a small, almost dwarfish figure into the shadows. As I moved to join them, I felt eyes on me. I looked around and saw statues against every wall. The statues seemed to be staring at me. There was an angel with a sword. A man with arrows in him. The Virgin Mary. Jesus with his hand upraised to give a blessing. All of them were carved out of wood, their faces painted. Their eyes seemed to follow my movements as I hurried past.

Up ahead, there was a raised altar with a carved pulpit. A wooden Jesus hung on a cross behind it. On the floor just below it, there were several tombs—stone boxes—set in a row against one wall.

Palmer and the dwarfish figure reached one of the tombs. They stood shoulder to shoulder on one side of it and began pushing at the lid. The heavy slab shifted with a grating noise.

I shivered, watching them. It seemed a gruesome enterprise: Palmer and that dark, small figure opening a coffin in this shadowy, mysterious place. I glanced around at the statues on every side of us—then up at the crucifix on the altar. Jesus seemed to be looking down at me. Man, I hoped he was!

I came up alongside the others. Now I could see: the dwarfish figure was a Catholic priest. He was a tiny, scrawny little guy with a wrinkled face and a downturning mustache that made his expression look mournful. In his black suit and white collar, he looked almost like a child playing dress-up. It didn't seem like he could possibly have enough strength to move that coffin lid.

But with Palmer's help, he did. The slab kept moving. In another moment, the tomb stood open before us.

"Come on," Palmer said in a harsh whisper. "Get in the coffin."

CHAPTER THIRTY-ONE

Meredith was the first to move. She stepped up to the tomb. Palmer held out his hand to her and she took it. He held her steady as she put one leg over the side of the coffin, then the other. She climbed in and lowered herself down until she was out of sight. Nicki came forward next. I could see the fear in her eyes even in the shadows. Palmer helped her over the side as he had Meredith. Again, I watched her as she sank down into the stone box. Jim took a deep breath and followed.

Then it was my turn. I swallowed hard as I approached the tomb. I had this idea in my mind that I would look over the side and see Meredith and Nicki and Jim in there all huddled together with a long-rotten corpse lying close beside them. I stepped up to the side of the coffin and looked down.

I breathed a sigh of relief. In fact, the tomb had no

bottom. It hid an opening onto a stairway. The stairs led down into a darkness lit only by a dim, red, wavering light.

I climbed over the edge of the tomb and lowered myself onto the first step. Then, clutching a metal railing to keep myself steady on the narrow stairs, I made my way down.

My sneakers touched a rough stone floor. The darkness was even deeper down here than in the church above, but by the small flickering red glow I could make out the silhouettes of Meredith, Nicki, and Jim standing nearby, their eyes gleaming. As my eyes adjusted a little, I could see they were standing at the entrance of a shadowy maze of vaulted corridors. I could see the halls going off into darkness in all directions.

Another moment and Palmer stepped off the stairs and stood beside me.

"What is this place?" I whispered.

"Catacombs," he said softly. "They've been burying people down here for five hundred years."

Now I heard stone grating on stone over my head. I looked up just in time to see the dim light of the church disappearing up there as the little priest—without any help at all this time—pushed the great slab of the coffin lid back into its place.

Palmer whispered, "This way."

We all followed him into the corridors.

We wound down one stone hall and then another. In moments, I had lost my sense of direction. I had lost my sense of the world outside. Out there, in the light, it was warm with summer. But here, it was dank and cold. The chill that I'd felt in the church upstairs grew deeper with every step we took. It seemed to creep under my skin and into my bones.

We took another turn. The wavering red glow grew brighter. In its flickering light, I looked at the catacomb walls. Now and then I'd see a little alcove in them. Some of the alcoves were empty. Some held what looked like coffins. In one, there was all that was left of a skeleton, grinning out at me through the red glow. Its hollow eyes spooked me as we went past. Then it was gone—and I told myself it had just been my imagination. But a few yards on, there was another skeleton lying embedded in the wall. Generally, I kind of think skeletons are cool. But it turns out I don't actually like sharing space with them.

At last, we turned a corner and came into a more open area—a sort of room where the various corridors came together. There was a large heater set against one wall here. A large electric fire was flickering in it, warming the dank air and giving off a bright red light. Nearby, there was a water-cooler with a stack of paper cups beside it. And there were sleeping bags rolled up neatly in one corner, as if the space had been prepared for us as a place of rest.

"All right," Palmer said. "We'll be safe here for a while."

I glanced over at him. His eyes glowed with the reflection of the heater.

"How did they know?" I asked him. "How did they know we would be coming?"

He shrugged. "It's a hard country with a lot of trouble. They knew someone would be coming, they just didn't know it would be us."

I was about to ask another question, but suddenly I didn't have to. I understood. The church was a sort of safe haven for people in trouble with any of the various violent factions in the country. Palmer had known about this just as he'd known about the temple in the jungle. Just as he'd known about the village where we found protection and food.

I guess there'd been no time for me to think about it before because only now, dimly and for the first time, did I begin to get a sort of picture of Palmer, an idea about who he was and how things had been for him these last couple of years.

He knew about these places—these secret safe havens around Costa Verdes—because he had been using them himself. Hiding from the authorities. Running guns to the natives so they could protect themselves from slaughter. Smuggling people to safety when they were in danger of being captured or killed. Fighting both the government and the rebels who opposed them—because one side was just as evil and murderous as the other.

Chased unfairly out of the Marines, Palmer had come to this hard and terrible country to hide away from the world and nurse his bitterness. I think he must've wanted to disappear, to stop being part of the human race that had treated him so badly. Instead, he had ended up helping the local people, protecting them when they had no other protector. Because he couldn't stop himself from doing that, I guess. He was still the same man who had joined the Marines to protect his country. Hard as he might have tried, he couldn't run away from his own nature, his own soul.

"There were people outside on the street," I said. "In the plaza outside the church, They saw us coming in here. Won't they tell the rebels?"

Palmer shook his head no.

"Why not?" I asked.

"Because they don't believe in the rebels anymore than they believe in the government," he said. "But they believe in this place."

"Yes," said Meredith. "I've seen that. They do."

"Fernandez Cobar says religion is the great oppressor of the people," Jim said—but he didn't say it in his usual way, as if he were trying to start an argument. He murmured the words softly, almost as if he were talking to himself. "He says people won't be truly free until all the churches are destroyed."

"Yeah, I bet he does say that," said Palmer with a tired smile. "There's a power here he can't get his hands on and he can't stand it. The old government was the same way. They murdered any priest who spoke up against them."

"They always do that," said Meredith. "It's always the voice of God they try to silence first."

"Who?" I asked.

"Tyrants," said Palmer.

I expected Jim to start making some sort of argument or other. I expected him to tell us again about what a brilliant guy Fernandez Cobar was and how he'd written a book and articles in the newspaper and so on. But to my surprise, Jim didn't say anything. In fact, I thought I saw him nodding a little.

"That's why the rebels will suspect we came here, whether people tell them so or not," said Palmer. "They're sure to come in and search the place any minute. I'm going back to the stairs to listen and make sure Father Miguel doesn't get himself hurt."

"You want me to come with you?" I asked.

He shook his head quickly and was gone into the shadows.

Left alone, Nicki, Meredith, Jim, and I turned and looked at one another in the flickering red light from the heater. The expressions I saw on their faces were grim: blank and exhausted. They all seemed to be wondering the same thing I was: How in the world had this happened to us? We had only come here to build a wall. We had been ready to go home. We had been laughing, kidding around in the cantina one minute . . . When was it? Three days ago? Four? I had lost count. And suddenly—so incredibly suddenly—there was nothing but death and brutality all around us—a kind of danger none of us had ever known before.

The people I saw looking back at me through the darkness were not the same people they had been back in the cantina. I mean, sure, it was still Meredith and Nicki and Jim—of course it was. But it was not the same Meredith and Nicki and Jim. They had changed. Or maybe it was I who had changed. Or maybe it was all of us.

Nicki let out a long sigh. As she passed close to me, it sent a pang through my heart to see the bruise disfiguring her pretty face. She moved to the wall and slid down it wearily, sitting on the floor. Meredith gave a little groan and joined her. Jim settled onto the floor cross-legged. I poured some water from the cooler and drank a few cups greedily. Then I joined them, sitting down next to Jim.

There we sat, it seemed a long time. We went on looking at one another, too tired to do much else, too weary even to speak for a while.

"Amazing," said Nicki then.

And the rest of us nodded. We all knew what she meant.

"What happened to you?" I asked her. "What happened to your face?"

"Oh," she said—as if she'd forgotten all about it. "Don't you like it? It's the latest look. All the kids are into it. I call it: getting punched in the head by a rebel guard."

I didn't know whether to laugh or not. I mean, it wasn't like Nicki to make a joke about something like that. She was more the complain-and-pity-herself type.

"A guard punched you?" I asked.

Now, even more surprising, she smiled at me in the half-darkness. It was a lopsided smile of . . . pride, I think it was.

She was proud of herself and her eyes were gleaming. And she said, "Yeah. He got mad because I cursed at him."

I have to admit, that was more surprising than anything. My mouth actually dropped open. Was this our Nicki talking? Our bawling, screaming, please-don't-hurt-me-I-want-to-go-home Nicki?

"Really? You cursed at a guard?" I asked.

She turned to Meredith for confirmation. "Didn't I?"

"She did," Meredith said with a small smile. "I was shocked," she added, not sounding very shocked at all. "I've never heard such language in my life!"

"You're kidding me," I said. "One of those guards with the machine guns? You cursed him out?"

"He was disgusting," she said. "The way he was treating us. The things he was saying. I told him exactly what I thought of him."

"Well," I said, "I'm not sure that was very smart, but it was definitely very brave."

Nicki looked down at the floor. I couldn't tell for sure in that red light, but I thought she was blushing. Then she lifted her gleaming eyes to me and said, "It was because of you, Will."

Really. She said that. I'm not making this up. "Me?"

"Yes. Because of the way you stood in front of me when we were attacked by that alligator."

"Crocodile," Jim said softly. "Or maybe a caiman, I'm not sure."

"Oh, like, whatever, okay? Giant-reptile-going-to-eat-me," said Nicki, rolling her eyes. It was kind of hilarious hearing her talk like that—talk just like the Nicki we knew before—here, in this skeleton-filled catacomb, with the gunmen all around us, looking for us everywhere and us with no idea how we were going to get out and get away. "After I saw you do that," she went on, "I just thought, if Will can do something like that for me, just, like, totally risk his life for me, then I should at least be able to stop screaming and crying all the time and making poor Meredith take care of me like I was a baby."

"You mean, me standing in front of the croc . . . the cai . . . the scaly green people-eater made you stop being afraid?"

"Oh no! Are you kidding? I'm still way afraid. Right this minute I'm so scared I think my head's going to just come off and roll down the corridor and then explode. I mean, did you see those skeletons in the walls back there?"

I laughed. She didn't sound afraid to me. "I saw them."

"I'm still *way* afraid," she said again. "But I just thought maybe I could stop *acting* so afraid. You know? I just thought, even if I wasn't really brave, I could start *pretending* to be brave so the rest of you didn't have to listen to me throwing a fit every five minutes."

"Yeah, but I mean . . . that *is* brave," I said. "I mean, like, we're all scared, right? We're all just trying to act brave."

"Oh . . . well . . . really? I don't know . . . ," said Nicki. "I don't think Meredith is afraid."

I looked at Meredith. We all did. She was sitting against

the wall, her head tilted back. She was gazing up into the darkness above us. When Nicki spoke her name, she glanced our way, but didn't say anything.

"No," said Jim. "You're right. Meredith *isn't* afraid."

"No," I agreed. "She's not."

"You should have seen what she did!" Nicki burst out. Her voice was animated and bright, as if she was describing some cool scene in a movie. "When the guard punched me? We were in that horrible, awful cell. And the guard hit me so hard, I fell down. I mean, I was, like, lying there against the wall, almost unconscious—all, like, dazed. And the guard gave this horrible laugh and he started to come toward me. And Meredith stepped in front of him. And he, like, grabbed her arm? And she just stuck her finger in his face and started screaming at him in Spanish—I mean, like, giving him a lecture, like he was five years old or something. And all the time, the guy is holding a machine gun, right, and grabbing her by the arm and ready to punch her too. Only he didn't. It was, like, he didn't dare."

I laughed. I could imagine that. "What'd you say to him?" I asked Meredith.

She tilted her head to one side a little. "I just told him that if his mother could see him hitting a defenseless woman like that, she would die of shame," Meredith said. "I told him Nicki might be his sister. I said, 'How would you like it if someone treated your sister like that?'"

Jim laughed too. "How did you know he even had a sister?"

She shrugged. "He knew what a sister is," she said. "That's the point."

"What did he say?" I asked.

"He didn't say anything!" Nicki said, practically giggling with glee. "He just finally sort of threw her aside and slunk out of the cell, grumbling."

I shook my head. "That's amazing. That's an amazing story."

"It is," Jim agreed.

"It was even more amazing to be there," said Nicki.

We all fell quiet for a minute. I could see the scene in my mind: Nicki lying on the dungeon floor . . . the guard looming over her . . . Meredith wagging her finger in the guard's face, ignoring his gun, lecturing him about his sister as if he were five years old . . .

"So why *aren't* you afraid, Meredith?" I asked. I looked at her. The red light from the heater played over her pale, still features. She turned aside a little, kind of rolling her eyes and smiling to herself, as if I'd said something ridiculous.

"No, really," said Nicki. "I want to know too. Why aren't you?"

"Stop it, you guys," Meredith said. "You're talking total nonsense."

"No, actually, they're not," said Jim, like a teacher correcting a mistake. "We can all see that you're not. We saw it from the beginning in the cantina."

"The rest of us are all terrified all the time," I said. "Maybe we're trying to be brave, or to act brave, or do what we think is right or whatever. But we're all afraid all the time. I know I am."

"So am I," Jim said.

"You *know* I am," said Nicki.

"But you," I said to Meredith, "it's like it makes no difference to you how things turn out. It's like you're . . ." I hesitated a moment because I remembered the word that Palmer had used when we were in that old temple, when he was whispering to her in the dark. I didn't want her to know that I'd been awake, that I'd been eavesdropping on them. But there was no other word to describe her. So I said, "Fearless. You're fearless."

I stopped there. We all stopped. We all waited, watching Meredith.

And Meredith—she just sort of gazed off into the flickering shadows, her features still, her eyes set on something far away we couldn't see.

Finally, not turning to us, not even talking to us it seemed, but just talking into the darkness around us, she said quietly, "I had a sister. Her name was Anne. She was five years older than me. I think she was . . . the single sweetest, gentlest, kindest person I've ever met in my life. I never saw her get angry. I never heard her say an unkind word. Really. I'm not just, you know, exaggerating or something. She really wasn't like other people. She was better.

"And, of course, I worshipped her. You know, little-sister style. She was nine, I was four. She was twelve, I was seven. She was sixteen and I was eleven. And I just wanted to do whatever she did, follow her around everywhere she went. And nine out of ten times, she let me. She let me tag along—to the mall, to get pizza, to the movies—even when it annoyed her friends, which was, like, always. She would tell them, 'Oh, let her come, she won't bother anyone.' Which almost certainly wasn't true. I must've been a terrible pain in the neck to her, but she never let it show. Really. Never once."

I saw the light gleam red on Meredith's cheek and I felt my throat get tight as I realized that she had started crying. It was a strange kind of crying. Her expression didn't change at all, the way it does with most people when they cry. Her features remained still, distant, sort of serene. Even the calm tone of her voice remained the same. The tears just streamed steadily down her cheeks as she talked. Now and then she moved her hand to wipe them away or she sniffed a little.

"When I was really little?" she said. "I used to think sometimes that she was secretly an angel. I really did. She would come into my room at night, when it was time for me to say my prayers. And she would tell me, 'Kneel down, and put your hands together, and point your soul toward the light of God.' And I would sort of steal glances at her while we were praying and she'd have her face lifted up, and her expression would be so still and peaceful, I would think: *She's going off to the angel place.* You know? Silly. I must've been three or four. You know the way little kids think."

The tears kept streaming down her face in the heater-light. But her voice continued quiet and unshaken.

"I was fourteen when she got sick. She had to come home from college. She'd been gone a year, and in that time I'd become this sort of . . . awful teenager. Always grim and complaining about everything. Nothing was any good. Everything was a 'bore' or a 'disaster' or a 'waste of time.'"

I had a hard time picturing Meredith ever being like that, but if she said she was, I guess she was.

"Whenever I could, I'd go online and chat with Anne about . . . you know, whatever was upsetting me that day. She was busy with school and her new life, her new friends, studying and all that, but she'd still make time for me. She was the only one who knew how to make me feel better. In fact, when she got ill and came home from school, I was, like, 'Oh good, now I'll have her around again until she gets better.' I didn't realize how bad it was. I didn't realize she wasn't going to get better, not ever."

She drew her sleeve across her face, drying her tears, wiping her nose.

"But she knew. Anne knew. And she never changed. The whole time the sickness ate away at her, she was the same as she always was. They had to give her chemo. She lost her hair—her beautiful, beautiful red hair. She got so thin . . . so thin and gray . . . but the way she was—that never changed. She was still Anne the whole time. Still my same sweet Anne."

Meredith turned and looked at us in the red glow of the heater. The light shone on her wet cheeks.

"That's what she said to me at the hospital, in fact . . . She had to go into the hospital at the end. And the very last time I visited her there, she said to me, 'Don't be afraid. Nothing has changed. I'm still who I am.' A few hours after that, she was dead."

Meredith shook her head as if to clear the old images from her mind.

"You think it makes no difference to me how things work out for us?" she asked. "That's not true. It makes a big difference to me. I don't want to die in this horrible place. I want to go home just like the rest of you. I want to see my mom and dad again. I want to meet my husband and get married and live in a big rambling house in the middle of nowhere and have more children than you'd think anyone would. That's what my sister wanted too. I just know that . . . the things you want don't always happen . . . sometimes terrible things happen instead . . . I've seen that with my own eyes . . . And you're right: since Anne died, I'm somehow not afraid of it anymore. I don't know exactly why. I can't explain it really . . ."

Her voice trailed off. She leaned back against the wall and looked off into the surrounding dark again.

"I don't get it," said Jim after a moment. "I mean, when you see something like that happen . . . like what happened to your sister . . . shouldn't that make you *more* afraid?"

"Maybe . . . ," Meredith said. "Maybe it should. But it didn't. I'm just telling you how it is."

Jim leaned forward over his own crossed legs, like a student asking a teacher a question. "Is it because you've seen the worst that can happen and it's not so bad?"

Meredith shook her head. "No. No, it's not that. It was bad. Losing Anne broke my heart. It still breaks my heart."

"Is it because she's in heaven?" Nicki asked. "I mean, are you not afraid because you know, if you die, you'll see Anne again in heaven?"

Meredith took another swipe at her damp cheeks. "Well . . . I do know that. But no—no, that's not it exactly either . . . Like I said, I want to live a full life before I die just like anyone."

"Well then, I don't get it," said Jim again. "I don't understand why seeing your sister die would make you fearless."

But I did. I didn't say anything, but I understood. I thought back to those terrible seconds when we were being taken out to face the firing squad. I remembered how I had looked at Meredith—and at Nicki—and at Jim—and even at the gunmen who were going to kill us—and I had thought how beautiful they all were, how beautiful they were all meant to be. Maybe not the rebel who was going to pull the trigger and snuff out an innocent life, but the man inside him who wanted to fight for justice and be a hero to his people. Maybe not the Jim who thought that fancy ideas and good intentions were the same as true goodness, but the Jim who wanted to think great thoughts and make the world better with them. Maybe not the Nicki who was vain and silly and weak, but the woman inside her who was so full of kindness and practically exploding with the joy of being pretty and alive. Those were the beautiful parts of them.

Their souls, I mean. I think in those moments, when I was so close to death, I was seeing their souls, the souls God had given them. And their souls were beautiful. And what Meredith knew, what Meredith had learned when her sister died, what her sister had taught her when she was dying, was that good things might happen to you in life or bad things might happen, sometimes terrible things, but no matter what happens, your soul is your own. It's in your power to point your soul toward the light of God, and no one and nothing—not even a man with a gun, not even death, not even the devil from hell himself—can stop you.

That's why Meredith was fearless. Because as long as she remembered what her sister had shown her, nothing that happened could ever hurt the most important part of her, nothing that happened outside herself could ever make her less than what God had meant for her to be.

I was about to try to tell the others this, to try to explain what I was thinking. But just then I sensed something nearby us in the darkness. And I turned and saw Palmer.

I'm not sure how long he had been standing there. Awhile, I think. He was just at the end of the corridor, at the edge of the little room we were in, at the edge of the brighter light from the heater. He was standing half hidden in the shadows. And he was gazing at Meredith.

Gazing is the right word. He seemed to be completely lost in the sight of her. I don't think I'd ever seen a man look at a woman like that, not even in the movies. In fact, it wasn't anything like the way men look at women in the movies. It was deeper, more serious than that somehow. His wry smile was gone, the mocking laughter in his eyes was gone. He stood and gazed at her and I could almost feel the heat of his sadness and his longing. He looked as if he wanted to somehow reach down into his own depths and draw out the very substance of himself and offer it to her in his two hands. He looked like he wanted to join his heart to hers forever.

Then the moment was over. He seemed to blink and shake off his trance. He stepped out of the shadows, stepped into the room, into the red light. The others noticed he was there for the first time and when they turned to him, they saw the Palmer they knew: relaxed and indomitable, the wry smile back on his lips, the mocking look back in his eyes.

Jim and Nicki watched him, waiting to hear what he would say. And out of the corner of my eyes, I saw Meredith quickly and secretly swipe at her cheeks one last time to make sure all the tears had been dried.

"All right," Palmer said. "The soldiers have come and gone. Father Miguel is a little guy, but he's tough as nails and he faced them down." He moved his eyes over each of us in turn, hesitating only slightly when he looked at Meredith.

When he spoke again, his voice was softer. "Get some rest," he said. "We're gonna wait for the rains to pass."

"Then what?" asked Jim.

"Then," said Palmer, "we make a run for the border."

CHAPTER THIRTY-TWO

We all arranged the sleeping bags around the heater and got into them. It felt so good to be warm and dry and relatively safe that after about a minute, I fell into a deep sleep.

The next thing I knew, I heard a noise—a sort of shifting sound. My eyes came open. I had been so soundly asleep that, for a moment, I couldn't remember where I was. Then I looked around and saw the others still snoring in their bags on the floor beside me and I remembered we were in the catacombs. The light from the heater was bright, and while it threw a red glow over our little area, it seemed to cast the corridors beyond into even deeper darkness.

I remembered that a noise had awakened me. I sat up in my sleeping bag and listened. The sound came again: something shifting, moving. I worried that the soldiers had come back—had maybe found the tomb with the secret passage and come down here to search the catacombs.

I didn't want to wake the others, but I thought I'd better check it out. I got out of my bag. Listened again. The sound was coming from the corridor to my right. I moved away from the heater, into the shadows at the corridor's entryway. I stood and listened. The shifting sound grew louder. Something *was* moving—moving toward me.

I stood there and peered into the dark. And my mouth fell open: I couldn't believe what I saw.

The skeletons. The skeletons from the catacomb graves. Amazingly, they had risen up from their resting places. They had joined their bones back together. They were slouching toward me out of the corridor shadows, a whole army of them, moving with the slow, limping, relentless tread of zombies. Their teeth were set in dead men's grins. Their empty eye sockets stared as they came to get me . . .

I woke in my sleeping bag with a gasp. Well, it was a dream, of course. And good thing. The living people in this country were dangerous enough. I didn't need the dead ones coming after me too.

I sat up. My heart was hammering in my chest so hard I couldn't catch my breath. I looked around me. I saw the others still sleeping in their bags, just as in my dream. The light from the heater made the corridors dark—also as in my dream.

And then—exactly as in my dream—I heard that same shifting noise. Something moving in the corridor shadows.

I thought my heart was beating hard before—I thought it was hard to breathe before—but now the fear went through me like a steady electric shock. Was I still asleep? Still dreaming? No. I couldn't be. I was awake this time. I was sure of it.

I listened, hoping I had imagined the sound. But no, there it was again. Something really *was* moving in one of the corridors.

I had this bizarre sense that I was living through my dream, that I was helpless to stop it from unfolding just the way it had before. I would get up. I would go to the corridor. I would see the oncoming skeletons . . . And there was nothing I could do about it.

And I did get up. What else could I do? Just as in the dream, I had to make sure the noise wasn't the soldiers searching the catacombs. I listened. I heard the sound in the corridor to my right. Just as in the dream. I moved into the corridor shadows. I stood there—just as in the dream—and peered into them.

No skeletons. Well, that was a positive development, anyway. But I did see a little glow down there in the dark—a small, flickering yellow glow. Candlelight—that's what it looked like anyway. I stared at it—and as I did, a shadow passed across it and it grew dim.

Someone was there.

I had to check it out. If it was a rebel gunman, looking for us, I had to find him before he found us. I had to raise the alarm and give the others a chance to get away.

I began edging slowly into the corridor, into the dark. As I traveled farther away from the heater, the dank atmosphere of the catacombs closed around me and I couldn't help but think of the skeletons I had seen lying in their alcoves—and the skeletons I had seen coming toward me in my dream. I listened—but the shifting sound didn't come again. Which only made me more afraid. Bad enough to know someone was there in the dark—even worse not to be able to see him or hear him. Because if I couldn't tell where he was—who knew?—while I was creeping up on him, he might be creeping up on me.

I had walked—I don't know—maybe thirty yards into the corridor when the shadows shifted. Someone moving. I held my breath. The dim yellow candle-glow shone clear again as if a person had moved out of its way. I saw that the light was coming through a narrow archway off to the right. There seemed to be some kind of little room or alcove in there.

I forgot I was holding my breath and now I had to let it out. I tried to keep it as quiet as I could, but I felt like my pulse was pounding so loudly that it would give me away in any case. I inched as silently as I could toward the archway. I pressed close to the wall . . . wound my head around the edge . . . peeked through.

What I saw was not as amazing as walking skeletons, I'll admit. But it was pretty startling all the same.

The little room beyond the archway was a chapel—maybe left there from the old days when they used to bury people down here. It was just a little closet of a place with smooth walls made of great blocks of stone. On the wall to my left, there was a cross with a small rickety wooden table beneath it. There was a big book lying open on the table—a Bible, I'm pretty sure. The candle stood next to the Bible, casting its glow up over the cross.

But that wasn't what was so startling. What really surprised me was that Palmer was there. He was standing very still, half turned away from me. His thumbs were hooked in his belt. His face was lifted to the cross. His expression was quiet and serious and intense, sort of the way it had been when he was watching Meredith earlier: the same expression of sadness and longing.

I stood there a moment, somehow riveted by the sight of him. Then it came to me what I was doing—kind of spying on him, you know. I felt my face get hot. I wanted to hurry back to my sleeping bag before Palmer realized I was there.

I turned away . . .

And I let out a high-pitched shout as a lightning flash of terror went through me—because there, right in front of me, was some small, weird, gnarled creature who had risen up out of the depths of this underground world, his eyes burning at me from the darkness.

I reeled backward in fear, my arms pinwheeling, my feet nearly slipping out from underneath me. The next moment, the corridor grew brighter as Palmer—hearing my cry— rushed out of the chapel, carrying the candle with him.

In the candlelight, I saw that the weird creature of the catacombs was only the little priest—Father Miguel.

Well, okay, I felt like an idiot for being so scared, but the priest really was a strange-looking little dude, what can I tell you? And he really did sneak up on me!

Behind the drooping mustache that gave the tiny little man's face its mournful look, I thought I saw him give a small smile.

"I fear I have frightened your friend," he said to Palmer.

Palmer shook his head, rolling his eyes. "No worries, Padre. The kid's a comedian. He embarrasses me wherever we go."

"Gee, thanks," I said.

The priest smiled again beneath that drooping mustache—and then the smile faded—disappeared. He raised his hands from his sides as if he were going to make some sort of offering. And he did—only it wasn't the sort of offering you normally expect from a priest: guns—an AK-47 machine gun and an old six-shot revolver of some sort.

"I'm sorry," he said to Palmer. "This is the best I can do on short notice."

Palmer took the weapons from him. He handed the revolver to me. I stuck it under my belt.

Father Miguel nodded. "And now," he said, "the rains are over. The dark is coming. It is time to go."

CHAPTER THIRTY-THREE

Everything happened quickly now. Palmer and I woke the others. Moving in silence, we all rolled up the sleeping bags in the light of the heater and stowed them in the corner of the room where we'd found them.

All the while, the priest spoke to Palmer in a low, urgent voice.

"The soldiers are everywhere, my friend. They are saying you murdered two of the guards during your escape."

"The guards and I had a vigorous discussion of the issues of the day," Palmer drawled.

"Yes," said the dwarfish little priest, his mournful expression never changing. "And you have put our mutual friend Señor Mendoza in a difficult position with his superiors. President Cobar seems to feel it is his fault that you and your companions have slipped their net."

"Bad news for Mendoza," said Palmer. "When Cobar asks for your letter of resignation, he usually takes your head with it."

"You joke, but it's true. If Mendoza does not return you to prison for trial and execution, he is a dead man. Therefore, he is, you might say, highly motivated to find you. And he has every available Volcano at his disposal to do the job. They have enough problems with people sending out the news on the Internet. They don't want American witnesses escaping to go on TV and tell the world what's happening here."

We finished stowing the sleeping bags and gathered around Palmer and Father Miguel in the heater's red light.

"Okay, Padre," said Palmer drily. "You've got me really scared now. Tell me some good news."

"We should move while we talk. There is reason to hurry."

So we moved. Father Miguel switched on a small flashlight with a red filter. The red beam pierced the shadows in front of us and we followed it.

We shuttled through the cold, damp atmosphere of the corridors in a cluster, the four of us tagging along just behind Palmer and the little priest. The red beam played off the rough stone of the walls and shot into the unseen depths of the corridors. I couldn't tell where we were going exactly, but I knew it was not the way we had come.

Father Miguel's voice trailed back to us as we traveled.

"Mendoza knows you are a flier, of course. He is expecting

you to try to escape by air. He has dispatched as many men as he can to guard the city's two airfields."

"That's tough," said Palmer. "We'll never make it out of here on the ground."

"No. This is why a certain gentleman who keeps his small Cessna in a private hangar has moved the plane to a little field not far from one of the catacomb entrances."

"Nice of him," said Palmer. "I assume he's a friend of yours."

"He is a friend of God's," said the priest. "And so he is a friend of freedom. But there is a problem."

"Somehow I guessed there would be."

"The field, as I say, is within reach of one of the catacombs' entryways. But almost as soon as this gentleman landed there, the rebels set up a checkpoint on the road nearby. It is one of many they have set up to keep you and other enemies of the revolution within the confines of the city."

"Great."

"You will need to cross the open space behind this checkpoint very quietly and without being seen in order to reach the plane."

We continued to move rapidly through the darkness, following the priest's flashlight. Now and then the light picked out the skull of a skeleton lying in its wall grave. It was pretty disturbing—like one of those carnival fun houses. We'd be rushing along and then suddenly there would be this skull, this empty stare, this grinning mouth—then it would sink again into the shadows as we hurried past.

"Let's say we make it to the plane," Palmer said. "What then? I gotta turn the engine on at some point. Won't the guards hear it?"

"They will," said the priest. "We must hope you fly away very fast."

Palmer gave a low chuckle. "We *must* hope, mustn't we?"

We went on through the corridors, turning this way and that, following the beam and the moving silhouettes of Palmer and Father Miguel. Already, I could feel the tension building inside me. I was thinking about how we'd have to sneak past the guards, get across the field, get to the airplane.

I told myself to stop thinking so much. *Suspend the imagination. Don't worry about anything. Pray about everything.* I did pray—and it was working pretty well . . .

Until I saw the stairway.

It was just up ahead: a rickety metal structure standing against one wall of the corridor, pretty much the same as the one we had come down. As we were approaching it, it seemed to lead up to nowhere, to the ceiling. But as we got closer, I saw there was a dark opening above.

Then the tension flared in me again. This was it. Our chance to get away, to get out of this country, to get home.

Our last chance.

CHAPTER THIRTY-FOUR

Palmer held the flashlight as Father Miguel climbed slowly up the stairs. The dwarfish man in black moved clumsily as if he were not used to so much exercise and every step was painful for him.

A moment passed. Our frightened eyes met in the red glow of the flashlight. Then we heard a heavy stone slab shifting above us.

I peered up the stairs into the darkness. "He's so small," I whispered. "How does he do that?"

"He's bigger on the inside," Palmer answered quietly.

The slab shifted again—and then gray light flooded down to us where we stood at the base of the staircase. I squinted up into the sudden brightness. My heart beat hard. I was glad to see daylight after so long underground, but I knew, too, that my life—all our lives—depended on the next few minutes.

I saw the priest's stunted shape above me. He peeked up through the catacomb opening. Then he came quickly back down the stairs to us.

"You must go now. Quickly."

Palmer shouldered his rifle. Stuck out his hand. "Thank you, Padre. Until we meet again."

"In this life or the next." Father Miguel shook his hand.

Nicki kissed the priest's cheek. "Thank you so much, Father." She headed up the stairs.

"I hope your country finds peace," Meredith said. She kissed Father Miguel too and went up into the light.

"Good luck," said Jim, shaking the priest's hand.

I was the last. I put my hand out and Father Miguel put his gnarled, claw-like hand into mine.

"Thanks, Padre," I said.

"Take care of Palmer," said the mournful-looking little priest. "He is a good man."

"I don't think he needs my help," I said.

"I know you don't think so. But you are wrong. Watch out for him."

"I'll do my best."

"Go with God."

I nodded—and let him go. And headed up the stairs into the light.

The stairs led up to another stone coffin. I had to reach

up from the top step to grab the top of the coffin's wall. I hauled myself up and over it into the waning daylight—and as I did, I felt Palmer and Jim grab me and pull me up quickly.

I dropped out of the grave and onto the muddy ground.

I looked around me to get my bearings. I saw my friends, all crouched low behind little house-shaped stone structures of various pastel colors. I started to stand, but Palmer gestured me down with his hand, and I remained on my knees, my head bent low. I scouted the scene.

We were in a graveyard. An acre or two of ground crowded with pastel monuments. The jungle pressed close to the cemetery border behind us, but in front of us, as the priest had said, there was a stretch of open ground—then more jungle on the other side.

I looked at Palmer. He was peering intensely over the top of a monument. I followed his gaze off to the left.

There was the road—and the checkpoint. Two pickups had been turned lengthwise across the paved two-way to block the passage. Four gun-toting rebels were posted in front of the trucks. Two of the rebels leaned against the trucks' sides smoking cigarettes and looking off into the distance. Two others paced and chatted. They were about a football field away, but close enough to catch our movements if we crossed within sight of them.

Where was the plane? I looked to my right now and spotted it. The edge of the jungle across the field sort of curved around away from us. The little Cessna was parked on the far side of the curve, so that the trees shielded it and the soldiers couldn't see it from the checkpoint. All we had to do was creep across the open space to the jungle, then make our way under the cover of the trees to the airplane.

That's all we had to do.

The afternoon rains were over now, but the sky was still steel gray. It was growing darker too, as the sun set behind the clouds. The heat of the morning had passed into a dense, humid chill. I could see my breath clouding in front of me as I waited, crouched behind the monument. The place was quiet. Very quiet. The insects buzzed. Occasionally a bird laughed in the trees. No other noise.

Palmer crouched even lower now so he could whisper to us.

"All right," he said. "The kid'll go first so we have a gun on each side. Then the rest of you will go while I wait here . . ."

"No."

Startled, we all turned toward Jim. His protruding eyes were fixed on Palmer, his thin lips pressed tightly together. "That makes no sense. You have to go first, Palmer. You're the only one who can fly the plane. If you get hurt, we're all finished. If you're already over there, whoever makes it to you has a chance of getting away."

Palmer hesitated. But then, to my surprise, he nodded. "Jim's right." He held the AK out to me.

But Jim reached out and wrapped his hand around the barrel. "Will's risked enough. I'll stay behind and cover you.

I'm a better shot than he is anyway. I got a marksman medal at summer camp when I was twelve."

Again, Palmer hesitated. And I was doubtful. I didn't want to shoot anybody else—not ever. But I knew I would if I had to. Would Jim? Was he really willing to fight against his cherished rebels?

I looked at him. He seemed serious enough. And however annoying he might have been at times, I didn't think he was the kind of guy who would betray his friends.

Palmer shifted the rifle toward him and handed it over.

"If they come for us, blast them," he said.

"I will," said Jim.

Palmer put his hand out to me. I drew the revolver out of my belt and gave it to him.

"All right," he said. "Watch me. Then follow one at a time."

Palmer moved. He stayed low and dodged in a crouch from one monument to the next until he was at the edge of the cemetery, at the edge of the open field. The rest of us remained where we were, watching him from around the edges of the little pastel gravestones. Our tense, rapid, nervous breaths plumed in the air.

Palmer waited, watching the guards at the checkpoint. The two who were pacing together turned their backs on us. They were a funny-looking pair, one tall and narrow, one short and squat. They walked away across the road. They passed in front of the other two, the smoking guards, blocking their vision a little.

Palmer chose that moment and broke cover.

I don't know how far it was from the graveyard to the jungle's edge—twenty yards? thirty?—but in those next few seconds—when Palmer was out in the open—when the guards could turn and see him at any second—it sure seemed like a long, long way. Bent over, carrying the pistol low at his side, Palmer rushed across the muddy grass without another look in the direction of the checkpoint.

But I looked. I saw the pacing rebels reach the far side of the road and start to turn. I glanced back at Palmer. He was only a few steps from reaching the protection of the trees. The pacing rebels turned around, chatting with one another. Then the skinny one glanced up—right in the direction of the open field.

By then, though, Palmer had made it across. He was crouched low within the cover of the jungle. He signaled us to follow, one at a time.

Meredith went next. She did just what Palmer had done. Stayed low. Dodged from monument to monument to the edge of the cemetery. Crouched there, watching the guards.

This time, though, the two pacing men stopped on our side of the road. They were chatting together and laughing, not particularly looking our way, but not looking anywhere else either. If Meredith moved, they would almost surely see her.

Finally, with another burst of laughter, the two guards turned around—and Meredith ran for it.

She kept low and moved fast. Before the rebel guards had taken two steps along the road, she was nearly across the open space. But she was *too* fast. The ground was too muddy, the grass too wet. Just before she reached the far jungle, her foot slipped. She tumbled down to one knee with a gasp.

The fall didn't make a lot of noise, but the little splash and Meredith's little gasp—they were different from all the other sounds of the surrounding jungle. They stood out.

The skinny guard must have heard them. He turned to glance over his shoulder. Luckily, he glanced over his left shoulder, toward the cemetery. He didn't spot Meredith. But then he turned to glance over his right.

By then, Meredith had scrambled to her feet, and Palmer had reached out of the trees to grab her arm and yank her into the jungle cover. When the guard looked in that direction, she was already gone.

But the skinny rebel was alert now. He turned to his squat friend. He gestured at the open passage between the cemetery and the jungle. The squat guard shrugged. The skinny guard spoke to the two others leaning against the trucks. They shrugged too.

Then the two pacing rebels—Skinny and Squat—began coming our way.

You could tell by the casual way they strolled toward us that they were not really worried yet. They were just being cautious, that's all, just checking things out. Jim and Nicki and I crouched low and breathed hard as we watched them come closer down the open corridor of grass between the jungle and the cemetery. I could see Palmer and Meredith watching bright-eyed from the trees across the way.

I tried to will the guards to turn back to their checkpoint—*Stop! Turn around! Turn around!*—but they just kept coming. I felt Jim shift beside me and turned to see him moving his hand on the grip of the AK, slipping his finger around the trigger. Getting ready for whatever happened next.

Another few steps and they were right across from us, only a few yards away. They scanned the graveyard, their eyes passing directly over the place where Nicki and Jim and I were crouching in fear. They didn't see us. They turned the other way and scanned the jungle—then the skinny one stopped and said, "Que es . . . ?" *What's that?*

I held my breath. Had he spotted Meredith and Palmer? No. He was moving away from where they were crouched in the trees, moving away from all of us. He moved to where the tree line started to curve away.

Then he shouted. He was waving to his squat friend. The squat guard joined him . . . And now I saw what they were both staring at.

"They found the plane!" I whispered.

The two guards were talking rapidly to each other.

"Can you hear what they're saying?" I asked Jim.

He shook his head. But then he answered in a very low whisper, "They're going to call Mendoza."

The squat guard nodded and started jogging back heavily

toward the trucks in the road. The skinny guard—a mean-looking, snarly-faced guy I saw now—moved in the other direction, toward the plane. He was looking it over, but also looking all around him in case someone else might be near.

"What do we do?" Nicki whispered. "Mendoza will send more soldiers . . ."

I nodded. She was right. In a couple of minutes, the place would be littered with rebels. They'd be sure to confiscate the plane—or set it on fire. They might even search the jungle for us. We had to get out of here—and we had to do it now.

But the skinny, snarly-faced guard was keeping watch, standing in the open ground, studying the plane, searching the surrounding area with narrowed, suspicious eyes. There was no way to get past him.

I peered across the open field to the jungle. I saw Meredith—I could see her eyes gleaming at me out of the jungle shadows. I saw her make a gesture—pushing her open palm out toward me: *Wait!*

I waited. I glanced over at the checkpoint. The squat guard had now made his breathless way back to the others. He was giving them the news about the plane. One of the smoking guards dashed his cigarette into a puddle by the side of the road. He took out his cell phone and held it to his ear.

I glanced back to check on the skinny guard over by the plane.

He was gone! He had vanished!

"Look!" Jim whispered.

At the same moment, a movement caught my eye. I turned. And I saw the skinny guard—or at least I saw his long legs—being dragged through the mud and out of sight, into the cover of the jungle.

"It's Palmer," Jim whispered. "He got him."

I looked across the way at Meredith. She was waving at me frantically, gesturing me to come over. But I already understood.

"We've got to move right now," I said. "This is the only chance we've got. Nicki."

She glanced at me—as if she didn't know what I was going to say!

So I said it: "Nicki, go! Go fast! Now!"

She went. And she did go fast. But she didn't stay low. She just dashed from our hiding place and started running. She raced full speed across the cemetery, leaping between the monuments like a deer.

"Nicki!" I said in a harsh whisper—but I didn't dare raise my voice and she didn't hear me. She didn't pause.

She broke out of the cemetery and barreled full speed across the open field toward the jungle.

I turned in fear to the guards at the checkpoint. Two of them were gathered around the third—the rebel with the cell phone. He spoke into the phone another second as Nicki ran full speed across the open space.

Then the rebel snapped the phone off. He was slipping it

into his pocket when Nicki's movement caught his eye and he turned.

And he saw her.

And he shouted. "Alto!"

Stop!

CHAPTER THIRTY-FIVE

After that, there was nothing but fear and gunfire.

The three remaining rebels unstrapped their weapons and ran toward us.

Jim shouted, "Go, Will!"

And I didn't hesitate. I leapt up from behind the grave and dashed forward, dodging like a running back through the headstones toward the cemetery's edge. The sound of the rebels' AKs rattled through the quiet jungle. Birds exploded out of the trees, screaming. Clots of mud leapt into the air as the bullets dug into the earth.

I was running across the open field, the mud squelching under my sneakers. I saw the three guards racing toward me, their rifles spitting flame.

But then I saw Palmer step calmly out of the trees in

front of me. He had a machine gun now too—the skinny guard's weapon. He opened fire and, at my back, I heard another coughing blast as Jim jumped up from behind the gravestones and starting shooting as well.

I only got a panicked glimpse of the onrushing guards as I made my crazy dash across the field—but so help me, if the situation hadn't been so insanely lethal, the looks on their faces would have been hilarious. One second they were all murderous intensity, rushing toward us like angels of justice ready to deliver the killing blow from their AKs. The next second they realized that *we* were armed as well, that we—Palmer and Jim—were actually shooting back at them. And the ferocity instantly went out of their expressions to be replaced by wild-eyed looks of terror.

The three rebels scattered. Two of them hurled themselves into the cover of the jungle on their left. The third, the squat one, waddled quickly behind the cemetery wall to his right.

I put on an extra burst of speed, trying to reach the cover of the trees before the rebels could start shooting again.

But that was a mistake. Just as I reached the spot where Palmer was standing, the ground seemed to fly out from under me. Like Meredith, I had run too fast and slipped. I went down—all the way down—landing hard on my shoulder, sliding through the mud.

The guards poked out from their blinds and started shooting again, trying to riddle me where I lay. Palmer and

Jim returned fire, trying to keep them pinned down. I struggled to get to my feet—and as I did, Meredith rushed out of the jungle to help me.

"No!" I shouted. "Stay back!"

But she kept coming—crying out and flinching as bullets pounded into the mud between us.

She rushed to my side. I leapt to my feet. She grabbed me to help me stand, and I grabbed her to push her back into the trees. Holding on to each other, we ran behind the firing Palmer until we were back in the cover of the jungle.

"Get in the plane!" Palmer shouted to us.

But the second he glanced back over his shoulder at us, one of the rebels leapt out of the trees and drew a bead on him.

Palmer faced forward just in time and fired. The rebel flew backward, dropping into the mud.

The squat guard seized the moment, jumped up from behind the cemetery wall, and took aim.

Palmer fired once and the squat guard ducked—but the next moment, Palmer gave a cry of frustration. His magazine was empty—he was out of bullets.

He threw the rifle into the mud and drew the six-shot revolver from his belt. He fired a single shot to keep the squat guard pinned down. He waved his free hand urgently at the cemetery across the way.

"Let's go, Jim! Let's go!"

Jim leapt up from the cover of the graves and let loose a burst from his AK. I heard a scream from the jungle and thought he might have hit another of the guards, leaving only the squat one left.

We're going to make it, I thought. *We're going to get away!*

But in the next few seconds—the next few terrible seconds—all our hopes seemed to unravel in awful slow motion.

I was in the trees with Nicki and Meredith. My hopes rising, I was shouting at the girls to get in the plane. I had my hands on their arms and we were all turning away from the gunfight, turning toward the edge of the jungle to where the Cessna was waiting.

I don't know what made me glance back, but I did.

I saw Palmer fire another shot from his revolver. Then I heard a burst of answering machine-gun fire. I saw a line of blood shoot out of Palmer's arm. He dropped into the mud, the pistol flying out of his hand.

"Palmer!" I screamed.

Then—still in the horrible underwater slow motion of a bad dream—I turned back for him. I took a step toward him out of the trees. He was already rolling to his feet, the wound just above his elbow spilling blood down over his forearm and wrist.

I broke out of the cover of the trees and grabbed his other arm to help him—and as I did, I saw a jeep screaming up to the checkpoint, turning off the road onto the open field, and racing straight toward us over the muddy ground. There was a rebel behind the wheel and another in the passenger seat.

I saw at once that this second rebel was Mendoza.

Now, as I helped Palmer into the trees, Jim made his

move. He broke out of the cemetery, shooting wildly, and rushed toward us across the field. The jeep swerved to get out of the way of his fire. Its tires lost their grip on the mud. It slowed as it spun round toward the jungle and then I heard the crunch of metal as its fender went into the trunk of a tree.

But Jim was out of bullets now too. He threw his rifle to the ground and started running toward us.

He got two steps before the squat guard rose up from behind the cemetery wall and shot him down.

The machine-gun bullets raked across Jim's legs. Jim cried out and threw up his arms and tumbled face-forward into the mud.

I didn't think. I let go of Palmer and ran to get him.

I dashed across the field and slid to Jim like a runner going into home plate. I grabbed his arms.

"Go!" he said. "I can't walk! I'll be all right! Go!"

But there was no way—no way—I was going to leave him there. I wrapped both hands around his arm and jumped to my feet, trying to haul him up with all my strength. He screamed in pain.

"I can't!"

"You have to!"

I saw the squat guard take aim at us and pull the trigger. Then he cursed and tore the magazine off. His gun was empty too. He fished a fresh magazine from his belt. I kept trying to pull Jim up.

And now Palmer rushed to us, bloody as he was. He

grabbed Jim's other arm. Ignoring Jim's screams of pain, we both dragged him to his feet. We draped his arms across our shoulders and began carrying him across the field toward the trees while his useless, wounded legs trailed through the mud behind us.

A troop truck was now barreling up to the checkpoint, rebels already pouring out of the back. I thought we might make it to the plane before they reached us. I even thought we might make it into the cover of the trees before the squat guard could reload.

But there was no way we were going to outrace Mendoza.

The rebel leader had leapt out of the crashed jeep. He had drawn his pistol. He was running toward us, screaming wildly in his desperation to stop our escape—in his determination to bring down Palmer Dunn.

As Palmer and I dragged the wounded Jim toward the jungle cover, Mendoza got close enough to take his shot—a good shot. He planted his legs. He lowered the pistol. He aimed straight at Palmer. No way he was going to miss at that distance. No way we could make the trees before he fired. No way we could escape if Palmer went down, leaving us no one who could fly the plane, and yet there was also no way Palmer could save himself—not while he was helping me carry Jim to safety.

I saw the wild rage for vengeance in Mendoza's eyes and I thought all hope was gone.

Then Meredith stepped out of the trees. In one swift and weirdly graceful motion, she bent down and swept up the pistol Palmer had dropped in the mud. She stood very still, very straight and tall, and took careful aim at Mendoza.

How long did she hesitate before she pulled the trigger? Some fraction of a second maybe? Even with all our lives on the line, I couldn't blame her. To kill a man, to send his soul to judgment—it's a terrible thing to do, a terrible thing to have to live with afterward, a terrible sacrifice to make even when you have no other choice. I knew that.

And Meredith did hesitate. And Mendoza saw her. And quickly he shifted the aim of his pistol from Palmer to her.

And Meredith pulled the trigger.

The blast of the pistol was loud even in the open field. The powerful recoil made Meredith's arm fly up into the air and even pushed her backward half a step.

Among all the crazy racing images around me, I saw Mendoza's face go blank with surprise as a black wound appeared in the center of his chest. I saw him lower his pistol and stagger where he stood. He gave Meredith a look—a look, I thought, of incomprehension—as if he couldn't for the life of him understand how she could ever do something as nasty as that to a sweet guy like him.

Then he toppled over—like a falling tower—and his body thudded into the mud.

The next moment Palmer and I had carried Jim into the cover of the trees and Meredith was with us, pale and grim, and Nicki was beside us and we were all racing through the jungle together, racing to the plane.

CHAPTER THIRTY-SIX

We had no weapons left. Meredith, in horror, I think, had dropped the revolver in the mud and left it there. Behind us, the squat guard had reloaded and was firing after us in short bursts. The bullets ripped through the leaves all around us. The rebels from the troop carrier—I don't know how many—were racing over the open field behind us, trying to get around the trees and cut us off to keep us from escaping. We were dragging Jim and dodging tree trunks and leaping over roots and pushing through foliage. Our pursuers were closing on us quickly.

We broke out of the trees and reached the plane. It didn't look large enough to hold us all, but it would have to. Meredith and Nicki, unencumbered by Jim, had rushed ahead of us. Nicki yanked the door open and bent the front seat forward. Meredith climbed in quickly so she could help pull Jim aboard.

Palmer and I brought the groaning Jim up to the plane and hoisted him through the door. Meredith grabbed him and dragged him through as he screamed in agony. His legs were a mass of blood.

Now Palmer was gone—around the plane to the pilot's seat. Nicki was climbing in and pulling the seat back to make room for me up front. I jumped in shotgun.

Even as I shut the door, the engine was roaring to life, the propeller turning and the plane starting to strain forward against the resistance of the muddy ground.

"Come on!" Palmer shouted at the Cessna. He was covered in mud and blood and his eyes gleamed white with intensity.

As if in answer to his cry, the Cessna went forward a little faster—then a little faster still.

There was no runway, but there was a stretch of dirt where the grass grew sparse. The earth was packed tighter here and the mud was not as bad. As the Cessna's wheels reached the spot, the plane sped up and turned.

I looked ahead through the windshield and saw the mountains to the west, the clouds breaking apart above them to reveal the dark-blue sky and the lowering sun.

The real shooting started now. The rebels from the troop carrier had come around the curve in the tree line. They had a bead on our plane as it rolled away from them. They were firing at us—their rattling blasts blending together into one solid death-dealing roar.

I didn't look back at them. There was no point. They would bring us down or we would outrun them, and there was nothing I could do to change the outcome. I sat in the plane facing forward, breathing hard from the chase but oddly unafraid, oddly calm about whatever was going to happen next.

Don't worry about anything. Pray about everything.

I remembered what Meredith's sister, Anne, had taught her:

Put your hands together and point your soul toward the light of God.

As the Cessna rolled faster, as the noise of gunfire rose above the noise of the plane, I clasped my hands together in my lap and faced the windshield.

I felt the plane take to the sky. I felt it wobble as if it might yet tumble back to earth—and then I felt it right itself and lift up faster and faster, higher and higher. I heard Nicki give a shout of celebration. And I heard Palmer laughing. I saw the sky surround us and I saw nothing before us but the mountains and the sun.

We headed for that light—with Costa Verdes, that country of tragedies, falling away below us.

We flew for the west.

America.

Home.

Freedom.

EPILOGUE

I never got to say good-bye to Palmer Dunn—or Meredith Ward either. I tried to, but it just didn't work out that way.

After we flew across the mountains, Palmer picked up a signal on the emergency band of the Cessna's radio. Voices guided us north to an airfield in Belize. We were met there by a small crowd of celebrating people. Father Miguel had told them we were coming. They all spoke English. They all slapped us on our backs as we stepped out of the plane. They had an ambulance already waiting. They helped us put Jim on a stretcher and they rushed all of us off to a nearby hospital, sirens blaring.

The next few days went by in a blur. We were taken first to one hospital, then flown to another in the capital city of Belmopan. At the second hospital, we were met by a woman named Mrs. Blake who was from the American embassy. Jim had to stay in the hospital another day while they worked on his legs, but the rest of us just needed some bandages here and there. Even Palmer: a bullet had torn a gash in his arm, but it hadn't stuck. He was fine. So Mrs. Blake had us moved to a hotel—an amazing luxury hotel with huge rooms and soft beds and hot showers and English-language television. It wasn't heaven, but for now, it was close enough.

I talked to my parents on the phone. My mother cried. My father laughed. They sounded good, I thought. I let myself hope that maybe they had stopped arguing with each other, but I wasn't sure and I didn't really know how to ask. I figured I would just have to wait and see for myself.

Mrs. Blake brought us new clothes. When we were all cleaned up and rested, she brought some reporters to the hotel. Some were local, some were from back home. We had lunch with the reporters in the hotel restaurant and they asked us questions about our escape and took video. Later I heard the interviews were on television and then on YouTube. I never watched them, but I hear they're still there.

Finally, Mrs. Blake brought us new passports and arranged our plane tickets home. By the fourth day, even Jim was ready to travel, though he was hobbling around on crutches.

We flew to Belize City and then to Dallas, Texas. From there, Jim and Nicki and I would fly home to California. Meredith was going back to Denver. Palmer said he was going to see a friend in Virginia, to ask about finding a new job. Something in law enforcement, he said, but he wasn't very specific.

I meant to say good-bye to Palmer and Meredith there at the airport. But as we were all making our way from the airport security checkpoint to our gates, I saw a sign for a chapel. I told the others I would catch up with them, and I went in.

The chapel was just a little room with chairs pointing at a podium. I guess it was supposed to look vaguely like a church, but only vaguely. There was no one there but me.

I sat in one of the chairs. I was planning to pray. I wanted to say thanks for our survival. I wanted to remember Pastor Ron, and ask God to take care of him and to bring peace to his family.

And I did start praying, but after a while, I just found myself sitting there, staring down at my sneakers, kind of lost in thought. I was a little nervous about going home, I realized. I was nervous about seeing my parents, about finding out if they had solved their problems and ended their arguments, or if their marriage was going to break apart and take my life with it.

I was nervous—but I realized I wasn't scared, not like I'd been scared before. I had gone to Costa Verdes to get away from them, to get away from the suspense of waiting to find out what would happen. But now I was back and I was not afraid.

Which was weird, you know. Because I still didn't know

what was going to happen. Not to my parents, not to me, not to my life or to the world. I didn't know the future, in other words. No one does. I definitely hoped there'd be some good news up ahead. But I knew there'd be some bad news sometimes too. And I won't say I was fearless about that like Meredith was—not yet—but I thought I understood now how a person might get to be fearless over time, if he set his spirit on the right path.

After a while in the chapel, I sort of came back to myself and realized I'd been sitting there longer than I'd meant to. I jumped up and headed back out to the airport concourse. I checked the departure signs and saw that my plane to Los Angeles was already beginning to board.

I didn't have much time before the plane took off, but I did want to say good-bye to Meredith and Palmer. I had learned a lot from both of them and they had both saved my life.

The gate for Meredith's flight wasn't far away. I ran down the concourse to reach it, weaving through the crowd. But just as I got to the right place, I pulled up short.

Meredith's flight to Denver was boarding now too. The line of passengers was moving through the door to the Jetway. But Meredith had not left the airport yet. She was still there, standing a little off to one side in front of the window facing the airfield. She was standing there against the backdrop of the runways, a 707 jet taking off into the sky behind her.

She was there with Palmer. He had her in his arms. They were lost together in a long, deep kiss.

So—yeah—what do you think?—I walked away. I walked off quickly to catch my plane home without saying good-bye to either of them. And I'll admit it: my heart felt a little heavy inside me. Because, you know, Meredith was with Palmer and would never be with me. And yes, yes, yes, I know: it was supposed to be that way. I was only sixteen, after all. I wasn't ready for anything that serious in my life. And Meredith and Palmer—well, they were made for each other. Anyone could see that.

But my heart felt a little heavy inside me all the same.

As I walked off to catch my plane, I tried to tease myself out of my mood. I told myself: *Hey, to win a woman like Meredith, you have to be a hero—like Palmer. And you're no hero, that's for sure. You're just an ordinary kid.*

I reached my gate. There was Nicki standing next to Jim on his crutches. She was waving to me urgently, telling me to hurry.

As I jogged toward them, I sort of answered myself. I thought, *Well, okay, I'm no hero now. But I'm still young. I might get to be a hero in time.*

And you know, I might. It's possible, anyway. I mean, that's the whole thing about the future, isn't it?

You just never know.

READING GROUP GUIDE

1. While in the jungle, Will remembers Ernest Hemingway's definition of cowardice: "a lack of ability to suspend the functioning of the imagination." What does this mean to Will? Have you ever needed to restrain your imagination to keep it from running wild?
2. Did Pastor Ron do the right thing by trying to reason with Mendoza and the rebels? Why or why not?
3. After being rescued from the firing squad, Will says, "It's too bad you can't always live as if it were the last moment of your life." What does he mean by this? How does Will experience the world right before he thinks he's going to die?
4. How do Nicki and Jim change throughout the story? What are the lessons they needed to learn?

5. Will acts heroically throughout this story, as do the other characters. In your opinion, which moments would have required the most courage and/or selflessness?

6. At first, Will finds Palmer Dunn to be arrogant and unlikeable; but by the end of the story, we know a very different side of Palmer. Have you ever met someone about whom your first impressions were completely wrong?

7. Will recalls Pastor Ron once saying, "Don't worry about anything. Pray about everything instead." How does this help Will along the way? How could this saying help you through trying times?

8. Meredith acts fearlessly on more than one occasion, and the people around her notice. Do you have to go through something tragic like she did in order to become a fearless person? Why or why not?

CHARLIE WEST JUST WOKE UP IN SOMEONE ELSE'S NIGHTMARE.

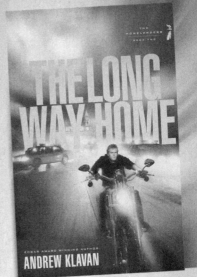

THE HOMELANDERS SERIES

AVAILABLE IN PRINT AND E-BOOK FORMATS EVERYWHERE

ABOUT THE AUTHOR

Author photo by Meredith W. Walter

Andrew Klavan was hailed by Stephen King as "the most original novelist of crime and suspense since Cornell Woolrich." He is the recipient of two Edgar Awards and the author of such bestsellers as *True Crime* and *Don't Say a Word*.